Tuscan Warlord

Book 5 in the Sir John Hawkwood Series

By

Griff Hosker

Tuscan Warlord

Published by Sword Books Ltd 2022

Copyright ©Griff Hosker First Edition

The author has asserted their moral right under the Copyright, Designs and Patents Act, 1988, to be identified as the author of this work.
All Rights reserved. No part of this publication may be reproduced, copied, stored in a retrieval system, or transmitted, in any form or by any means, without the prior written consent of the copyright holder, nor be otherwise circulated in any form of binding or cover other than that in which it is published and without a similar condition being imposed on the subsequent purchaser.
A CIP catalogue record for this title is available from the British Library.
Cover by Design for Writers

Contents

Tuscan Warlord i
Prologue 3
Chapter 1 7
Chapter 2 18
Chapter 3 32
Chapter 4 43
Chapter 5 52
Chapter 6 64
Chapter 7 75
Chapter 8 86
Chapter 9 101
Chapter 10 109
Chapter 11 118
Chapter 12 130
Chapter 13 142
Chapter 14 152
Chapter 15 167
Chapter 16 176
Chapter 17 188
Chapter 18 200
Chapter 19 213
Chapter 20 222
Chapter 21 233
Epilogue 250
Glossary 252
Historical note 254
Other books by Griff Hosker 257

Tuscan Warlord

Real People Used in The Book

Sir John Hawkwood- Captain of the White Company
King Edward Plantagenet
Prince Edward of Wales and Duke of Cornwall- his son (The Black Prince also known as Edward Woodstock)
King John II of France
Crown Prince Charles, the Dauphin of France
Pope Urban V[th]
Pope Gregory XIth, - Pierre Roger de Beaufort
Pope Urban VIth - Bartolomeo Prignano Cardinal Gil Álvarez Carrillo de Albornoz – Papal envoy and general
Robert de Genève - Cardinal, papal legate and general, later Pope Clement VIIth, an anti-pope
Queen Joan (Joanna)I - Queen of Naples, and Countess of Provence and Forcalquier
John II - Marquis of Montferrat
Amadeus - Count of Savoy, known as the Green Count
Bernabò Visconti - Lord of Milan
Ambrogio Visconti - his son and leader of the Company of Ambrogio
Ettore Visconti - an illegitimate son
Rodolfo Visconti – a legitimate son
Donnina Visconti - an illegitimate daughter
Galeazzo Visconti - Duke of Milan and brother of Bernabò
Gian Galeazzo Visconti- son of Galeazzo Visconti and Duke of Milan
Pellario Griffo - Chamberlain of Pisa
Luca di Totti de'Firidolfi da Panzano - Florentine warrior
Ranuccio Farnese - Florentine leader
Sir Andrew de Belmonte- an English adventurer
Heinrich Paer – German Mercenary leader
Giovanni Agnello – Merchant and doge of Pisa
Albert Sterz - one-time captain of the White Company
Annechin Baumgarten – Leader of the Star Company
Sir John Thornbury - English condottiere
Sir Edward de Berkley – English knight and diplomat
Geoffrey Chaucer - poet and diplomat

Prologue

I am Sir John Hawkwood, leader of the White Company. Whilst we have not always emerged from battle the victors, we have never been badly defeated and many men put that down to my skill as a condottiere. I am an arrogant man but people whose opinion I value have told me that is true. However, one of my skills is finding the right men to lead the company and over the years I have found men who knew my mind and would do as I ordered. I suppose I was an old-fashioned warlord. We were employed by city-states but every military and strategic decision was made by me. My right-hand men were Giovanni d'Azzo who commanded the lances, the men at arms and spearmen, and Robin who commanded my archers. I had been an archer but Robin was in a different class from me. I was happy to defer to him about the dispositions of our most potent force when we fought. Sir Dai, who had been my squire, and Sir Andrew Belmonte, an English knight, were Giovanni's lieutenants.

It had been December when we had defeated Paer and the Florentines. It had resulted in two things: firstly I made another fortune both from the battle and from the Florentines and secondly, my reputation and that of my company was made once more. The first battle of Cascina had damaged it but the second saw me held in even greater esteem. Bernabò Visconti, the Lord of Milan, was my partner and paymaster. He and his brother, Galeazzo, jointly ruled Milan. Galeazzo had the title of duke. Bernabò was, of course, delighted for it made him master of the north of Italy. He was an opponent of the Avignon pope and the victory ensured that the Papal League could do little about their enemies, the Visconti brothers.

I had not planned on returning to my sons in Bordeaux but I had lost men in the campaign and I needed to hire more men. More importantly, I was keen to bring my sons with me to Italy. I had promised them as much more than a year ago. Now it was time to deliver on that promise. I had learned over the years that if I had youths whom I could train then they made better leaders than many who had more experience. Dai had been my squire and was now a more than competent leader. Michael was still my squire but he had thus far refused my offer of spurs. I wanted my sons, who were now youths, to be the clay I moulded into future leaders. I always planned for the future.

My fortune was in the bank we owned in Pisa and my army and I returned there for it was also our home. The Pisans were more than happy to accommodate us for although they were not currently our paymasters, they knew that our presence would stop their avowed enemies, the Florentines from trying to take land from them. William, who was my treasurer and Dai, who had been my squire, had both married into the nobility of Pisa and they had fine homes there. It meant I knew that my fortune was safe. Old soldiers who no longer campaigned were now the guardians of our coins and it would be safe from predators. I went on my return to visit with the doge, Giovanni Agnello. It was due to my White Company that he was the doge and we had kept him safe from any potential coup that might threaten his position. He was a nice man but not a strong leader and he had many enemies in Pisa. There was a faction that thought an alliance with Florence would make them the strong power they had been before being defeated by Genoa.

He liked me and had tried to marry one of his daughters off to me. He had failed for I needed no wife, not yet at any rate, "You have won a great victory, again, and Bernabò is delighted with you."

I shrugged, "And why should he not? It was my men that won the day and not his Milanese soldiers."

The doge frowned, "It would not do, Sir John, to bite the hand that feeds you." He and Bernabò were great friends. I knew that my words would get back to the Lord of Milan but as he was often times slow to pay us it would do no harm to remind him that we were the best company in Italy.

"And I would not but the Visconti family have not always been friends of mine and I will be wary in my dealings with them."

My tone left the doge in no doubt that I was not in the mood for debate. He changed the subject, "And now, do you find time for yourself? Perhaps take a wife?"

I smiled as I shook my head for the doge was ever keen for me to marry one of his many relatives. He saw it as a means of securing his position, "I am not yet ready. I will, however, return to Bordeaux to hire more men."

"Be careful, Sir John. Genoa has a long memory and her leaders know that you bloodied their noses the last time you sailed in their waters."

"And that is why I am here. I need a good ship and cunning captain."

He rubbed his beard. He had the largest fleet of merchant ships in Pisa, "Giacomo Benvenuti is the cleverest. He is not the most experienced but he manages to evade the Genoese and travels the western Mediterranean as and when he wishes. His ship has one more voyage to make to Narbonne and then he will be in port until Easter."

I nodded, "That will do. I will need berths for six of us and I will need return berths for Easter."

"It shall be so." He scribbled on the wax tablet. I smiled for he was getting old and his memory was not what it was.

I left and headed for my home. I was rarely there and it had nothing to mark it as Sir John Hawkwood's. It was a place to store my clothes and armour and somewhere I could sleep when I was in Pisa. Michael, my squire and my four bodyguards awaited me.

"Prepare to leave for a few months in Bordeaux."

Harold commanded my bodyguards. He was a man at arms who had shown me many times that he was one of the best men at arms in the White Company. He nodded, "Arms and horses?"

"Arms and horses but not Ajax. He deserves some rest. Use Remus. He is young and the journey will help me to see how he does after a long ride."

Harold would choose well. I had lost bodyguards in battle. Harold and the other three had lasted longer than most, six months. He had been promoted to the better-paid position and had no intention of losing it.

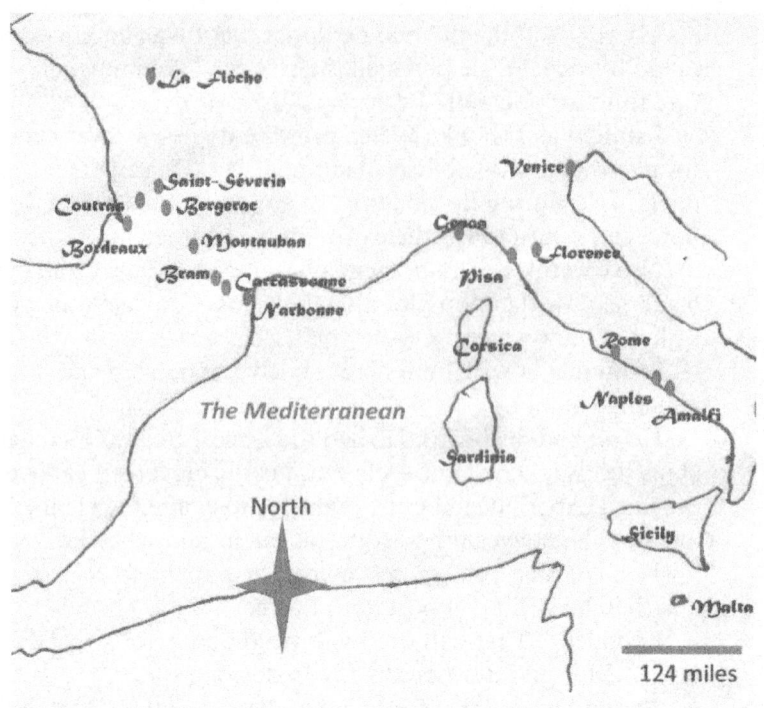

France 1369

Chapter 1

Giacomo was everything the doge had said and more. His father had been a sailor and had lost his life and his ship to the Genoese. Rather than simply making him bitter and resentful, which he was, it made him determined to outwit the Genoese at every turn. When he was able, he hurt them but as they had the most powerful fleet in the Mediterranean he would not spit into the wind. He took satisfaction in using his mind and his great skills as a sailor to best them.

"Of course, I can get you to Narbonne unseen, Sir John, and I would be honoured to do so. I was told how you and your archers drove off two Genoese ships, killing many of her crew. I know that we cannot do that now but I was happy about your victory. Hopefully, we will not need your archers." He nodded at the handful of men I had brought with me, "I can see you have no archers this time so we will have to rely on my methods." He peered over the side, "We have missed this tide for it will take time to load your animals but we can leave on the next one."

I left that to the crew and stood on the sterncastle to watch the loading. Horses are always difficult to load. The harbour was busy for despite its recent decline Pisa was still a port and had a mercantile fleet that was only rivalled by the Genoese and Venetians. That said not all those at the port were Pisan. There were enemy spies who lived in the port and were paid to send messages. They eked out a living and lived parlous lives. Often bodies were found floating in the harbour with slit throats. I knew that the Florentines kept spies here. They wished to rule Pisa as it would give them the port that they needed. There were also, tied up, ships that were more piratical than mercantile. They were hard to identify but I tried. They were the ones that had a larger crew than was necessary and had the lean and hungry look of a predator. When I spied the waddling cog that left just as the tide was right, I looked and saw the two smaller ships that left soon after. They would not need the highest tide to leave the harbour. Unusually one of them looked to have metalled men aboard. Normally pirates did not wear mail as it was too great a risk at sea. I wondered about that. It would not concern us as we would be leaving on the next tide. I had wanted our own horses this time and this was the price I would have to pay. The cog would be lucky to survive more than a mile or two from the coast.

We left in the early hours of the morning when the port was quiet. Few ships would risk landing in the early morning tide and most watchers had departed the port. I stood with Giacomo as we headed out to sea. He nodded in a satisfied manner, "I had not planned it this way but it is better than had we left last night. I am carrying the friend of the Doge of Pisa as well as the leader of the White Company. Many men would wish you dead."

He was right and I merely nodded.

Michael was with me and he asked, "So, Captain Benvenuti, how do you get us safely to Narbonne?"

He grinned and tapped his nose, "The cargo we carry is not perishable. It is spices from the east and valuable. Better that I get to Narbonne safely than hurry and fall foul of pirates or the Genoese. The usual course, and the quickest, is along the coast but there are watch towers and many ships. Instead, I take an extra half a day and head through the channel between Corsica and Sardinia. That means that we approach the French coast during the hours of darkness and from the south but once we pass those islands then there is little danger and we can use full sail. We will reach Narbonne by dawn." He shrugged, "Sometimes we have to wait for the right tide but that is not much of a problem."

He knew what he was doing. "And you will be back here at Easter?"

He nodded, "I like to clean the hull of my ship over winter and clean the weed from her. I also like to see my wife and make more children. It is why a man marries, is it not?"

Michael nodded, "So you usually carry spices?"

The captain nodded, "We specialise in spices and we store them in the warehouse. The doge and I have an arrangement with Giovanni Dini who fetches the spices from the east. All three of us profit. We carry other goods but spices are the most profitable cargo. I leave at Easter knowing that there will be a great need for spices." He smiled, "The ones I carry now will fetch a high price for Christmas looms and people like to indulge and celebrate. They will have used all these spices by Easter and be ready for more. It is another way that I can have my revenge on Genoa for I have the spice trade and it is the most lucrative."

He was right and we had a safe crossing. We would have landed in Narbonne a whole day earlier had we managed to make the earlier tide but there was no rush. We unloaded the horses and then strapped the panniers on the sumpters. I had promised my sons' hauberks and the ones I carried were well made. They were also heavy. We could have waited to give them the hauberks in Pisa but this would make a good Christmas present and make up for the little time I had spent with them. All of them knew what to do and they packed and prepared with little fuss. We did not ride the horses but led them to the small inn on the outskirts of the port. As we passed the sweepings of the port, I watched for any showing undue interest in us. We were noted and I knew that the information would be sold but by then we would be on the road to Bordeaux and we could watch the trail behind. We went to the inn run by Jean du Pont. The villainous-looking former man at arms ran a successful business that included smuggling as well as protection for merchants. I had used him before and I trusted him. I saw the looks on my bodyguards' faces as we entered the less-than-salubrious inn.

"Fear not, Harold, this man can be trusted."

Jean du Pont grinned as we approached. I saw Harold frown for the grin merely made the innkeeper look more evil than when he scowled. "I am guessing, my friend, that you wish the services of Arnaud, Georges, Guillaume and Pierre and horses?"

"The former yes but we brought horses this time."

He affected an outraged expression, "Mine are not good enough for you? I am disconsolate."

I laughed, "No, but as I brought more men, I wanted no delay in leaving."

He nodded, "I fear that you will be delayed by one night at least for the four men you wish are busy this night. You can have them tomorrow. For how long do you need them?"

"We will return by Easter."

"They will be pleased for they like you and enjoy Bordeaux. I have rooms for you." He scribbled a price on a wax table and showed it to me. I nodded. "Good. Marie, take these men to their rooms, 1, 3 and 4." The serving girl wiped her hands and approached. Jean continued, "I will have food prepared. It is all included in the cost. I will join you if you do not mind as I wish to hear of the Battle of Perugia from your own lips. The version I heard was too fantastical to be true. I was a soldier and I like the truth, no matter how unpalatable."

I knew what he meant for many victors exaggerated what they had done in battles. When we had secured our chests in our room we descended to the main room where people ate. I knew that we were safe so long as we were in the inn but had I been a stranger I would have feared for my life as the clientele looked to be made up of the sweepings of the gutter. The food was good and the wine was well selected. Harold and my bodyguards kept a wary eye and drank sparingly but Michael and I were comfortable for we had been here before. I told him of the battle without hyperbole or exaggeration and I saw his eyes widen. When I finished, he said, "Your victory was as fantastic as I had heard. I would have stayed in Pisa, my friend, surrounded by your White Company. Even with my four extra men, this will be a perilous journey you make." He leaned over and said quietly, "Surrounded by your company you are safe but there are many lords and captains of companies you have defeated who would like your head."

"I know but it will be the last time. I know that my sons are still young but I would have them with me rather than far away being raised by a man I no longer respect. Once I am back in Pisa then I will stay there. You are right but I hope that my enemies have not had the time to make plans to stop me."

The four men who would guard and lead us were tired when they were woken the next day and told what was needed of them. I was flattered when despite their tiredness they enthusiastically accepted the commission.

Georges spoke for all of them when he said, "Our choice is escorting boring and tight-fisted merchants who treat us like the leavings of a gutter or with you, a soldier who we know will keep us regaled on the road with stories that quicken our hearts and you pay well. Besides, Bordeaux is an easy place to earn extra gold. The whores there like real men."

Despite the fact that we chatted as we rode, I was with professionals and they were vigilant. We rode with coifs and helmets. They were well made and did not hinder conversation. We wore our mail too although our plate was back in Pisa. We had no intention of battling. With daggers and swords in our baldrics, we were ready for any bandit who made the mistake of attempting to rob a small band of travellers. The decision to use the same route we had before, through Carcassonne, Bram, Montauban and the rest of the places we had used was because of familiarity. We knew the inns where we would not be rooked and having travelled the road twice, we knew the places to be wary of an ambush.

The road began to grow easier after we had passed Valence and we were more than halfway home. Ahead lay Marmande, a town built by Richard the Lionheart, it was a shadow of its former self. Amaury de Montfort, Simon de Montfort's brother, had captured the town and massacred its inhabitants. Even after the Count of Toulouse took over the town it did not recover well. It was like Bram, a place of ghosts and people were too scared to peer out of their doors when strangers approached. We would have no choice but to stay there. There was no inn and we would have to buy food and cook it ourselves. There was a sombre mood amongst us as we descended towards the setting sun. All conversation ceased.

Georges and Guillaume rode at the fore while Arnaud and Pierre brought up the rear. The horses' hooves clipped clopped and echoed on the cobbles in the town but none peered forth from their doors. It was understandable. To them, all strangers were a threat. I turned to Michael, "Perhaps they have found more food and do not need our coin." When we passed through Bram we were asked for help by people who had nothing. We were pleased to help. "That is good. I hate to see people like this suffer."

My bodyguards had not been with us the last time I had passed this way and their hands were on their weapons as we neared the small square built by King Richard when he had been lord of Gascony. There was a water trough there and, if memory served, a deserted house that we could use. We had just dismounted when the fourteen or so mercenaries appeared from the shadows of the buildings. Their horses had to have been elsewhere for our animals had not given us any warning of danger. Eight came before us and I heard a curse from Harold when he realised that six were behind. They had the advantage over us for they had weapons drawn and some of them, the leader included, wore plate. This was not an accident. We were trapped and from the drawn weapons, they meant to cause us harm. My mind began to think and I dropped Remus' reins.

The leader had an open helmet and he was grinning at me as he walked towards me. I took some steps in his direction so that I was between Georges and Guillaume. I did not like others to have to fight my battles. As soon as he spoke it was clear that they were German. He spoke to me in atrocious Italian. At first, I did not recognise him but his words soon made it clear who he was.

"Take off your helmet, Sir John, I would see your face when you die."

I heard swords drawn behind me as Harold and the bodyguards began to draw weapons.

"Tell your men that if they draw their weapons they will die where they stand."

I slipped my dagger into my left hand as I took off the helmet and turned. I said, "Sheathe your weapons. There will be a time for bloodshed but first, we talk." I held the eyes of my bodyguards as I said, in English, "Do as I do when I do!" Harold saw the dagger next to the helmet and nodded. They sheathed their swords and, as I faced the mercenary leader, I took the helmet in my right hand and dropped my left hand to my side. The German's attention was on my right hand which held my helmet. So long as I held my helmet, he thought me defenceless.

"What is it, apart from my death, that you want?"

He smiled, "Why, the treasure you carry, of course, as well as your horses and your mail. Heinrich Paer sends his compliments. Thanks to you he will never hold a shield again and your victory at Perugia means that it is unlikely that we will be employed again in Italy." He took a step forward and spoke a little quieter. His tone was no longer bantering but threatening. He smiled, "You have made enemies, Sir John. The Doge of Florence has paid us well although we would have done this for nothing. Heinrich is still recovering in a monastery but we, his oath brothers waited in Pisa and when we saw your ship was delayed, we seized our chance. We have been waiting here knowing that this God-forsaken spot was the best place to ambush…"

He got no further for I had seen that his sword was lowered and he was close enough to me for an attack. I used my helmet as a weapon and stepping forward I smashed the helmet into his face while at the same time stabbing him in the thigh with my dagger. As I had expected, my men all drew their weapons. I had my back protected. I hurled my helmet at the man behind the mercenary leader and drew my sword. My helmet smashed into the man's face and slowed him a little. I could not afford to be charitable and, indeed, I had no inclination to do so. I brought my sword across the neck and shoulder of the mercenary. My archer's arm was enough to break the bone. I rammed my dagger into his eye and left it there as his lifeless body fell back. I was wearing gauntlets and I ran at the man I had hit in the face with the helmet. He had recovered and was bringing his sword over his head to strike at my coifed skull. Had he connected then I would be dead. An archer has a powerful right arm but his left is stronger than most men's. I held his sword close to the hilt. Few men sharpen a sword there. As he tried to bring the sword down, I stabbed down at his foot, driving through the leather boot and into the soil between the cobbles. He screamed in pain and resistance went from his right hand. Stepping back I drove the sword through his mail hauberk, twisting through the links to enter his flesh. Pointing the sword upwards I tore through his organs and into his heart.

I heard hooves as four of the attackers, seeing their leader dead, fled back towards Montauban. There were none ahead of me and I whipped my head around. Michael was finishing off a mercenary but only Harold of my bodyguards remained standing. Even as I turned a German smashed his mace into Harold's skull. I saw red and I drove my sword through the mercenary's back. All thoughts of taking a prisoner evaporated when the last of my bodyguards died protecting me. I was panting heavily and I stared around to look for another I could kill. All were dead or dying. Pierre had been wounded and Georges was tending to him.

"Guillaume, find their horses. Michael, see if any of them can talk." As they rushed to obey me, I knelt for some last words with Harold. His brains oozed from his skull and he would talk no more. My bodyguards, it seemed, did not live long. I had lost four in battle and now a second four had fallen in this ambush. Michael shook his head and I sheathed my sword. Cupping my hands I shouted, "Come forth, you will not be harmed. I swear it."

At first, none emerged but then a door opened and a man I remembered as being the headman, stepped nervously out. I waved for him to come closer to me. "When did these killers come?"

I heard the terror in his voice. His eyes were on the bodies of my bodyguards and the five men they had slain. "They rode in last night, lord and asked if a party of men had passed through. We told them that they were the first. It is almost winter and few use this road until spring. They said we would not be harmed if we stayed within our homes." I knew why he was afraid. He did not wish me to take my revenge upon him.

I nodded, "You could have done nothing else. Is there a church here?"

"Aye, lord, but we have no priest."

Tuscan Warlord

"It matters not. We will bury my four men in the graveyard." I was not asking permission. I was taking it as a right. "The men brought food?" He nodded, "Then have your women use it to cook us a meal. We will leave in the morning."

Guillaume approached. "There are just six horses left, Sir John. The four who fled took the others."

There was still light in the sky and I said, "Bring Harold and the others. We will bury them." We slung their bodies on their horses and led them to the church at the corner of the square. Behind it was a cemetery. There were no stones there for this was a poor place. Arnaud found the spades and picks and, Pierre apart, we dug the graves. I ensured that when we laid them out they had their swords on their bodies and their helmets were next to them. They had been oathsworn and kept their oaths. They deserved to be buried with honour. We covered them with earth and the others looked at me. I was no priest but I would have to use the right words. They deserved nothing less.

"Lord, welcome the souls of four brave men, Harold of Bath, Edward son of John, Walter of Warrington, and James of Parr. They were brave men and died doing their duty. Any sins that they may have committed were not intentional. I swear that I will pay indulgences for their safe passage to heaven. Amen."

While we waited for the food, we stripped the bodies of the dead and made a pyre in a nearby field. I ensured that the wind would take the stench of burning flesh away from the village. We burned them. I let the four guards take their pick from the mail, weapons and treasure from the dead and then we ate the food brought silently by the women of Marmande.

We were silent as we ate. When we had finished Georges said, "Once more we have become richer through your service, Sir John, but I would rather be poorer and these four brave men alive."

I nodded, "As would I and I tell you this, I will travel to Bordeaux no more. I had intended to let the mother of my sons raise them a little while longer but I see now that was a mistake. I should have fetched them back the last time.

Travelling alone not only puts me in danger but my companions." I put my hand on Michael's shoulder, "If anything had happened to you…"

"But it did not."

"Nonetheless, we hire men for our journey home and I care not if we look like a warband, I will have my sons safe and you Michael too. When I reach Italy then I will be safe for the White Company will be my surety. I will make the other mercenary leaders fear me. I will rule northern Italy."

Arnaud shook his head, "That sounds, Sir John, as though you would be a warlord."

I smiled, "Perhaps that is a good thing. Doges and dukes, counts and popes all seek to serve themselves. Why should I not? The difference is that I will do things that are right. I have enough money now and I will make a home for my sons where they will be safe. I will make a land where the White Company ensures that there is peace."

Michael asked, "Through war?"

"If that is what it takes, then, aye."

As we completed our journey my active mind pieced together the events that had led to the deaths of my bodyguards. The mercenary leader, I had found nothing to indicate his name, had obviously come to Pisa with revenge on his mind. When he discovered I was due to sail to France it would have been simple enough to hire a boat. He and his companions had plenty of gold, payment from the Doge of Florence. I stored that in my mind. There would be a reckoning. He had assured me there would be no attempt on my life and he had lied. Giacomo's decision to take a longer route had delayed us more than enough for the mercenaries to get ahead of us and they had chosen their place of attack well. It was the most sparsely populated place on our route home. I had learned a valuable lesson, at the cost of four good men at arms.

Tuscan Warlord

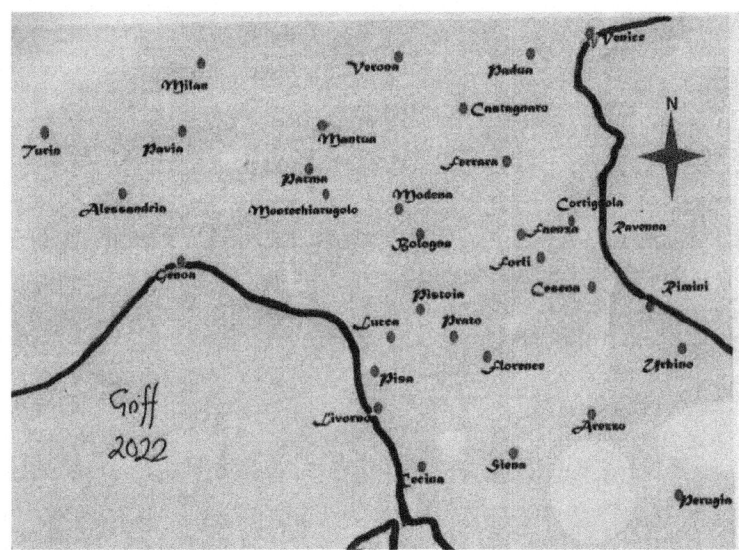

Northern Italy 1368

Chapter 2

I had not written to the mother of my children. That was not my way and it was clear that we were not expected as we rode into my yard in the late afternoon. The flurry of activity as servants ran indoors to tell Roger and Elizabeth of our arrival was clear evidence. As Michael and I dismounted Georges said, "If you do not mind, my lord, we will seek to augment the coins we are paid by you and seek employment in the town."

I smiled, "Stay here, there is room and enjoy the time off."

He shook his head and waved a hand at the others, "The deaths of your bodyguards, not to mention Pierre's wound, have shown us that we are no longer young men. When we return with you, to Narbonne, we will tell Jean that we wish to retire. We will buy land and let others work for us."

I looked at them and saw that they were about my age. I had no inclination to retire, why were they? "I respect your decision. Let me know where you stay although as I intend to hire men our paths should cross."

They left so quickly that Roger and my sons had not emerged by the time they did so. Elizabeth came out nursing another baby. She and Roger now had a family of their own. My boys ran at me and hurled themselves into my arms. They were much bigger now and almost bowled me over. I saw Michael smile.

"You have the hauberks?" John did not wait upon pleasantries. I had promised them hauberks and children remember such promises.

I adopted a serious face, "Aye, but they are dependent upon Tall Tom's report on your archery skills."

Frowns appeared and then Thomas said, "We have worked hard, father."

"We shall see." I turned to Elizabeth, ignoring her husband, "We stay until a fortnight before Easter." She nodded. "The boys will return with me to Italy," I said it firmly to remove any doubt that it might be open to debate.

"But…"

I held up my hand, "My mind is set. I shall come here no longer for this journey cost me four invaluable men. You and your husband can continue to run the manor for me and send me the profits but after Easter, I shall see neither this manor nor you, any longer."

I saw that Roger was pleased by the comment but not Elizabeth who rushed inside. My sons led us upstairs to the rooms we always occupied. They jabbered on, as we ascended the narrow stairs telling me of their prowess with sword, shield and bow. They helped us to unpack but I left the hauberks wrapped in their sheepskins. Patience was a skill that they would need.

We ate in the dining hall I had once enjoyed. If the mother of my sons thought that a stony silence and baleful glares would make me change my mind about taking my sons then she knew me even less well than I thought. I ignored her and interrogated, instead, Roger about the profits from the manor. It was another source of income for me. I had lands and manors in England and the money I accrued there was managed by my father-in-law, John. I would be taking back the recent profits with me.

I nodded when he had finished, "As this is the last time I shall be here, from now on you shall send a copy of the accounts and the money by ship to England and my father-in-law. His offices are still by the river in London. I trust John and he will act as my bookkeeper."

I saw that my barb had struck home, "And that means that you do not trust me, Sir John."

I gave him a thin smile, "Not really, Roger. You changed from the warrior who stood hard by me and defended me when you bedded Elizabeth. I do not blame you but I do not like change." Our eyes locked and he nodded. He understood. It was better to be held in contempt by me and yet retain a fine home and have a living that was free from danger. In many ways, the new arrangement would suit him. I would not be making infrequent visits to criticise him. I knew that I was risking smaller profits from the manor but that did not worry me. On the voyage west, I had already begun planning where to raid and make more gold in Italy. The news that the Doge of Florence had reneged on his word added fuel to my desire to take from Florence and her allies.

I did not see Tall Tom until the next day. John and Thomas looked fearful as Michael and I approached the archer. "Well Tom, how are they?"

The boys held their breath but Tom smiled, "They have worked hard, my lord, and given that they continue to practise every day then within seven years they will be able to draw a war bow."

I smiled and nodded to Michael. Like a conjurer, he produced the two cut-down hauberks made for me by my weapon smith. They had been taken from two dead Perugians. The youths were a little older than my sons and little adjustment had been necessary.

"You may try them on although your mother will need to make you a padded smock to wear beneath."

They donned them and taking their wooden swords and shields began to spar. There would be bruises and perhaps blood, but they would harden. I saw, already, the effect of Tall Tom's daily efforts. Still young, they were filling out more than the other boys on the manor and as I had discovered when they had greeted me, they were far bigger than they had been the last time. Elizabeth was feeding them well.

"I thank you, Tom, for your work." He nodded but I saw that there was something preying on his mind. "Speak Tom. I am not Master Roger and I play no games here."

"I would return with you, Sir John, to Italy. I had thought I tired of war but I have not." He looked around and then came closer, "The archers here are lazy and do not work. Most could not hit the shortest mark we have in England."

"I thought you wanted a family."

"I did but the woman I chose did not choose me. She ran off with a soldier heading to join Sir John Chandos in Spain."

"I heard he was back in Poitou. Up near Poitiers."

"He is and she is still with him."

"Of course, you may come and you can come with me to Bordeaux when we hire archers and men at arms. You still have a good eye for archers, I take it?"

He laughed, "I thank you for the compliment, Sir John, but yours is the best when it comes to choosing warriors. However, I fear that you will find few."

John had used his foot to trip Thomas who cried out, "Unfair! You tripped me."

I shouted, "There is no fairness in war, Thomas, use your eyes and your mind."

"Aye, father."

"Why will I find few? Bordeaux still has ships arriving from England does it not? There is neither civil strife nor border wars in England so why will I find few warriors?"

"Because the French are winning in Poitou and King Edward is bolstering Sir John's army. He has enforced the terms of service initiated by his grandfather, Longshanks, and every decent archer now works for the crown."

I believed Tall Tom. "Nonetheless we will try. There may be men who wish to line their own purses rather than work for their lord of the manor."

"Such men often prove to be untrustworthy Sir John."

"And that is why I need you, to see through the veil of deceit."

Christmas was but a week away and I needed to begin to seek men before that. There would be little point in trying to recruit during the twelve days of Christmas. We left a few days later. I left the boys with their tutor. They would continue their education in Italy but the journey back there would be devoid of lessons, save those of survival. They were unhappy but they knew that I was not a father who would relent on such matters.

Georges had sent word that the four men had found employment guarding the inn and whores at the *'Prince's Feathers'* by the harbour. It was a good place to begin. My name was well known in these parts despite having spent the last few years in Italy. There were men who had fought at Poitiers who remembered my knighthood. I was accorded respect as well as fear for my reputation as a man who did not mind offending popes was also well known.

The four men and the innkeeper, Gaston, confirmed all that Tall Tom had said. "If there are ten archers in the whole of Bordeaux, Sir John, I would be surprised."

"And knights? Men at arms?"

The five of them shrugged and looked at each other. Gaston said, "Knights and men at arms stay in the better parts of Bordeaux, my lord."

"Spread the word that I seek archers and men at arms, not to mention, knights. I will pay them a daily stipend until we leave for Italy and they shall be fed and housed."

Michael had been silent but he spoke up at my words, "The ones you attract will be the ones with nothing, Sir John."

I smiled, "And often they prove to be the best of men for if a man is drowning and someone throws him a rope then that ties them together. I am a good judge of men, Michael, do you not remember Karl von Sturmz?"

He smiled, "Aye, I do."

I stood, "Tom, stay here and seek archers. Michael and I will visit the seneschal in the castle. If I do not let him know I am back in Bordeaux he might become offended."

Michael shook his head, "You managed that, Sir John, the last time we were here and you refused to join Sir John Chandos."

He was right, of course, and I headed for the castle in low spirits. When I saw the standard of the Black Prince flying from the tallest towers of the castle then my spirits fell even lower. I knew Edward of Woodstock and the meeting would not be a pleasant one. I steeled myself and spoke, first to the sentries and then the pursuivant who reported to the seneschal. We were made to wait in an antechamber with other nobles seeking an audience with the future King of England. That I did not need to seek the audience and was merely paying my respects mattered not. I was viewed with suspicion.

We cooled our heels for an hour. We were served wine and brought titbits to eat but I was not good at waiting. The pursuivant eventually beckoned us to a small chamber. Edward of Woodstock was there with his secretary, a priest, who was making notes. "Your squire can wait without, Sir John."

I waved Michael back outside. He would keep his ears and eyes open. The last time I had been with the man known as the Black Prince, had been before I had become a mercenary. I had served in the Rhone Valley. My parting from both the prince and his father had been bitter. Having knighted me after Poitiers he and his family thought that they had bought me. They had not.

"Are you still a mercenary, Sir John, or have you come to your senses and realised that you are an Englishman who should serve his country?"

"I am contracted, Prince Edward, to serve the Lord of Milan and defend his land. Until I am released I cannot, in all honour, leave his service." I did not add that I did not wish to leave.

His eyes narrowed, "You have lands here, I believe?"

"I do, my lord."

His face broke into a grin, "Then I call upon you to come to my parliament in January at Saint-Émilion for I wish to have a hearth tax."

I kept a straight face for the tax would not affect me, just Roger and Elizabeth. I also knew that the parliament would just be a way to try to make me fight for England again.

"I shall be there, my lord."

He viewed me suspiciously but my words had not hinted at objection. He smiled, "This is better, Sir John. The wars in Italy are petty little disagreements. Here in Aquitaine, we fight the old enemy, France. With men like you and your company, we could take the whole of France and reclaim the land that was stolen from us."

"My lord, I command but a few hundred Englishmen. We are called the English Company by some but that is because I lead them. We call ourselves the White Company and there are Italians, Germans, and Hungarians in its ranks."

The prince had an astute military mind, "Yet it is your English archers who make you supreme, is it not?"

"And you, Prince Edward, have twenty times the number of archers that I command."

"But are they commanded by the hero of Crécy, the archer who was knighted after Poitiers?"

"You flatter me, Prince Edward, for there were other archers there and we all served England."

"Perhaps." He turned to the priest, "Include Sir John's name amongst the lords summoned to the parliament." The priest nodded and Prince Edward dismissed me, saying, "You may leave."

As soon as I re-entered the antechamber every head switched to view me. I sought Michael and saw him speaking with, by his spurs, a knight. I headed for them. Michael looked animated, "Sir John, this is Sir Richard of Telford."

I nodded to him. He said, "Sir John, I have heard much about you."

I was noncommittal, "If they were my friends, they would have flattered me and my enemies, of which I have many, would call me a scoundrel."

He smiled, "They were from both camps but I like to make up my own mind."

Michael said, "Sir Richard has fallen on hard times, Sir John. He has been ordered to come here with his five archers and serve Prince Edward."

I asked, "And this does not please you, Sir Richard?"

He looked around nervously, "We should talk away from this place, Sir John, for there are ears. Let us walk by the river, eh?"

Intrigued I led the two of them out of the castle. Outside we were greeted by his squire and his five archers. I had not seen them when we had entered for I had been distracted by the standard of the Black Prince.

"Michael, speak with these men. Sir Richard and I will walk some steps ahead." Michael knew what I wanted, privacy. He would ensure that the squire and the archers were not privy to my conversation with Sir Richard. "You may speak openly for no matter what my enemies have said I never betray a confidence."

He chuckled, "That was not a criticism levelled at you, Sir John." He sighed, "I have a small manor close to Telford. We were prosperous but when the pestis secunda came, it wiped out my whole manor, including my family. I was here, serving with Sir John Chandos and we escaped."

"Pestis secunda?"

"The Black Death. The disease not only robbed me of my family but also my income. I am without funds. I sought permission from the prince to return to England. There are money lenders there from whom I could find the money. I would replant what was taken from me."

"The prince refused."

"He did. He said England's need was greater than mine."

"Join me and you need no bankers. Serve with me for a year and you will have coins. Serve for longer and you will return a rich man."

He stopped and stared, "A mercenary!"

I shook my head, "Do not be so offended, my friend. We fight as knights and we are honourable. The difference is that we are well paid for our service. When we win, we profit. When you fight for England, it is the Plantagenet family who benefits. Trust me I fought at Crécy and Poitiers. I know."

"It is tempting but what of my archers? They have stood by me and I would not abandon them."

"Sir Richard, with respect, they are more valuable than you and your squire. In a perfect world, you would also have some men at arms but the seven of you would do. Do your archers ride?"

He shook his head, "No matter, we have time to train them."

"What of the prince? He will expect me at the muster."

"Leave that to me. All I need is a decision from you."

"I need to speak to my men."

We had reached the inn and I said, "I will go with my squire and enjoy some ale. If your answer is aye then come and join me, I will buy you and your men food."

I knew, by the lean looks on the seven faces that they had been living on short rations. "Thank you, Sir John. I think that those who speak well of you have the right of it."

Tuscan Warlord

After our eyes had adjusted to the gloom of the inn I saw more good news, or what I hoped was good news. Tall Tom was speaking with two archers. Both looked like veterans. As I neared them, they stood and I waved them back down, "Sit. I care not for ceremony."

Tall Tom said, "This is Garth and this is Egbert. Both are archers and served in Spain. They were here to seek a ship home." I cocked my head to the side asking the obvious question.

"I am Garth, my lord, and we served Sir Geoffrey of Brough. He died of the pestilence in Spain and we were left without funds. We were abandoned."

That surprised me, "Were you not needed as archers?"

"We fell out with his son who took over and he dismissed us. He owed us pay. We have taken three months to reach here. Until we met Tall Tom here, we had decided to return home."

He paused and I added the question I knew was coming, "But…"

"But Tom said we might sign on with you and make our fortune." I heard the doubt in his voice.

I put my hand in my purse and pulled out a handful of coins. They were all golden florins. "This is the loose change that I carry about with me. You know that I was an archer once?" They both nodded. "As archer to archer, I tell you that you will earn twelve of these for one year of service and if you sign now then your pay begins today as well as your board and lodging."

Egbert said, "And if we like it not?" He saw my frown and said, "We hear that many of your men are Germans and Hungarians. We trust only Englishmen."

I smiled, "You will find the German, Hungarian and Italian warriors are good fellows too but rest assured, you will serve with English archers. To answer your question. You leave whenever you wish but you will only have the pay for the time you have served." They looked at each other and nodded. "Tom, take them back to the hall. I have more men to see."

The two new archers both gave a half bow and Garth said, "Thank you for this chance, Sir John, we will not let you down."

"Believe me, you will earn the gold I pay you but you will be fighting in the finest company of warriors, commanded by the best condottiere in the whole of Italy, nay, Europe."

They all left smiling. I had sounded vain but I knew that I was speaking the truth and a man who does not know his own worth makes a poor leader.

When, as Michael poured our second goblets of wine, Sir Richard and his men walked in I knew we had made a good start to recruit the men I needed. We ate and drank well. Sir Richard and his squire had horses but the archers walked. By the time we reached my hall the effect of the drink had worn off. Tom had taken charge and accommodated the men in the warrior hall. I had no idea what Roger would use it for once I no longer visited the manor but for now it was a warrior hall once more. I saw his frown when we arrived. He would have to find more food. The stablemaster would have more work and fodder would be needed. I cared not. Roger had an easy life compared to many men.

We found no more men before Christmas but the nine we had hired were nine more than I had expected. I told Roger that he would be needed to go with me to the parliament at Saint-Émilion. He was not happy about it, "But you are the lord of the manor, Sir John. Why am I needed?"

"Because, Roger, I will be an absentee lord. You will become the constable of this manor and any commitment made to Prince Edward will be fulfilled by you. Surely you would like to be able to voice your opinion and know, first hand, what is expected?"

He could not argue with that. The three of us left on the last day of December. Saint-Émilion was just twenty-five miles away. Had this been England then the short days would have meant leaving and arriving in the dark but we managed to make the journey beneath a weak winter sun.

The other nobles who were in Saint-Émilion were not happy to be summoned as we all knew that the prince would not call a parliament unnecessarily. He would make demands and that would involve either labour or expense. The parliament was held in the Great Hall of the castle. Our names were noted when we arrived and written on a wax tablet. They would be written down for posterity at the end of the meeting. I pointedly told the clerk that Roger was the constable of the manor. He wrote it down and that meant Roger could not evade his duty. It gave me satisfaction. Roger had given up the sword when he had taken Elizabeth to his bed. He would now endure the consequences.

Prince Edward was business-like. "We have a war to win against France and it is right that Aquitaine, Poitou and Gascony pay the price. It is not far in the future when I will ask for the warriors in your manors to join me in battle." He smiled, "That will not be until after Easter. However as we will have to hire mercenaries," his eyes coldly lit upon me, "and we know how expensive those men without a country are, I am imposing a fouage, or hearth tax, of ten sous for five years to pay for such hired swords."

There was an audible gasp not only for the amount but the time scale. One Gascon shouted, "That is unfair!"

The prince was in no mood for debate, "Call it the price you pay to live under English rule. Any who refuse to pay will have their manors confiscated." That effectively silenced all debate.

His chamberlain said, "Before you leave you will each be given the numbers of men at arms, archers and billmen that you are to provide when we go to war."

We queued with the other lords of the manor. I was the most philosophical about the whole matter. Roger would have to find the men and the coins. Bearing in mind the gold I would earn, ten sous was a drop in the ocean but Roger would have to tighten his belt. He was already chuntering away to other lords as we queued.

Before we left, an equerry summoned me back to the prince, "I would still have you fight for me Hawkwood and that door is always open."

"I have made a bed here, my lord."

His face hardened, "There are some in England who demand that you be punished for crimes against the church here in France. Thus far my father and I have resisted the demands that charges be brought against you. That may not always be so. Think about that."

I was being threatened. I had always thought that one day I might retire to England and my estates and daughter. The words of the Black Prince filled me with disquiet. Over the next years, those thoughts often entered my head and made sleep impossible.

I decided to give him more bad news at the same time, "I should tell you, Prince Edward, that I will be in Italy at Easter. You shall have the men due to you from the manor but all the men I have hired and will hire in Gascony will come with me."

One thing you could not say about the prince was that he was stupid, he was not and he understood the implications of my words immediately, "You would steal lances and archers from under my nose?" I said nothing. "Then I shall initiate proceedings so that when you step ashore in England you shall be arrested."

I nodded, "That is unfair but it is your right and when I do land I shall have my day in court before my peers. Let us see how they view what I have done." I had no intention of visiting England any time soon. I wanted to see my daughter Antiochia but she was being well cared for and did not know me. When the time was right then we would meet.

We left for home immediately. I had no intention of spending another night in an inn. We would arrive back after dark but I would have a bed that was free from wildlife. As we rode Roger said, "Where will I get five men at arms and ten archers? The billmen are easy but I only have Tall Tom now."

"No, you do not have Tall Tom for he returns with me to Italy. You need ten archers but only four men at arms for you will lead the men, will you not?"

"You are taking Tall Tom? I need him."

"Tall Tom wishes to come with me and you only have yourself to blame. You neglected the training of archers.

Tuscan Warlord

From what Tom told me you do not even insist upon a Sunday practice. I have no sympathy for you Roger."
 The rest of the journey was in silence.

Chapter 3

By the time we left Bordeaux to return to Italy, I had managed to hire another five archers and four lances. Each lance had a man at arms, squire and spearman. I had the expense of horses but that would be paid back to me when we reached Pisa. The lances came because of the meeting at Saint-Émilion. Some men decided that pay was better than conscription into an army where victory was not guaranteed. What they knew about the White Company was that even when we lost, they would be paid and as our defeats had been few and far between, if the White Company was not paid by our employer then I paid and everyone knew that.

Elizabeth was upset when John and Thomas left without a backward glance. Her new children now demanded her attention and my sons had been more neglected of late. The tears that flowed as we clattered out of the yard were too late. They never saw their mother again.

Our four guards were even more alert than on the journey west. Two of them rode ahead to scout out every town, no matter how big or small. They looked for danger of any kind. Allied to the training of archers who were unfamiliar with horses it added two days to our journey, but as I had left four days earlier than anticipated it did not harm us. The reason I left early was to avoid killing Roger. Since the parliament, he had moaned and carped about everything. If it was not for the fact that his wife had borne my two children, I would have thrown him and Elizabeth from the manor. As it was it did come to blows. Roger lost his temper and swung his fist at me. It was a mistake for he was an unfit and overweight warrior who had not had to fight for nine years or more. It showed. I blocked the punch and the one in return laid him out, unconscious on the floor. We left the next day.

When we reached Narbonne, I paid off my sentries and gave them a bonus. They had ensured my sons survived their first major journey unscathed. Indeed, the two youths grew as a result of it. Georges and the others spoke to them constantly. Jean had barely enough room for us to stay in the inn and half of the archers had to make do with the stable. They had food and ale and I knew, from my time as an archer, that sleeping in a stable was warm and usually less infested with wildlife than some of the chambers.

Each day Michael and I took my sons to the harbour to watch for the ship. I knew that Giacomo was careful and he might not arrive exactly when he said he would. Michael and I used every step to and from the sea to teach my sons. They could read and write. They could speak French, Gascon and English. They even had a smattering of Greek and Latin but they had been sheltered and cossetted in the manor and we were giving them lessons in life. We showed them the beggars and taught them to differentiate between those who were genuine and the able-bodied who simulated wounds. They learned to recognise old soldiers. I always gave them coins. When ships arrived, we told them what the flags at their sterns meant. We showed them the difference between merchant ships and pirates and smugglers pretending to be merchantmen. We drank in inns other than Jean's partly because they were closer to the port and partly to show them the rougher side of life. Living with Elizabeth and Roger had kept them cloistered. They needed to meet the worst of people for, in my experience, they would meet more of them than kind and generous souls.

When the ship appeared on the horizon, we hurried back to pay our bill and make our way to the port. Giacomo knew that we would have horses but I had not specified how many. It would take time to load them.

Jean was sorry to see us go. We had paid well and behaved ourselves. He also knew that this would, in all likelihood be the last time that we came to Narbonne. He promised to send any soldiers seeking work to Pisa. "I know that they will have a condottiere who will bring success and treasure. What soldier could ask for more? There are no certainties in battle are there, Sir John?"

"Indeed there are not."

It took a whole afternoon and night to load the horses and my men as well as the cargo of pots that Giacomo was also transporting. It meant we left on the early morning tide and that suited the Pisan captain. We took the reverse of the route we had taken west. It was longer but this time there would be no ambush waiting for us in Tuscany.

Northern Italy and Tuscany were now my land. Even though it was not that much further south than Bordeaux, the sea was warmer and that seemed to make the land warmer. Certainly, my sons felt the warmth as they stepped down from the gangplank. I knew I could leave the unloading of the horses to Michael and my new men. I strode through the town with my sons, heading for my home. People knew me in Bordeaux and I think I was welcomed but it was nothing like the reception I received in Pisa. There were smiles, waves and even cheers as I walked the few hundred paces to my mansion. There might have been noble families who did not like either me or my company but they were the ones who wished for new masters, Florence or the pope. My home felt welcoming as I walked in with my two sons. I employed old soldiers as my servants. I was not just being benevolent, these men knew my ways and were an added protection for my home. We employed a cook who came from the town each day and orders were sent for food. Before I had left, I had ensured that there were two bed chambers for the boys. One task would be for them to have new clothes bought that befitted their status. Dai's wife, Caterina, could be left to that task. I was not a wet nurse. I sent one of my men to find William. I needed my treasurer. I sent Jack White, who ran my household, to show the boys their room and give them a tour of the house which dwarfed the one in Bordeaux.

By the time I had changed from the clothes I had worn at sea and was seated with a glass of wine, William appeared. Each time I saw him, these days, he looked more and more like a successful merchant. His waistline had grown and his thinning hair grew greyer. There had been a time when he had come on campaign with us but those days were long gone. He was no longer needed there and I knew that he was far more valuable looking after the finances of both the company and me. Marriage to Bianca had changed him. He was already a father and I expected a regular supply of children. It was the Italian way and even though we were both English born I knew that we had become Italian.

I waved him to a seat and, without preamble told him of everything from the attack on the road through the meeting with the prince, the parliament and then the acrimonious parting of the ways from his sister and her husband. William was not a sentimentalist and he merely nodded. "My sister and her husband are lucky to have been gifted a fine manor in which to live. This might be the making of them." That was the extent of the concern for his sister. "I am not surprised by this news of killers. Paer will never be a warrior who will face you in battle. It remains to be seen if he can keep hold of his company. As for the Doge of Florence," he smiled, "we both knew that his word meant nothing." He gave me a warning look, "Little would be gained by trying to get revenge. We fight for money, Sir John and not vengeance."

He was right and was one of the few men from whom I would take such words. "Nonetheless when we seek contracts then one against Florence has my approval already. What of Bernabò? What are his plans?" We had allied with the Lord of Milan. The most powerful lord in northern Italy, he challenged even Pope Urban.

"He has allied himself with Cansignorio Della Scala, the Lord of Verona, and intends to make war on Mantua."

I frowned, "That seems unlikely as his niece married its lord, Ugolino Gonzaga."

William smiled, "If Bernabò had intended to take Mantua then we would be preparing to join him in the spring. No swords will be unsheathed. He does this to make the emperor intervene. The empire has no desire for war. They are still embroiled in disputes with the pope. Your partner seeks to show his influence. Besides, his wife is related to the Della Scala family. I believe she has encouraged him to help her brother."

I sipped the wine and nodded. With his brother Galeazzo, the Duke of Milan, the Visconti family were like an octopus whose tentacles wriggled and writhed to control larger stretches of Italy than the small size of Milan might suggest.

"Then we have time to recruit more men and to train them."

"We do. I had more barracks built in anticipation of recruits."

"I would like to get to five or six hundred English archers once more and at least fifteen hundred lances."

He shook his head, "We do not have that number yet. Your news of this Sir Richard of Telford is interesting. Perhaps we will acquire more lances if the effects of the plague continue to hit those who work the fields." William had never been a landowner but he understood better than any that the prosperity of a manor lay not in the lord's hall but in the ones who worked the field. The pestilence had barely touched the nobility but it had wiped out whole swathes of England. I had thought the first plague, twenty years earlier had been the extent of the plague but the second coming would mean more manors would become impoverished. Perhaps the plague might benefit us. He finished his wine.

"I will send word to England that the White Company is hiring."

Nodding my approval, I said, as he rose, "John and Thomas are with me and I will need a tutor to teach them Italian. You have one for your children do you not?"

"I do."

"Then I will have him for an hour each day. Make it early in the morning." He frowned for it would upset his routine but he knew better than to argue with me. He would have neither income nor a life but for his partnership with me.

The next day I went through the correspondence that had arrived in my absence. William's tutor appeared and the boys had their first lesson. The lesson and my reading finished at the same time. As the tutor left, I said, "When they are both fluent in Italian there will be a florin for you." The coin would be worth six months of tutoring and he smiled and bowed. Turning to the boys I said, "Fetch your cloaks and strap on your daggers. You are now part of the White Company and we all walk armed." If they thought that they were in for an easy time they were wrong. I took them to the training ground just outside the city. There was a gyrus, a circular enclosed ground where horsemen could practise and there were permanent marks set up for the archers. I took them to Long Tom who was there with Sir Robin, the captain of my archers.

Robin was one of the original men who had followed me. I had knighted him but he never used his title. He was still an archer. He beamed when he saw the boys, "Tom here told me that they had begun to tread the path of an archer."

I nodded, "And I hand them over to your charge, Robin. You have them until the noon bell. After they have eaten hand them on to Giovanni. The afternoon can see them learn to be horsemen and men at arms."

He nodded, "The archers you sent are welcome but we need more." He lowered his voice, "You can train Italians to use swords but they make piss-poor archers."

I nodded, "The new archers will need lessons in horsemanship. The journey across France was a beginning only."

That done I turned and left my sons. They would find it much harder than in Bordeaux. There they had their mother decide that they had worked enough. There would be no relenting from Robin. He had to mould them into archers and at their age, every day was an opportunity to do so.

Bernabò was still my paymaster and when he arrived in Pisa, a couple of weeks after my return I knew that I would be called to fight once more. I was happy about that for the new men I had brought and the trickle of reinforcements had yet to be blooded. You could only judge a warrior when you saw him fight. Even a defeat could teach you much about a man.

The Lord of Milan met me at the home of his friend, Doge dell Agnello. It meant that by the time I had arrived, they had enjoyed a private conference. I was ever suspicious of such meetings. Italy did that to a man. You were constantly looking for hidden meanings and were wary of allies becoming enemies. This time, however, all seemed well and I was greeted with smiles.

"My friend the doge tells me that, thanks to you, Sir John, he is secure in Pisa."

"When the White Company is present then no one would dare to cause trouble."

Bernabò went directly to the heart of the matter, "The Perugians are still causing trouble. They demand that the pope intervene and restore lands taken from them after our last victory. I believe it is at the behest of the Florentines. They need to be taught a lesson."

I waited for elaboration. I got it but not from the source I expected. The doge said, "We cannot allow Pisan soldiers to be involved in this. We have too small an army for such a war. It must be the White Company that does this."

"Then it cannot be done for I lack the numbers."

He nodded, "My son and his company, the Company of St George will accompany you. That should be sufficient to bloody their noses."

I knew the size of the company as well as Ambrogio's strengths and weaknesses. We could, if we chose the right target, do as we were ordered but I was intrigued by the use of two mercenary companies. I knew Visconti well enough to know that his mind worked differently from others. There would be something for him from this but I could not see it. However, I would have his son with me and I hoped that meant there was no treachery intended towards me.

"When would you like this lesson?"

He smiled, "There will be Perugian and Florentine spies in this city. They will report my arrival and departure. They might suspect that I come to order you to attack one or the other. Leave it until summer. That will give time for my son to reach here and for you to do that which you do best and plan for victory."

"And my pay and that of the company?"

"You mean in addition to that which you take from the Perugians?"

I shrugged, "That could be a fortune or a handful of copper coins. The White Company fights for pay in advance."

Tuscan Warlord

He took a wax tablet and wrote a figure upon it. He pointedly hid the amount from dell Agnello. He was a careful man. The amount was worth the effort and I nodded. "It will be paid in September by which time you should have been successful and returned here to Pisa." He smoothed away the figures and put the tablet on the table then sat back and smiled, "The Doge tells me that you are not yet wed. Are Italian women not to your taste?"

He was blunt. He had married and sired more children than was good for one man. He had also sired children with women to whom he was not married. The blood of the Visconti was embedded in many Italian houses. "If I want a woman then there are many I can choose,"

"And family? I have been told that your sons are here in Pisa. Daughters? They can be useful. You can marry them into noble families. Think about it. William and Sir Dai are both happily married are they not? A married man is tied to the land. I would prefer it if you were married."

I had never liked taking orders and I would certainly not take them from a man who had spread his seed across Italy. "When I am ready, I shall marry and as for being tied, two of my leaders are tied to Pisa. They are shackles enough for me."

We chatted for a while about less contentious issues and I learned more about the politics of this land. Visconti had heard that the pope wished to return to Rome. That was something he would fight. The Emperor, Charles V[th] was also a threat to the Visconti stranglehold on northern Italy. The key seemed to be Tuscany and I stored that information. If there came a time when the White Company was without an employer then that might be a fruitful land to control. Romagna was ostensibly under papal control but as the pope was still in Avignon the cities there lived autonomous and peaceful lives.

After I left, I went back to my home. I took my maps and with a pitcher of wine spent the afternoon examining them. I needed a target that was close enough to Perugia to serve as a warning but one that might not be as well defended. It took some time but by the time John and Thomas returned, accompanied by Michael, I had a target in mind. I returned the maps to their chest and chatted with my sons about their day while we awaited food. They were exhausted, bruised and battered but had never been happier. Life in Bordeaux had been dull in comparison. I had made the right decision but I now wondered if I should have made it earlier. If I had then the four dead bodyguards might still be alive. There was little to be gained from regret and from debating decisions made in the past but the deaths of Harold and the others weighed heavily upon me. Other bodyguards had died in battle. The last four were on a personal matter of mine.

I drank too much that night and woke with a thick head. I resolved to throw myself into the planning for the raid and the task of finding four more bodyguards. The former was the more urgent and I summoned William, Sir Robin, Giovanni d'Azzo and Sir Dai. They were the inner core of my leaders. Sir Andrew was a sound soldier but I knew he would have little to offer in terms of constructive advice.

I outlined what we had been tasked with. I let William know about the funding. He would need those figures to calculate the profit we might make. He seemed satisfied, "We have enough in our bank so that we can pay the men for two years if we choose to. The odd setback has been offset by great riches from our successes."

"And that is why I have chosen to attack Brufa." I spread the map out and jabbed a finger at the target.

Sir Dai nodded, "Five miles from Perugia as the crow flies but luckily for us more than twelve miles by road. Trasimene is the only danger that I can see."

The lake, Trasimene, we had used the last time to deceive our enemies meant that we had to decide before we raided it, whether we would return to the east or west of the lake.

"Giovanni, take half a dozen men, in disguise of course, and scout out the roads and the city. I would know the strengths and weaknesses and your judgement about the best way there and back. We have time. We do not travel until summer."

Sir Robin picked his teeth with a splinter of wood, "And we fight with Ambrogio again?"

Tuscan Warlord

I knew that Sir Robin did not trust other companies, "They are there for numbers. The main targets will be taken by our men, Robin. I will use the Company of St George to protect our back. Dai is quite right, the road from Perugia will take a relieving army time to reach Brufa but it can be delayed on the road. That is a task for Ambrogio but depends upon Giovanni and what he discovers."

They all seemed satisfied with the plan. "It goes without saying that all this remains secret. Giovanni, choose your men well. As for the rest of the company, we tell them that we will be raiding in summer but know not where." I smiled, "It will do no harm to let them think that this is a vengeance raid on Florence. I have already begun to make noises about the treachery of the attack in France."

Michael had not accompanied my sons and when my leaders had left, he remained. "You can still have your spurs, Michael? I value you, your opinion has as much merit as any."

My squire shook his head, "I am still learning and besides I assume that John and Thomas will be with us on the Brufa raid?"

I had hidden that thought from myself. It lurked in the dark recesses at the back of my mind and Michael's words brought it to the fore. I said, "I am loath to leave them here and yet such a raid has dangers."

Michael agreed with me, "I know. When we travelled to Narbonne from Bordeaux, I gave thought to this. Both can ride. That was one skill they learned well from Roger. The exercise and the food they enjoy means that they are much stronger. I suggest we use them as pages. They can wear hauberks and helmets. We can give them a sword and they can ride with me."

"Not holding a banner."

He laughed, "Not holding a banner. I thought that when you choose your bodyguards one could take on that task." I saw a frown flicker across his face, "Sir John, how old are you?"

I was taken aback by the question. In another, I might have thought it impertinent but Michael, I knew, was not like that. I chose to answer, "I have seen more than forty-odd summers. It is twenty years since Crécy and then I was a young man. What is the point you are trying to make?"

"That which you have just made. Twenty years ago you were a young man. You are now a condottiere. It is you who leads. Why put yourself in danger? There is not a man in the White Company who doubts your valour. Surely you must see, Sir John, that if you can distance yourself from the front line then you will have a better view of the battle and be able to make better decisions."

My eyes narrowed, "You are suggesting that I have made bad decisions?"

I saw his face stiffen and saw in him Robin and Giovanni d'Azzo. They were the only two who might have the impudence to say what he said next, "No man is perfect, my lord. let us say that some of the battles we lost might have not been as bad had you been at the rear. At Cascina, you were closer to the rear and what might have been a disaster was not."

I stared at him. My mind ran through all the battles I had fought. He was right. Sometimes I had been too close to the fighting to see the bigger picture. "You may be right. Yes, have my sons as pages. Perhaps their presence might make me less inclined to make rash decisions." It was not just Michael's words that made me agree. I was also wondering at the reason I was being sent one hundred and forty miles south of Pisa in the height of summer.

Chapter 4

Giovanni d'Azzo was an able leader. Indeed he could have easily led the White Company but he seemed to like living in my shadow. It was he who suggested a route to the west of Trasimene Lake. It would avoid paths we had trodden before. The walls of Brufa were not particularly high and he had spoken to men in the inns who had laughed off an attack on their town. They felt that the proximity of mighty Perugia kept them safe. We had sat in my hall and planned a night attack on the gates. This time I would not lead the attack. Giovanni and Dai would attack two gates at the same time. Robin and the archers would be ready to unleash death on its walls. The time we had was used well to explore every possible way of hurting Perugia and not getting hurt ourselves. By the time Ambrogio joined us in the middle of May the plans were in place. He was no longer the young inexperienced leader who commanded a company only because of his father's money. He had endured defeats as well as victories. I knew that defeats were as valuable as victories and he had learned from each one. More importantly, he was quite happy to be given the role of the rearguard and would protect our backs.

"And the division of the spoils, Sir John?"

"So long as our backs are protected then your men will be given an equal share. As for the payment from your father that is between you and him. I have negotiated a price for my men."

He nodded, "I am content then." He looked at the map, "Are there any other companies employed by Perugia? I hear Paer has but a small force."

"It is von Bongarden who commands in Perugia and has still to make up the numbers we slew in our last raid there."

"And our escape back to Pisa?"

It was my turn to smile. Men called it the smile of the wolf and perhaps they were right, "You and your men can lead the return and sack every Perugian town we pass. We will, of course, share the profits."

Tuscan Warlord

He clasped my arm and I was a happy man for he would share the dangers and that was a good thing.

I knew that our route, towards Florence, would have the Florentines panicking. They would expect us to attack them. The journey to Perugia would, perforce, be longer but that would deceive the Perugians. The land to the east of Trasimene lake was wild and untamed land. An army, so long as it had enough supplies, could disappear there. It would only be when we arrived at the village of Sant'Andrea delle Fratte, six miles from Perugia that the Perugians would be alerted to our presence and we planned to pass through that village just after dark. Ambrogio would secure the village and use it as a bastion in case we had to make a hurried escape from Brufa. Like all plans, it looked perfect when we spoke about it but I knew that many things could go wrong. Perhaps Michael had been right and I needed to distance myself more from the front line of battle. The warrior in me did not like that but I took solace from the fact that my sons would be safer if I heeded the advice of my squire.

The two companies were like a long metal snake. Ambrogio's had fewer horses and so, when we entered Florentine territory, he took some men and raided for them. It added to the illusion that Florence was our target and also increased our speed. By the time the Florentines had mustered their army, we had passed and disappeared into the uplands to the west of Arezzo. As with Florence, the warriors of Arezzo thought they were the target and they barred their towns and gathered in animals. We had our own supplies and we pushed on. Once south of Arezzo, we travelled through a land devoid of walls and, largely, people. It was rough land and the people knew they were safe as they had nothing for us to take. We made a camp on the side of Trasimene lake. We took over the small village of Magiore. When we left, we knew that they would send word to Perugia but by then it would not matter. We would be leaving before dusk and any messenger that reached Perugia would be too late to stop us for by then we would hold Sant'Andrea delle Fratte and be preparing to attack Brufa.

Tuscan Warlord

I took the opportunity of the wait to speak to my sons who had been with Michael for the whole of the journey thus far. "Tonight, when we ride, I will have no time to watch out for you and Michael will also have tasks he needs to perform. You understand this?"

They nodded. John, the elder, added, "We know that we are part of the White Company. Uncle Will told us that we are paid and we have to earn our pay. There are no passengers in the White Company and being your sons buys us no extra privileges."

It was strange to hear William referred to as Uncle Will. He was their mother's brother but I always saw him as my treasurer.

"I want no reckless acts from either of you. You both stay behind me and, if he is present, Michael."

Thomas looked disappointed, "We will be spectators only?"

I nodded, "As will I. If we are called upon to draw swords then it will be because something has gone wrong." I leaned into them, "You need to think on your feet if you are a mercenary."

"Roger told us that mercenaries were like bandits, father."

John's words were innocent enough but I became angry inside. I had known that Roger and Elizabeth had been trying to undermine me with my sons but I had not imagined it as hateful as this. "We fight because the men who live in these places do not wish to fight. We are, to many people, the law for without us they might be subject to attacks from their neighbours. Brufa will suffer because she is part of the Perugian commune and Perugia is an avowed enemy of the White Company." I was not sure I believed what I said but I knew we were not bandits. The next time I saw Roger he would suffer more than the edge of my sharp tongue. I would teach him that my Italian name, Giovanni Acuto, was more than symbolic.

It was Robin and my archers who swept into Sant'Andrea delle Fratte and took it without either inflicting a wound or suffering one. I think Robin was unhappy at his supporting role in the attack on Brufa and wished to show the others that he and his archers were still a powerful force. Leaving Ambrogio to fortify and defend the village the White Company rode on. Giovanni had been quite right. The walls of Brufa were too low and the night watch was manifestly inadequate. We spied out the walls from the safety of the woods. Giovanni knew the town better than any and led his half of the assault force to the east of the town. Dai and his men dismounted and prepared to attack. The walls of Brufa were so low that ladders were unnecessary. Men could hold shields and boost warriors to climb the defences. The trick would be to get close to the walls so that the alarm was not raised. Dai chose his men well. We counted just eight sentries on the walls. Four were on the gatehouse and two pairs of two walked to the corner towers. These were the town watch and not a professional garrison so that instead of walking apart, they walked together and it was simplicity itself to calculate when their backs were to us. Dai divided his men into four and each group scurried in the dark, using whatever shadows that they could to reach the walls. Dai took the gatehouse. They all began their ascent simultaneously. This was the part where I held my breath for if Giovanni's men made an error and the alarm was raised too early then we would have to battle to take the gates. Robin and his archers had strung their bows and loosely nocked an arrow as we waited in the eaves of the forest. There was noise on the walls, that was inevitable but there were no cries. Those who died did so silently but most were just taken such was the surprise by the attack. The lantern swung from the top of the gates told us that we had the walls and Robin and his men hurried to the gates which soon loomed open. Michael and I had just two hundred men left and we led the archers' and men at arms' horses through the gates.

"Michael, stay here with the boys and ten men. Guard the gates."

It was not a simple ruse to keep my sons safe, we had to guard an escape route in case things went awry.

Tuscan Warlord

In the event, it was almost a bloodless action. Less than a dozen men were killed and we lost not a one. We had caught them at night and most were abed. We confiscated every wagon that we could find and emptied the treasury and the recently filled granaries. The men of the town were disarmed and we had two wagonloads of weapons and armour. After sending a message to Ambrogio we set sentries and enjoyed hot food and rooves over our heads. We left the next morning. Although we had taken every horse from Brufa I knew that men would be running along the roads to reach Perugia to let them know that the fox was in the henhouse. It was now a race.

The Perugians sent an army out to stop us. Moving with wagons meant we were slower than we might have wished. They had roused every noble and soldier from Perugia. Every man who could hold a weapon was pressed into service and they outnumbered our small company. However, what we lacked in numbers we more than made up for in quality. Our vanguard, led by our two new recruits, Garth and Egbert warned us of the host that marched towards us and were between us and Ambrogio.

"Dai, take my sons and your half of the men, guard the wagons. Robin, tether your horses to the wagons and deploy before us. Giovanni, I want your men mounted here with me." There was no panic for the army from Perugia was more like a mob. The nobles led them much as they might a pack of hounds when out hunting and like hounds, the mob, seeing how few we were, bayed for blood.

I surveyed them as they charged towards us. They had not waited for orders but saw their chance to destroy us. Their lords sounded horns. I know not if they were intended to give orders but the cacophony merely created confusion. Perhaps they were to encourage the mob. It did not upset Robin and his archers who each nocked an arrow. There was no need for me to give a command. Robin knew better than any the perfect time to do so. Giovanni had the wit to fetch lances from the wagons. His squire offered one to me but I shook my head. I was mindful of Michael's words. Even if I charged with the horsemen I would not be in the fore.

"Michael, keep your horn close. When we charge, I would not have us go too far."

The Perugian fanfare must have been ordering the charge for the nobles lowered their lances and hurled themselves at us. The whoosh of the arrows would not have been heard by the helmeted nobles whose hearing would still be filled with the sound of horns. Five flights were enough to unhorse half of the nobles and to make the rest rein in. Many riders and their horses stumbled and fell over those hit before them. The mob behind kept coming and met the wall of horseflesh. As Robin switched to war arrows and sent the archers' arrows vertically more men died as arrows fell from the sky. The effect was devastating. The Perugians fell in their dozens and then, to add insult to injury, Ambrogio, having heard the noise of the horns had brought half of the Company of St George to charge into the rear of the Perugian army. They broke and fled. It was a complete a victory over Perugia as I could remember although we were not fighting mercenaries but ordinary men led by arrogant nobles. It had an unequal battle. We did not even need to use the lances. The dead nobles were stripped and the captured horses were added to our own. Confident that the threat from the east was over we reorganised the wagons in Sant'Andrea delle Fratte and left even more heavily laden than we had been. Every wagon and draught animal for miles was taken.

With Robin and his archers as our rearguard, Ambrogio and the Company of St George led us north and west. This was not the wild country east of Trasimene lake. This was fertile land filled with crops and the Company of St George took everything in their path. Each night we stayed in a defensible position, normally a village or small town. The Perugians made one more attempt to take us but Robin's acute sense of danger warned him of pursuit and the ambush of six hundred archers emptied more than eighty saddles. Perugia pursued us no longer.

It was August when we rode into Pisa. My sons were disappointed as they had expected a battle or a fight at least. They had seen nothing but for my part, I was pleased. The new men had performed well. We had suffered no losses and

Tuscan Warlord

we had taken more treasure than the pay we would receive from Visconti. Our coffers were swollen and we could enjoy our victory and enjoy a peaceful autumn and winter. William was more than pleased. He was in a good mood in any case as he had a new son. Dai was equally happy as his wife was with child too. Such domestic bliss was not for me. Despite Bernabò's encouragement to me, I had no inclination to take on a wife. Antiochia had been the woman with whom I could have set up a home but that had not been meant to be. I suspect I might have tired of even her. Elizabeth had been a comfort only when I was young. I had no desire to be married.

Our success drew more men to our white banners. Many had deserted other companies. Von Bongarden apart few enjoyed the success of the White Company. The winter passed with training and gathering recruits. I was determined not to become a fat old warrior like Roger and so I trained with my sons every day. I doubted that I would draw a bow in anger again but the exercise was the best that I could enjoy and my sons took great pleasure in trying to beat me at the mark. They never would. As Tall Tom and Robin told me, they would both be acceptable archers but neither had that skill that marks a captain of archers. Giovanni, on the other hand, was well impressed with their sword skills. I put that down to the sibling rivalry from Bordeaux. The cuts and bruises had made them all the better for it.

We had enjoyed success but I could not see the real purpose of the raid. The following year when I was summoned to Milan to attend the wedding of Lionel, Duke of Clarence and a son of King Edward of England to Violante, the daughter of the Duke of Milan, Galeazzo Visconti, I gained more insight into the reasons. I knew, from the others who were invited, that I was in elevated company. Everyone else was a duke, prince, count or marquis. I was a knight. Having said that I was sought after. Such political marriages were an opportunity for the great and the good, as well as the not-so-good, to share gossip as well as secrets. My success was noted.

Tuscan Warlord

After the speeches at the wedding feast, I sat with the brothers Galeazzo and Bernabò along with Ambrogio. Having fought alongside the young Visconti I now considered him as close to a friend as I had. The wine flowed and I ventured, "My lord, what was the real purpose for our raid last year, to Perugia?"

He smiled and the rosy glow told me that the Lord of Milan had consumed a large amount of wine, "You and Ambrogio made money did you not? Lost not a man?"

"Aye, but why?"

He leaned in and tapping the side of his nose said, "There are other parties who are interested in hiring you. I wanted a demonstration of your skill. You and I are allies now. Pisa pays you a small stipend but the doge is quite happy for you to serve me. I am negotiating for Perugia to hire your companies and to fight against the pope." He held up a hand, "The negotiations are at an early stage. I am the broker and I have to have my own fee. It will not be until next year but do you think that you can go to war with the pope?" Both Bernabò and I had been excommunicated once by the pope and I would have no problem fighting him if I had to but he was no Perugia. He had mercenary companies of his own.

I looked at Ambrogio, "What do you say?"

He nodded, "My company are all Italian and the thought of fighting a Roman pope would not appeal but this pope is from Avignon. I would need, as would you, to recruit more men but it could be done."

I nodded. Bernabò smiled, "Then keep this to yourselves for the negotiations are at a delicate stage. The Perugians fear you both and that means that half of their council wants nothing at all to do with you while the other half are desperate to hire the dogs of war that savaged them so."

As Michael and I headed home the next day I now knew why we had been ordered to raid Perugia. It was to weaken them and encourage them to make an alliance with Milan against the pope seem more attractive. I had been told to keep the news secret but that did not, in my mind, include my inner circle. I spoke with Michael as we rode south. He had a wise head on his young shoulders, "The pope is a different prospect to Perugia, Sir John. He has allies and professional armies."

"Are they as good as we are?"

"No, but they know you. You have a reputation and your methods are well known. What do we know of the leaders of the papal armies."

I nodded, "You are right. We need to make it our business to discover their strengths and weaknesses."

The others were of a similar mind. The contract was seen as a good one that would add to our coffers but like Michael, we needed intelligence about their leaders. William was not only our treasurer but our spymaster. Our company made money even when we were not fighting. He traded and he had merchants who worked for us. It was they who were given the task of bringing back information about the leaders of the other mercenary companies.

We kept recruiting and a steady supply of men came from the west. The Black Prince and his father were not having the success that they hoped. His lieutenant in Gascony, Sir Thomas Wake, the high steward of Rouergue, had been badly defeated by the French and the Gascons were unhappy at the drain on their purses and their warriors. English men at arms and archers who had come to France to fight for the Black Prince were disillusioned and the White Company seemed to be a better alternative. Our numbers swelled and our Pisan camp grew larger.

Chapter 5

Pisa 1369

Bernabò himself came to see me in the spring. This time he came to see me directly and I knew that it would involve some direct action and that we would be fighting for the Lord of Milan. "Sir John, Emperor Charles is making war on me and I have heard that he intends to take my fortress of Borgoforte." I had a good knowledge of the lands around Pisa and knew that the fortress guarded a major crossing of the Po as well as the south eastern approach to Milan. "I want your company to augment the garrison there. They are good men who guard it for me but yours are better."

"I command?"

"Of course, that goes without saying, but time is of the essence and you must leave within the week."

"Has the fortress and town been well supplied?"

"They have. The emperor hopes to take the town in spring before crops are gathered in but I have diverted what we have to the town."

"And the pay?"

"One hundred and fifty thousand florins for the company."

"And if the fortress falls?"

"Nothing." He said bluntly.

This was a test of my skill. I agreed but while the Lord of Milan visited his friend the doge, I called a hurried council of war. Unsurprisingly my leaders were all more than happy to accept the contract. As Robin pointed out our archers would enjoy the chance to stand behind walls and rain death on an enemy while Dai and Giovanni were happy that they would not be risking horses. I told Bernabò and we made the arrangements.

Had we travelled on the better roads, the ones built by the Romans then it would have been a journey of almost two hundred miles. Worse, it would have taken us close to Bologna and the Emperor would have known that we were coming. Instead, we used the smaller roads through the mountains and only joined the Roman road to the north and west of Parma. We reached the city and the fortress quickly and without too many being aware of our arrival. We entered the city at dusk. I had sent Giovanni ahead to inform the lord of Borgoforte, Antonio delle Rivergaro, of our imminent arrival. The beleaguered Lombard lord was more than happy to both facilitate a secret entry through a side gate and to give my men the best of accommodation in the fortress proper. His garrison was just two hundred strong. With just fifty crossbows and one hundred and fifty men at arms had we not arrived then the bulk of the fighting would have been done by the citizens. Imperial troops would have made mincemeat of them.

The next day I was given a tour of the town and defences by Antonio delle Rivergaro. I took Robin, Dai and Giovanni with me. Michael and my sons followed behind. The three of them had wax tablets and I shouted out comments for them to scribe. The walls were well made but I knew that it would be hard to defend them all. We would have to risk them breaching the walls. I had planned to counteract that. The bridge over the Po was the obvious route for the enemy to take but they could also approach it from the east along the Roman road. As we toured, I did not divulge my plans for I was still formulating them. Apart from the ones with me the rest of the White Company was hidden inside the fortress. When we stood on the mighty gatehouse guarding the bridge over the Po, I turned to the Lord of Borgoforte, "Men still come and go from the city?" He nodded. "Then the enemy will know of my presence but not my company. There may be rumours but arriving as we did at a side gate after dusk and not travelling through the city will make the information murkier. Keep it that way. Tell your people that I have been sent by the Lord of Milan to advise you on the defence of the city."

Antonio delle Rivergaro frowned, "To what end, Sir John?"

"I want them to think I am waiting for my company. Spread a rumour that Ambrogio Visconti will soon be arriving with the company of St George. I would have

Emperor Charles send his men sooner rather than later. I want a rash attack." I nodded to Robin, "You have plenty of arrows?"

He nodded, "We brought wagon loads. Half are bodkins."

I turned to Antonio delle Rivergaro, "And what of handguns and cannons, do you have any?"

"A few but I am not experienced in their use."

"Neither am I but I want what we have concentrated here on this gatehouse. If we can make the bridge a killing ground then we can hurt them early on and discourage them from prosecuting an attack."

Once back in the fortress I sat and studied the wax tablets and the scribblings of my squire and sons. Giovanni d'Azzo could easily have led the White Company but he always deferred to me. He offered suggestions as I formulated my plan. It was he who came up with the idea of mounting half of our men at arms. It meant that if the walls were breached then we had a force that could reach the walls quickly. They would not fight mounted, their squires would hold their mounts, but the men at arms would be able to add their strength to the townsfolk who would bear the brunt of any attack.

It was almost midnight by the time the plans were finished. We would brief the men the next day. Lord Antonio delle Rivergaro had scouts and spies spread in a half circle around the countryside and we would have warning of the approach of an imperial army. It would be slow in its approach. Unlike my company, an imperial army was made up largely of men on foot. The mounting of my men gave us an advantage. The Perugian horses we had captured had given us an abundance of horseflesh.

I had the garrison improve the defences the next day. Along with the townsfolk, they cleared the ditches and repaired any damaged masonry. Dai, Giovanni, and Robin ensured that every man knew his task. They hated being confined inside the fortress but understood the effect of surprise. When our white tabards and surcoats appeared on the walls it would be a blow to the attackers. I gambled that they might expect me but not the whole company. Our secret arrival would be the key to any chance we had of victory. As I walked the walls my constant companions were Michael, John and Thomas. My sons had learned not to chatter but the questions they asked and the comments they made showed me that they were becoming thoughtful warriors. It was Michael who was my rock. He could have had his spurs a dozen times over but he seemed to enjoy my company and had, it seemed to me, little ambition. I had not been the same. I had always been ambitious, and I still was. I was far more arrogant than any other man I knew. Perhaps it was a character flaw, I know now that a man cannot change his nature. Michael was the one who brought me down to earth, who while not curbing my ambition, gave it parameters. I was pleased that my sons were in his company so much. I could not give as much time to their education and however it turned out, it would be down to the influence of my squire.

We had cleared the ditches and repaired the mortar as well as finding timbers to strengthen the gates when the imperial army arrived. They camped north of the river and I saw that they had come prepared for a quick assault. I saw neither trebuchets nor bombards. I presumed that they were coming but such weapons are slow to move. Whoever commanded the imperial army had opted for speed and not power. Antonio delle Rivergaro asked, "Do we now reveal your men, Sir John?"

I shook my head, "Let us see what your people can do. They may not know that my men lie hidden in the fortress but they see me and my bodyguards." I shrugged, "My reputation may add to their resolve."

The north wall of the town and the gatehouse bristled with handguns and crossbows. They would provide an instant and spectacular response when the troops attacked. The attack did not come immediately. The imperial troops made camp and built a defensive stockade to prevent a sortie. I saw that they had hewed trees and intended to make rafts to cross the Po. It was what I would have done and I could not fault their commander. He thought he was fighting townsfolk with a stiffening of professional troops.

Tuscan Warlord

The next day the attack started with a mist upon the river. I had slept in the gatehouse and the sentry woke me to tell me that men were crossing the river. I sent Michael to fetch my men. John and Thomas helped me to dress for war. Antonio delle Rivergaro waited for me with his own bodyguard. He pointed, "It is a determined attack, Sir John. I estimate he is sending a thousand men." I heard the fear in his voice. We had less than four hundred men on the walls and most were militia.

"Fear not, the White Company comes but I want them encouraged by our apparent weakness. I do not want them to attack at many places around the walls. I want to hurt their first attack. Your people are ready?"

"When you give the command then every handgun and crossbow will fire or release."

The handguns were a primitive weapon, little more than a tube that sent a lead ball at the enemy but a hand gunner could be trained in an hour and the sixty or so handguns would make a spectacular noise. The mist had not cleared and explained their urgent attack but we knew the range to the river. I gambled that the rafts would reach the south bank of the Po at roughly the same time. I saw shadows as men disembarked and I gave the command. The rolling cracks of the handguns were augmented by the sound of crossbows banging too. We could not see the effect but we heard the result. Screams, cries and splashes told their own story. I yelled, to give encouragement, "Well done, men of Borgoforte, you have bloodied their noses. Do not relent. Send them to their deaths."

I was aware of white shadows moving as my archers ascended silently to the walls. The mist only hid the river and their leaders would have seen that it was just militia on the walls. Robin's men stayed hidden, helped by the mask of smoke. The second volley was more ragged and there were fewer cries for men had shields before them. Carrying ladders, they raced at our walls.

Raising my arm I shouted, "Now, Sir Robin, unleash death!"

Tuscan Warlord

The mist obligingly began to clear and my six hundred archers had the luxury of choosing targets. They were professionals to a man and knew when a bodkin was needed and when a war arrow would do. The crossbows, handguns but largely my archers, hewed down swathes of the imperial troops and they fell back in great disorder. The cheers from the townsfolk told me that I had been right. Letting the men of Borgoforte bear the brunt of the initial attack gave them confidence. Of course, the imperial leader would now know that a quick attack was not going to work. He would bring up bombards and trebuchets and batter our walls into submission. I already had a plan to deal with that. The rash attack defeated, the imperial commander set about surrounding the city and building siege works.

We watched as the imperial troops spread to the east of the city. They used the rafts they had made but wisely crossed the river further upstream and out of range of our missile weapons. We saw more troops arriving from the direction of Parma and Bologna. That made sense as the land of Milan lay to the west and the last thing the imperial troops needed was an attack on their rear from either the Lord of Milan or his son, Ambrogio and his Company of St George. We did nothing to hamper their movement as I had a plan already in my head. It refined it as I stood watching with Michael, Robin and Giovanni.

Despite the fact that we were under siege there was an ebullient mood among the defenders. The attack on the walls had been repulsed without loss and while I knew that the majority of casualties had been caused by my archers the townsfolk felt that they had driven off the attack themselves. I did nothing to disillusion them. It was late in the afternoon when we saw the bombards and trebuchets ferried across the river. They were cautious and only took one at a time. They left one trebuchet and three bombards on the north side of the river while two trebuchets and six bombards were ferried across the river. It would take time to build the trebuchets and mount the bombards.

I had seen enough and I retired to the Great Hall for a council of war with my leaders and Antonio delle Rivergaro.

His presence was a courtesy only. I began without preamble, "They have shown me their plans clearly now. I can see that they will pound our walls until they fall," I gave an apologetic nod to Antonio delle Rivergaro, "I fear they will crumble, despite our repairs, in under a week." He nodded his agreement. "It will, however, take them all day tomorrow to assemble them and put them in the right position and prepare them. Tomorrow night I will lead all of our horsemen to attack the siege weapons that lie to the south of the river and to disrupt their camp as much as we can. Robin, you and your archers will aid us by closing with their camp and loosing your arrows before we attack. You will withdraw into the walls and defend us from the battlements."

Michael asked, "Is that wise, Sir John? Surely Sir Dai and Sir Giovanni could lead the attack."

"They could but I would have the imperial troops know who it is that attacks them." When the others nodded, I saw Michael's shoulders slump. He had done his best. "I will lead the horsemen from the south gate. Robin, you and your archers will use the sally ports and the east gate. Our foot soldiers will guard the two gates."

We spent an hour or so refining the details and apportioning commanders. Sir Andrew Belmonte would act as a deputy to Sir Dai in case he fell and as Sir Richard of Belmonte had covered himself in glory at the battle of Brufa, he would act as Giovanni's deputy. I needed no deputy for both Dai and Giovanni would be leading the two halves. I was a symbol. Riding Ajax, my war horse, encased in my silvered armour and covered in my white surcoat, I hoped to draw every eye to me.

As we retired to our chamber I said to Michael, "You need to come with me, Michael."

He snorted, "Just because I think you are foolish Sir John does not mean that I lack courage. I will carry your banner and be there to guard you." I smiled and he shook his head, "What happened to your resolve to watch your leaders do the hard work?"

"I still intend for that to happen but in this battle, we either win or lose. Nothing that I could wish to change from the walls would be possible. When we fight again, I will stand in a wagon and direct the action but tomorrow night I need to be there."

I had, of course, to repeat everything for my sons who were most unhappy that they would not be with me but took consolation in the fact that I said they could watch from the east gate where they would have the best view of the night battle. One refinement that Giovanni made, the next day as we told the men their instructions, was that he suggested we had ten men in each company, at the rear, with lighted brands. Gunpowder would explode and the trebuchets could be burned. I was annoyed that I had not thought of this.

The imperial troops must have thought that our inactivity was a sign that we despaired. An envoy was sent to the bridge with a white flag to discuss our surrender. Antonio delle Rivergaro and I did not rush to the gatehouse. We stood and I allowed the castellan to speak to the envoy, Gerhard von Getz. He spoke Italian at first but when he recognised me, he switched to English. I interrupted him knowing that it would annoy him, "You may continue in Italian, my lord as I speak it fluently and I am just a guest of the castellan." My words made Antonio delle Rivergaro smile.

"You are surrounded, my lord, and tomorrow we will begin to reduce your walls. It will not just be the archers of the White Company who will die but the citizens of Borgoforte. The emperor does not wish civilians to die. If the Lord of Milan had more honour, then he would be here defending its walls rather than a condottiere and a few hundred archers." I kept a straight face but inside I was beaming. We had deceived them and they knew nothing about our lances.

Antonio delle Rivergaro spread his arms, "My lord, I have given my word to the Lord of Milan that I will defend this city against all enemies. To do other would be dishonourable. Sir John has kindly come at my request so that his archers can defend the walls. You have already seen their efficacy. Perhaps it is you who should withdraw."

The German became angry, "What arrant nonsense. I too have given my word. If that is your final answer then the slaughter that will result when we take your city is on your head, castellan."

As we walked back to the Great Hall I said, "Well done, castellan. You are a fine actor."

He shook his head, "I spoke with a courage I did not feel. If your attack fails then I might be sentencing many of my people to an early death."

"Fear not, my lord, for you have the White Company and we will teach the emperor a lesson."

The men at arms were eager for action. They had cooled their heels in the fortress during the first attack and the archers, in the usual bantering way of warriors, had let them know that they had done so. After an afternoon of rest, we led our horses to the gates we would use. Giovanni and I had concocted another surprise for the Germans, Italians and Hungarians who surrounded the walls of Borgoforte. It would be a trick and many leaders would not stoop to use such tricks. I would use any means in my power to enable a victory. Robin could be relied upon to do his part and, as the town bell tolled the hour we walked our horses from the gates. The last men had their brands, hidden by their horses and their cloaks. They would only mount once our attack began. It was a cloudy night and the lack of moon helped us. They had campfires close to their siege weapons which had been brought as close as they dared to our walls. We had no campfires before us as we emerged from the south gate. We walked our horses until we were clear of the walls and could see the campfires. We formed our lines but did not mount. We were now reliant upon Robin. I could smell the brands behind us but when I turned, I could not see them.

The first we knew of Robin's attack was when there was a sound like a flock of birds taking flight followed by the cries as the arrows descended into the camps. It was our signal. I mounted and Michael handed me the lance. I took my place as the two columns of men behind me formed up. I would lead with Michael and my banner, while Giovanni and Dai would lead two columns of men twenty men wide. Our plan was to cut two swathes through the disordered camp. I waved my lance and we moved off. I was counting the flights. Robin would send twelve flights and then fall back. Almost five thousand arrows would cause great destruction not to mention chaos in the camp but they would react. We had time to get closer to them before we charged. I wanted them to spread out with their attention on the archers. They would be desperate to get close to the Englishmen who, I hoped, had caused such destruction. When the flights stopped, I raised my lance. It was the signal for the charge.

First Dai and the men he led all chorused, "The White Company and Sir John Hawkwood."

Then as the sound echoed across to the imperial camp Giovanni and his men shouted, in Italian, "For Ambrogio Visconti and the company of St George."

I hoped, by this simple ruse, to make the enemy think that we had twice the number of horsemen than we really did. I was known to work for Bernabò and had fought alongside Ambrogio and his men twice, it was a natural assumption that they would be with us.

I am not sure how well it worked but there was a wail from before us as the men who had been pursuing the archers realised the threat from their flank and turned to face us. Few of the imperial troops had enjoyed the time to fully prepare for battle. Helmets, the occasional breastplate and the nearest weapons to hand were all that they had. As we slammed into isolated men our lances struck flesh each time they were pulled back and thrust. Any fallen and wounded men were trampled to death by the hooves of the horses. The imperial horns sounded and men hurried back to form lines. In doing so they presented their backs to us and we reaped a fine harvest. As I pulled back my broken lance, having struck eight men, I saw that they had chosen to form a line closer to the river where Robin's arrows had little effect. It was beyond the war machines and I shouted, "Michael, sound fall back."

As the horn sounded, I threw away my lance and drew my sword. Rather than fall back all the way to the walls our men knew that the signal meant to attack the camp and the war machines. The men with the brands were already piling faggots close to the trebuchets and laying trails of powder.

Tuscan Warlord

We rampaged through the camp slaying any who managed to stand against us. As the first trebuchet burst into flames there was a loud crack and bang as the first powder was ignited. The imperial horn told me that they had mounted their horsemen and would pursue us. I saw that the trebuchets were afire and would be rendered useless while the powder needed for the bombards had exploded, showering us with shards of wood. The bombards no longer had carriages, they had been burned and Sir Andrew Belmonte had attached ropes to some of the weapons and he and his men were dragging them to the ditch. Once there they could not be used against us and any attempt to recover them would result in losses.

"Sound the retreat!" The strident notes had an instant effect. My men all turned and headed back to the east gate and the south gate. The thundering hooves that followed us would not reach us before we entered the city for they had to negotiate bodies and the wreckage of the camp. They did try. I turned when we were just one hundred paces from the east gate and saw the horsemen eager to get at us and have their vengeance. The arrows from the walls emptied their saddles and we were able to walk through the gates. Leaving Michael to look after Ajax I hurried up to the walls to view the destruction.

The trebuchets were burning and they were no longer upright. Their bases had burned and the arms and throwing mechanism now smouldered on the bonfires. I saw at least four bombards in the ditch and another couple lay just a hundred paces further away. There would be no bombardment of the walls. The camp was wrecked. The powder fire had sent burning wood to set fire to tents. Already the smell of burning flesh was added to the stink of saltpetre as those killed in their tents burned.

I nodded to Robin, "A satisfactory end, eh Robin?"

He nodded, "And Sir Andrew has gone up in my estimation for that was clever of him. The city can recover the bombards and use them to defend the city."

I was too full of the thrill of battle and success to sleep. I walked the walls. Michael fetched food and wine and Dai

Tuscan Warlord

and Giovanni joined me. It became clear that our victory was far greater than we could have hoped. As the sun rose, we saw a gaggle of imperial leaders engaged in what was clearly a heated debate as men combed through the camp to salvage what they could. As the church bells tolled the ninth hour, I saw that the enemy had decided that they had lost and were packing up their camp. It was over and we had won.

Chapter 6

I think that the leaders of the defeated enemy were keen to leave quickly for they abandoned their camps as quickly as any army I had ever witnessed. My company spent a day picking over the detritus they had left. We also helped the castellan recover the bombards. They could be mounted over the gatehouses and would deter any future attacker. We left for the long ride back to Pisa. We followed the same route we had taken when we had travelled north for I was wary of an ambush.

The payment for our service was swiftly delivered. I am not sure that the Lord of Milan believed we would defeat an imperial army so quickly but he was grateful and, for once paid us promptly. We had lost but a handful of men. One had died when his horse had tripped over a hidden guy rope while the other casualties had suffered minor wounds. Some of the men with brands had endured burns from the exploding powder and two had been hit by flying debris. They were more than acceptable losses. Dai, of course, was keen to be with his wife and I noticed that Giovanni also left my side with great alacrity. He was courting a Pisan woman, the daughter of a rich merchant. Michael and I, along with my sons, enjoyed a bachelor's existence.

That ended when Bernabò made another visit, this time, directly with me. He had me dismiss my servants and even Michael. I knew that whatever he was going to divulge he wished it kept secret. As soon as he explained to me the reason for the attack on Perugia it confirmed what I had already surmised. "I have made an alliance with Perugia. We will aid them in their fight against the pope and his tentacles."

My attack had been to show Perugia the value of my company. The defence of Borgoforte had been to establish that the White Company was the pre-eminent band of mercenaries in Italy and that explained the prompt payment. If Perugia wanted to hold out against the pope, then it was not von Bongarden's Germans and Hungarians they needed but the Englishmen and Italians of the White Company. While I felt used, I was also flattered. Bernabò's plan had been both convoluted and inspired.

"And how much are we being paid?"

"One hundred thousand florins."

"For?"

"For a year. The pope is gathering his men to send them against Perugia. It is all part of his plan to gain the territory that lies closer to Rome so that he can return there from Avignon."

"And that is why you ally with them for you do not wish that to happen."

He beamed, "Every day, Giovanni Acuto, you become more Italian. Marry one of my daughters and the transformation will be complete."

I laughed, "When I am ready then I might consider your proposal. What happens next? My men have just had a hard march north to defend your city. Their animals need time to recover."

"I understand that but you must go to Perugia and prepare to defend the city. I know that you have attacked it before now. The Perugians need you to assess how best to defend it. The company can follow in a month or so. It will take you some time to see all the weaknesses."

I nodded, "And my fee will be ten thousand florins."

His eyes narrowed and then laughing, he nodded, "An Englishman who can negotiate. You truly are changing. Very well. You will need to leave within the week. As soon as the news gets out that you are to take command then the pope will rush men to take Perugia before you have the chance to make it defensible."

I knew he was right. As soon as he had gone, I sent for Michael and William. I explained to them what I would be doing. "I will need just my new bodyguards, Michael."

"And John and Thomas?"

"I am not sure."

William said, "They will be most unhappy to be left behind, Sir John. They should be safe enough travelling to Perugia."

I turned and snapped at William, "As someone who never leaves the safety of the walls of Pisa, I hope you do not mind if I totally ignore your advice." He recoiled and I snapped, "You are a good bookkeeper but you know nothing about aught else."

I saw Michael hiding a smile. He had commented before now about the airs and graces now adopted by William. I suppose it was understandable. He had married the doge's daughter and was accustomed to associating with the wealthy families of Pisa.

In the end, I did take my sons but the main reason was that since I had taken them from Bordeaux I had found that I actually liked being in their company. They were both hardworking and reminded me of Dai and then Michael when they had been youths. I did not want to spend months apart.

I told Robin, Giovanni and Dai what we would be doing and asked them to bring the company to Perugia in August. That would be the time that the pope's men would seek to ravage the land when the harvests were being gathered in. Jack of Nottingham led my new bodyguards. They had been the four men who had shown the greatest courage in the battle of Perugia. They were paid extra and accorded more privileges. Bearing in mind the fate of Harold and the others, they would earn the extra pay. We went nowhere near Florence for obvious reasons and we took the road that led close to Arezzo. I was not a fool and we avoided every major town, stopping when we had to, in small towns or large villages. I rode Remus and did not wear my usual livery. We travelled incognito. Two bodyguards rode before us and two behind. One led the sumpter with our war gear.

It was pleasant to ride through land which, unusually, was peaceful. We rode early in the morning and in the early evening to avoid the heat. We tried to find a shaded town with an inn at noon. We had ridden hard to get beyond Arezzo and found a village which, whilst it had no inn, had an obliging farmer's wife who was happy to provide us with food while the farmer had a porticoed veranda where we could eat.

Tuscan Warlord

The two crossbow bolts that killed Lemuel and Hal came from some trees and the six Germans who burst from the interior of the farm had their swords at our throats before we could react. Another twenty men emerged from the trees. I had to admire their ambush. It was well-planned and I could not see how it could have failed. The farmer and his wife had been complicit in the action but I could not blame them for it. I would, when I had time and freedom, punish them but for the moment I handed my sword over as a sign to the remaining bodyguards that more bloodshed was unnecessary. Their faces told me that they wished to fight but I knew the futility. I also had my sons to consider. They might not be the targets for the Germans' weapons but in a close fight, they might be hurt.

"Wise, Sir John." They must have been shadowing us and knew us for the leader turned to Michael and said, "Take your two men and return to Pisa. The ransom for Sir John and his sons is one hundred and fifty thousand florins." He smiled. They had known how much we had been paid and that meant a spy in Pisa. Michael nodded. "You will bring the gold to Florence. The doge is anxious to speak to Sir John."

I said, "I take it we can finish our food first?"

He nodded and then laughed, "You have courage, Sir John."

I shrugged, "And I am guessing signora that as you have been well paid by these papal mercenaries that there will be no charge?"

She put a cloth to her mouth, "We had no choice, my lord. What could we do?"

I said nothing but began to eat. I had been well and truly caught. Had my sons not been with me then I might have attempted an escape but they tied me. I would have to go along with what they said and wait for the ransom to be paid.

My two bodyguards left with Michael glaring at the Germans. They would seek vengeance. Michael was more practical. With luck, I could be freed in a week. To ensure that I did not escape the three of us had ropes tethered to our bridles and we were each flanked by two men. The leader,

Tuscan Warlord

Gerhardt von Stroheim, knew his business and was taking no chances. He avoided Arezzo and made directly for Florence. I knew that he would be safe for I had no allies along this road. At best the people might be neutral toward me. I put my mind to the problems of a spy in Pisa and what I would do about Perugia. All sorts of plots and plans filled my mind like a nest of vipers suddenly awoken. Was the Perugian alliance a trick to lure me, alone, away from my army? That seemed likely but I could not see Visconti allying himself with Florence, then again, I had not envisaged an alliance with Perugia. The Lord of Milan was a chess player and might be thinking five or six moves ahead. When we stopped my sons were kept apart and that was deliberate. I was known for my sharp mind and they wanted no devious plan concocted to help us to escape. I had no opportunity to speak to my sons save on the road and there we had six pairs of ears to hear what we said.

As we neared the walls of Florence Thomas said, somewhat fearfully, "What will happen to us, father?"

I tried to reassure my youngest son, "We have been trapped but they want money. William will send the coins and then we will return to Pisa."

The snorted laugh of the German next to me made me turn to stare at him. He said nothing but I saw, in his eyes, knowledge. He knew something that I did not and I did not like it.

Despite the fact that I was not wearing my white surcoat I was recognised. I had been a thorn in Florence's side for many years. I had taken coins from them each time I had fought them. I had paraded outside their walls and they knew me. I also suspected that the doge had been forewarned of our arrival and spread the word for there were more people on Florence's streets than I might have expected. Surprisingly there were few jeers and catcalls. It seemed to me that they were curious about the man who had caused them so much financial hardship and inflicted military disasters upon them. They wanted to see the monster who had now been caught and curbed.

Tuscan Warlord

We reached the palace and our horses were taken away. I took a coin from my purse and flicked it at the stable hand who led Remus away, "Care for him well and when we leave there will be another." He nodded. I had given him six months' pay.

We were taken into the largest room of the palace and I expected it to be crammed full of Florentine nobles but, instead, there was just a cardinal, whom I did not recognise, and the doge of Florence. There were, of course, guards who stood at the doors and flanked the two men on the dais but that was all. As we were led before them I saw why they had done this. It was to make us feel small. The huge hall dwarfed us and the two men on the thrones stared down at us. Even if we were not kneeling it felt as though we were. This had been well thought out and my mind wondered when the trap had been set.

"Thank you, von Stroheim." The doge threw a purse at the German who deftly caught it. The cardinal threw a second.

The mercenary nodded, "Gold is always acceptable, my lords, your eminence, but I would have done this for nothing. This Englishman has been responsible for the deaths of many of my friends and family." He turned to me and said, with an evil grin upon his face, "Enjoy your incarceration, Sir John."

I did not like the tone or the implications.

When he had left, I spoke, "The German said incarceration but my ransom will be here within the week. This will be but a brief sojourn."

The two men exchanged a knowing look and the doge said, smoothly, "It may be longer than that, Sir John. In your absence, there has been a change in Pisa. Giovanni delle Agnello is no longer the doge. He and Griffo have been expelled and now reside in Milan. It was a bloodless coup." He was enjoying himself, "Had you been there perhaps you might have prevented it but you were busy trying to make war on the pope. I do not doubt that your ransom will be paid but your company has been expelled from Pisa and I suspect your William Turner is a little busy. That is the problem with marrying into noble families is it not, Sir John, when disaster strikes it spreads like the ripples on a lake?" He nodded to the guards, "Take them to their chambers and have them provided with clean garments and washcloths. They stink." It was an insult but I bore it. Riding sweaty horses in the hot Italian sun would make any man stink. Such insults could be borne but the disaster of a coup was another matter. As we were led away, I once again regretted bringing my sons. If they were not with me then I would escape. Their presence guaranteed that I would not.

We were taken to different rooms. I was taken to my room first and that made sense. They did not want me to know where my sons would be kept. "Do not worry, John, Thomas, you know that Michael, Robin and Giovanni will be working out a plan to free us. Trust in our men."

"But the ransom, father?"

"Trust to my friends." I was pushed inside but John's words made me wonder. Our money was in a bank in Pisa. It was guarded but the security relied on the presence of the White Company. I also wondered if Dai and William had left Pisa with the doge. The daughters of the doge were now a leaden weight rather than a ladder. I undressed and washed. I saw that they had provided me with a bag of lavender to wear beneath my clothes, a swete bagge. When I had washed and dressed, I sat on the bed and considered my situation. Either my company would come for me or the ransom would be sent. Both would take time. Robin, Giovanni, and Michael were all clever and would not risk a full assault on the city. If they came for us, it would be quietly and using stealth. That could take a month or more. The ransom might be forthcoming but that, too, might take a month. I had to be patient and learn as much as I could in that time. I needed to be ready to flee whenever the opportunity arose but first, I had to find out where my sons were being held.

I discovered that when we were taken down to eat. The guards who took us were not the German mercenaries but Florentines. Unlike the Germans, they did not speak English. The smile I adopted as I spoke to my sons made them assume that my words were innocent. "Where are your rooms?"

John spoke and he took his cue from me, he smiled, "There is a guard room next to yours and we are in the next room. A guard has his bed in the room. Do we escape?"

"Not yet but be ready."

It was a small victory but I revelled in it.

The high council was at the feast. My sons were at the lower end of the table and I was seated next to the doge. He beamed the whole night as though it was he who had ridden to take me. Men gloated at my fall from grace. There was open laughter when they spoke of my vaunted company being evicted from their home and that the ransom might not be coming. One said, "You may become a permanent fixture here, Sir John. How do you feel about that?"

Emboldened by my victory I slowly sipped the wine, wiped my mouth and said, "It could, of course, save me one hundred and fifty thousand florins if the White Company and the Company of St George come to take me hence. How do you feel about that?" While it wiped the smile off some of the faces the cardinal and the doge were unperturbed.

The doge reassured the noble who had asked the question and now looked fearful, "Fear not Don Giorgio, the White Company will do nothing. The pope has ensured that his men are ready to pounce if the White Company heads for Florence."

That told me much. The papal lands were not concentrated in one place. Cities like Ancona, Urbino, Gubbio and the like supported either the pope or the emperor but they were controlled by neither. Imperial cities lay further north but papal enclaves lay dotted between the great city-states. Usually, papal troops ensured their safety. The pope had clearly concentrated his forces in northern Italy to thwart the White Company. Every piece of information, intelligence and knowledge that I could gather was valuable. William's merchants had once been our spy network but since his marriage, he had concentrated more on mercantile matters. I saw now that was a mistake. Hindsight was always perfect. When this was over, I would have Giovanni create my spies. I had been caught because I was blind. A lesson I would learn would be to keep spies in every city in northern Italy. The spy in Pisa who had betrayed me had been one of the Pisan council. Poor Giovanni delle Agnello had been the one who had been duped, not I. I saw, as I was taken back to my room, that I had not been betrayed by Visconti. He was the enemy of the pope and seeing the cardinal identified my enemy clearly. They had used Florence to get what they wanted, the thorn that was Sir John Hawkwood removed from their side. They now had free rein to do as they wished.

Having spoken once I was able to speak to my sons each time we were taken to our rooms and to dine. We were allowed to exercise once a day in the courtyard. We were watched and loaded crossbows guarded us but we could talk. My words gave them reassurance. Surprisingly Thomas was not the more fearful of the two, it was John who kept as close to me as he could when we walked. I used the opportunity to teach my sons how to observe. The first morning I nodded up to the crossbows on the walls, "They watch us with loaded crossbows but that is a mistake. Like a bowstring, the cord on a crossbow becomes weaker if it is kept taught. It will not send the bolt as far. Now if they used archers which, thank the Lord they do not, then they could nock and loose an arrow in a heartbeat."

I taught them about the armour of the Florentines. Only the nobles wore plate and mail. Most of the guards who watched us wore court bouillon, boiled and hardened leather. It was effective against bladed weapons but even a war arrow could pierce it. I told them of the weapons that we might fear, the glaive, the long, curved pole weapon that was similar to an English billhook and could take a horse's leg or pull a man from his mount. The lessons I gave them would make them better leaders. Tall Tom and my men at arms had trained them to use a sword and a bow but when they led men they would need to think of how to use the different arms to their best effect. My words also seemed to make John less fearful.

By the end of the first week, we had established a routine and it helped to stop my sons' spirits from sinking into their boots but even I was becoming despondent. I had hoped that the ransom would have been on its way but when we dined it was clear to me that the doge knew the ransom was not forthcoming. He took delight in taunting me with that knowledge. I had told my sons that every scrap of news was valuable and so it proved. My company was still a formidable body. They had been evicted from Pisa but they had not deserted. Delle Agnello was in Milan as was Bernabò Visconti but his son was in Borgoforte. The Doge of Florence told me that to dishearten me but it did not. Ambrogio had been north of Milan the last time I had heard of him and now he was moving south. Perhaps we might be saved the expense of one hundred and fifty thousand florins. I had my sons exercise when we walked around the courtyard. To the great consternation of our guards, we began to run. Their fear that we might be trying to flee made my sons laugh, for we were just exercising as we ran along the cobbles in boots that were designed for riding and not running. We endured the laughter for I knew that the running would harden my sons.

    A fortnight later Michael and Giovanni, escorted by Sir Andrew and twenty men at arms brought a wagon with the ransom through the streets of Florence. That it was unexpected was clear from the faces of the cardinal and the doge both of whom looked as though they had eaten bad fish. They pointedly counted out every coin and ensured that every florin had been paid. Their snarling dismissal gave me great satisfaction. They had expected to hold us longer.

    While I was desperate for information from Giovanni and Michael, I made sure that I rewarded, when my horse was brought, the stable hand. Remus' coat gleamed. I gave him two gold coins and said, "Thank you, my friend, you, at least have honour. When I return to Florence, I will reward you again."

    I saw the look of fear on the face of the doge. Giovanni was smiling when he said, "You had better hurry, Sir John, for our archers are anxious for your return. I would not like them to loose five thousand arrows into the city. We have

Tuscan Warlord

paid the ransom and despite the discourtesy shown by the doge I would not have unnecessary deaths."

I saw then that my company had remained loyal and not let me down. We rode through streets filled with fearful faces. The Doge of Florence must have told his people that I would be a permanent fixture. Now I was free and they would fear my revenge.

Chapter 7

I waited until we were reunited with Robin and a hundred of his mounted archers guarded our rear before I let loose the torrent of questions that I had in my head.

Giovanni answered most of them, "The coup was well handled, Sir John. We trained the Pisan army too well. They took William and Sir Dai, as well as the doge and they surrounded the bank. They could not, of course, get into the bank but they could stop us from taking your ransom. Von Bongarden and his men appeared at the same time." He shook his head, "We were defeated by deceit. We could have fought but that would have resulted in many deaths. We withdrew to Lucca where we were welcomed. Delle Agnello is still popular there."

"William and Dai?"

"Still held but they have not been harmed."

"How did you get the ransom?"

Robin answered that one, "The men had the pay you gave them and the men of Lucca found the rest. You will have to pay it back, of course, but you are free."

"And I will see that they are all repaid every florin. Did you find the spy?"

They all looked at me, the questions now on their faces, "The spy?"

"Yes, Giovanni, they knew we were on that road and when we were travelling. As the doge was removed from office and Visconti lost an ally it cannot be those. We have someone to find."

"That could take time, Sir John. We know, from the coup, that there were many Pisans opposed to the doge and therefore you."

I nodded, "Then we will need to be wary when we return to Pisa. They will expect us to cool our heels in Lucca and lick our wounds. Let us surprise them and do that which they do not expect."

Robin laughed and held out his hand, "I told you that he would not take this lying down. Gold, Sir Andrew." The

English knight handed over five florins. Robin knew me better than any of my other leaders, Giovanni included. "What do you plan, Sir John?"

"We strike immediately but not at Pisa. You are quite right Giovanni, there is little point in fighting Bongarden. A softer and more lucrative target will be the papal lands hereabouts. Sir Andrew, you go to Lucca and fetch the army. We will meet you just outside Pisa."

He galloped off with the other men at arms. Giovanni said, "We are not welcome any longer in Pisa."

I shook my head, "That was when they thought that Sir John Hawkwood was a prisoner. Michael, did you bring my banner?" He nodded. "Then we unfurl it outside the east gate and let them know I am alive. I want the new doge and his leaders to be nervous. When we have met with the rest of the company I will send a couple of men to Bernabò. I assume that is where the doge took refuge?"

Giovanni nodded, "And all his family. William and Dai are still in Pisa."

"Good, then we know where their loyalties lie. I am glad now that I did not take up the offer of a daughter of the doge. And the bank is still in our hands?"

Robin laughed, "Aye, Sir John, the men we pay to guard it value their income and none dare breach its walls. However, it may be that putting all of our eggs in that particular Pisan basket may not be the best idea."

As we rode towards Pisa Giovanni and Robin interrogated me about my plans. I had not expected to be freed so quickly but I had already planned what I would do. We were now without an employer. Technically it was Pisa and Visconti who paid us. I now had the freedom to choose my own targets. We would become a warband who raided for profit but it would also ensure that our enemies knew we were far from finished.

"I intend to raid every papal town, city and farm. I will become a warlord and use the power of the White Company to hurt the pope. He values his income. We shall deny him that which comes from Emilia-Romagna. Cesena and Faenza shall be our first targets and we shall spread our net wider until we can return to Pisa. We will take the florins we are owed from the pope."

Michael said, "You sound confident, my lord, did not your incarceration give you doubts?"

I laughed, "If anything it made me more confident. We should not have been taken but the lengths to which our enemies went show me that they fear me more than I fear them." I gestured with my thumb towards my sons who were riding flanked by Tall Tom and eight archers. "They were my undoing. If I take them to war then the whole company will be there to guard them. I feared that the Lord of Milan was party to our abduction but I can see now that is not so. He would not wish to lose his buffer city of Pisa."

"Buffer city, my lord?"

"Yes, Michael, Pisa has not been an important city for more than a hundred years. Her defeat at sea lost the sea power she once enjoyed but she now acts as a barrier to the Florentines holding the land to the sea. The main road to the north passes through San Miniato which is under Florentine control but the road to the sea and the north is guarded by Pisa, Lucca, and Livorno. This new doge must be a Florentine puppet and Bernabò Visconti will not like that."

We camped in full view of the city. We took over a small farmhouse. The family had fled at our approach. The change in government might not have been of their making but they knew that they might suffer my vengeance. My banner was unfurled and my archers paraded themselves before the walls. The men of Pisa knew better than any the skill of my archers. Von Bongarden and his men would be equally wary too. We did not have to draw an arrow such was our power. They barred their gates and manned the walls but did nothing. Robin was taking no chances and he had stakes embedded around the camp. Sentries were placed on the extremities and also on the house used by my sons and me. We ate in the farmhouse; the family had taken their gold but left their food and we ate well.

Giovanni was a practical man, "My lord, it is more than a hundred miles to Cesena and we risk an enemy barring our way."

"And who is there in this part of the world that could do that? The Florentines will be filling their breeks when we pass close to their city for they will fear my vengeance. That will be a treat for later. You, Giovanni, will scout out whichever of the two targets you think is stronger and we attack that one."

John was listening and he put down his knife, "Attack the stronger one, father, why?"

Robin ruffled John's hair, "Because, young man, when we take that one the other will sue for peace quicker. The less fighting we do the better. We go to make money from the pope and make him rue the day that he sent his Germans after Sir John Hawkwood."

When Andrew arrived the next day and joined us in our camp it did not take long to evoke a response. An envoy came from Pisa. It was Pellario Griffo who was with two German mercenaries. I recognised neither of them but they knew me and I knew that they had come to confirm my presence.

Pellario Griffo was smiling. "You did not go with the doge to Milan?"

"I have always served Pisa, my lord, and while I am no longer the chamberlain, I am considered valuable by the general and the doge. No one knows better than I how the city functions." I noticed that he was speaking Italian and that meant the Germans spoke no English. "I am here on behalf of the general and the doge to beg you not to attack the city that gave you a home for so many years." I saw the twinkle in his eye. He knew I had no intention of attacking a city that held my gold. "Both men urge you to consider this. It was just Doge Agnello who was their enemy. Your gold and your homes are safe. They have not been touched and will remain safe so long as you do not make war."

"Then I can enter at any time?"

One of the Germans spoke, "You and your sons can enter but your company has to stay without."

I had known that would be the case but I had to be certain. "Send out William Turner and Sir Dai so that I can confirm what you say." I looked pointedly at the German who had spoken, "They will have safe passage in both directions." He nodded. "When I have spoken with them you shall have my decision."

They bowed and Griffo smiled and said, in English, "It is good to have you back, my lord." The Germans glowered.

John asked, "Do you intend to attack Pisa, Father?"

"No, my son, but they do not know that."

William, Dai, and his squire rode out to us. William especially was shamefaced, "I am sorry, Sir John. I could do nothing about the ransom."

"At the moment that is a moot point. Is our money safe?"

"It is, my lord, they have made no attempt to either take it or damage our properties."

"Yet if Robin and Giovanni had not secured my release who knows what might have happened? Return to Pisa and tell them that I have decided not to attack Pisa for the present but I wish them to reconsider who defends it and who is the ruler. Dai, I need you to stay in Pisa."

"My lord, I am one of the White Company and I should fight at your side."

"Your situation means that you might jeopardise our enterprise."

"Situation, Sir John?"

"You are married to the daughter of the former doge. Besides, I need you to keep an eye on my home and to discover as much as you can about the new doge and Bongarden. Discover their plans."

"I am loyal, Sir John."

I said nothing, "You had better return now. We will leave on the morrow and that should make the Pisans feel less threatened."

"And where do you go, Sir John?"

"Away from here, Dai," I said enigmatically.

As soon as they had entered the city, I sent Sir John Gardener and his lances with an oral message to Bernabò. I trusted Sir John who had been with me for some time and, more importantly, he was a friend of Ambrogio Visconti. In these treacherous times, such friendships were to be used and not ignored. We broke camp early the next day. As we

Tuscan Warlord

headed east, I heard the tolling of the celebratory bells in Pisa. I knew that my departure would create debate and my message to Visconti might effect a change while we profited.

I deliberately led the company towards Florence. It was the most direct route to Cesena and I wanted the Florentines to see that my company had not deserted me. I rode Ajax and wore my white armour. I rode to within crossbow range of the gates almost daring them to send a bolt at me. It was extreme range and my armour was the best that could be found. Michael held my banner and I simply stared at the walls. The gates were closed and the walls were manned by the town watch and armoured nobles. I waited an uncomfortable few minutes and then simply wheeled Ajax's head around and led my company around Florence's walls. Until we disappeared to cross the river, they would fear an attack and only when their scouts had ensured we were not moving to attack the other side of the city would they relax.

Michael smiled as we crossed the river, "They will think that we go to the aid of Perugia." I nodded. "You are a clever man, Sir John. You keep offering me spurs but so long as I am this close to such genius why should I choose knighthood?"

The city of Cesena had been captured by papal forces under Cardinal Albornoz. Although the warrior had died and been buried in Assisi his conquests for the pope had paved the way for a papal return to Rome. I knew the man and his skill. He had tried to use me to fight for the pope once before. In his battles, he had destroyed the walls of the city and as far as I knew he had not rebuilt them. He had begun to build a mighty fortress before he died. Had it been completed then it would have made the capture of the city much harder. As it was the foundations, half-built walls and the two towers were not really defensible. His death had prevented him from achieving all that he hoped for Pope Urban.

We waited for Giovanni in the woods to the west and south of the city. Every single member of the company was anxious to get back to what we did best, raiding. While we awaited the return of our spies I gathered my leaders. I had learned to use trusted men to lead groups of lances. Robin had appointed centenars, archers who commanded one hundred men. It was this outer core of leaders that I addressed. Giovanni already knew the city and his visit was to confirm what he had told me. I was flexible enough to change if I had to but my aim was to attack the next morning. Every moment we delayed increased the likelihood of discovery and we needed surprise.

"It is the men of the papal armies who are our targets. Archers aim for those in papal livery. This time I will not lead the attack on the gate, Giovanni and Sir Andrew will have that honour. Once we enter the city the aim is to take the citadel quickly. I care not for papal prisoners but I would prefer none of the citizens to be hurt. We will be taking their gold, let us leave them their lives. From what I understand they have little love for the pope."

Sir John Thornbury asked, "Does that mean they will seek to rejoin the Empire?" Sir John was a skilled soldier who had recently joined us. He knew war and always asked pertinent questions.

I shrugged, "Perhaps. That does not concern me. Speed is key to this. Now go and tell your men what we intend. Unless Giovanni brings new intelligence, we attack at dawn, as soon as the archers can clear the walls."

It was after dark when Giovanni and his six men rode in. Michael handed him a wineskin and I waited patiently for his report, "There are two hundred papal troops in the town." He smiled. "The commander is one you know: Gerhard von Getz."

I remembered the envoy from Borgoforte. "And the townsfolk?"

"Do not like the German nor his troops. The pope is bleeding the town dry. They have just collected in the taxes and there is unrest in the town."

"Then my plan has a good chance that it might work if we do not harm the citizens."

"It will Sir John."

Our movements from Pisa had been secretive enough for the papal troops in Cesena to be unaware of our presence. I suspect that the Germans who had captured us had reported to their masters that we had been taken and the White Company was no longer a threat. My speedy release had taken them all by surprise. That was clear from the murmur of conversations we heard drifting from the walls. Sentries who were alert to danger did not congregate to talk, they walked their walls and tried to spy out danger. Chatting was a sign that they thought they had an easy duty, The best archers we had were led by Robin and they darted ahead, shadows flickering across the semi-open ground before the gates. When a horse further along from me snorted I gripped my reins tighter but the sentries seemed oblivious to what should have been an obvious sign of danger. The slight creak of the yew bows should also have told those on the walls that they were being hunted but the murmuring continued. More shadows followed my archers and I saw men at arms race to the walls and use their shields to prepare to boost men over the walls. The flight of the arrows did have an effect. I saw white faces turn. The sentries saw their death approach. No matter how good an archer is he cannot guarantee that his target will die silently. There were, inevitably, cries. I waved my arm and my line of horsemen moved from the cover of the trees. I had personally briefed every leader and I was confident that my men knew their task. As we trotted across the ground, dotted with mean homes and smallholdings, I saw my men ascend the walls. The clash of steel preceded the tolling of the bell but by then we were almost at the gates which opened invitingly to allow us entry to the city.

    As I passed beneath the gatehouse, I drew my sword and spurred Ajax to head for the citadel. The last thing I needed was a standoff with papal troops holding the heart of the city. Such was the speed of our attack that, as we reached the castle in the middle of Cesena, we saw the papal garrison of the city running, armed and mailed, to the walls. They had acted as they had been ordered but as my white-coated warriors galloped towards them they made the mistake of hesitating. Hesitation can lose a battle. In this case, it lost a city as we drove through the men who were caught in the open. I slashed down with my sword at the mail-clad man at arms to my right. His glaive came up to stab at me but he was a heartbeat too late and my sword struck the side of his helmet so hard that I dented it and broke his pate. He fell to the ground. Around me, my men at arms used their lances to good effect and when I entered the outer bailey of the small castle, I realised that we had Cesena. The tardy garrison should have stayed in the castle where they could have negotiated a truce but by trying to evict us they had ensured their own end. We had been too quick for von Getz. I know that many of the free companies had earned bad reputations for wild behaviour and savagery, The White Company was never such a company. They obeyed my orders to the letter. The papal garrison was slaughtered but not a citizen was harmed. Even those who emerged from their homes with old swords and helmets were simply disarmed and allowed to return to their homes. We had taken their city but as we had freed the city from the iron grip of Pope Urban were seen as liberators rather than aggressors. Gerhard von Getz proved to be a cowardly commander. As we searched the bodies we did not find his. It was Tall Tom whose sharp eyes spotted him as a horse galloped from a stable just outside the castle walls. The red papal livery was clear evidence of the identity of the rider and Tom's arrow knocked him from his saddle. It was the German Commander. The pope would get to hear of the loss of his city but not for some time.

    As dawn came up the stripped bodies of the pope's troops were gathered outside the city and burned. The air would be filled with the stench of burnt bodies for days. We had no need to take from the citizens of Cesena as the garrison had granaries filled for the winter. We took the supplies intended for the papal troops in this part of Italy. Similarly, we took the treasure, the taxes taken by von Getz, intended for Avignon, from the storerooms. The first thing I did was to repay those who had used their own coins to pay my ransom. There was none left for me and my leaders but the men appreciated the gesture and it was money well spent.

    We stayed but one night and then headed to pass Forli, which, whilst a papal city, had no papal garrison, and make for Faenza which did. This time we would make a daytime attack. Robin and his archers led. The pall of the smoke from the bodies as well as the news which always flew, like clouds in the sky from place to place, must have forewarned the red-liveried garrison. I heard horns as Robin and his archers rode towards the gates which stood invitingly open. Michael's sharp eyes spotted the column of men leaving from the west gate as we neared the south. Robin had seen them too and I saw him wave an arm. He led half of the archers to pursue them while the other half continued through the open gates.

I waved and shouted, "Giovanni, take your men and secure the town. We will deal with those who have deserted Faenza."

He waved his understanding and we galloped after the horsemen. I knew that there would be men left in the city for fewer than half of the garrison would be mounted but the leaders would be horsemen. They might escape us but the lightly armoured horsemen led by Robin would catch them. We did not gallop at full tilt but kept a steady pace as we passed the west gate and then the north gate. No more horsemen emerged and I saw Robin and his archers close with the papal troops. My archers knew how to use swords and they began to catch and kill the fleeing men. The ones who had left from the north gate must have been led by the garrison commander. Perhaps he had realised, when my archers closed with him, the futility of flight but still refused surrender for they found a farmhouse, dismounted and took shelter behind the walls.

Robin simply dismounted his archers and they leisurely strung their bows, Pope Urban's garrison was not behind the walls of a city but the fences and drystone walls of a farm. By the time we reached them, half of the men were dead and the rest had raised their arms in surrender.

We had taken two papal cities without loss and we had destroyed one garrison and rendered a second ineffective. The pope had been given a message.

We made the message as clear as we could. The garrison was disarmed. Their purses were taken and they were sent to head to Rome. Pope Urban and his brother Cardinal

Tuscan Warlord

Angelicus Grimoard had returned to Rome from Avignon. He was trying to re-establish his power in the traditional papal residence. It would take the red-liveried men many days to reach it and I knew that some of the survivors would desert. I did not doubt that they would swell the numbers of other companies. That did not matter as what they would do was spread the stories of Giovanni Acuto and the White Company. Our reputation would be enhanced and that could bring victory sooner.

Faenza was not as anti-pope as Cesena but we were welcomed. Perhaps that was out of fear, I know not. We emptied the garrison granaries and the treasury and then began our chevauchée. The land between the two cities had many rich farms. When Cardinal Albornoz had captured this part of Romagna for the pope, he had given the best farms to supporters of Pope Urban. Leaving the other manors alone we systematically took animals and treasure from all those who had supported the pope. We burned the farmhouses and the survivors, like the garrison, headed for the safety of other papal refuges. The other farms we pointedly left alone. I wanted us seen as saviours and not oppressors.

Three weeks after we had begun a message came from Dai. Our raid had had an effect and the news had reached Pisa. Doge delle Agnello had been restored to rule and the city was in the hands of Bernabò Visconti. We packed wagons with our loot and headed back to Pisa. That part of Italy had learned a lesson. If you took on the White Company you had better have a plan to deal with the warlord who led them. I had learned a lesson too. I had power that went beyond the numbers of the White Company. Our name had emptied Faenza. We did not flaunt our treasure at Florence for I wished to return to Pisa without having to defend the wagons and sumpters that carried our profit. We used back roads until we neared the city and then marched down the road to the open gates with banners flying. We entered Pisa like conquering heroes.

Chapter 8

The Battle of San Miniato 1369.

Visconti had another reason for staying in Pisa. He had restored his friend to power with a small force, just his son's company and his own bodyguards. I was ushered into the doge's palace as soon as I arrived. Dai's father-in-law gushed his thanks. I smiled for I could see from the look on Bernabò's face that there was something else on his mind. He took me to one side,

"Sir John, the pope is a beaten man but we cannot take advantage of that. He is in Rome and attempting to gather an army to take the cities in northern Italy that support either the emperor or us. The Marquis of Montferrat is becoming ambitious and seeks to take some of my lands. I believe that he has been suborned by the pope. I have to return with my son and deal with him." I nodded. I had fought for Montferrat and the reforms I had put in place meant that they were a more formidable force than when I had served them. "I have spies in Florence and you should know that Giovanni Malatacca is heading for Pisa with a Florentine army. The pope cannot fight Pisa but his allies can. The Florentines thought you were still in Faenza and Florence. They wish to take Pisa in your absence. You need to take the Pisan army and fight him." He nodded to Chamberlain Griffo, now restored to office. "I have left the information with the chamberlain. My son and I will be gone by the morrow. You need to plan."

"I will deal with this man but you should know, my lord, that I will not fight for Perugia against the pope. I now fight the pope for the White Company and Sir John Hawkwood."

He gave me a sharp look, "But you still work for me?"

I smiled, "I will work with you, my lord. Perhaps if the ransom had come from Milan or Pisa I might be a more loyal leader but…"

"My hands were tied. I am financially constrained."

"I have been honest with you."

"I know and I shall not neglect our relationship in the future." He turned and left.

Waving Griffo to follow me I led my leaders to my home. Jack White had heard of our return and all was ready when we reached my home. William and Dai were waiting there. Any recriminations would need to wait until the Florentine threat was over. When it was, I could meet with Bernabò and work out how to defeat the pope. His abduction of me told me that he saw me as a threat. So long as Pope Urban was head of the church then there would be enmity between us.

"Giovanni, you are well known in this valley. Ride to San Miniato. You know what to do."

He grinned and nodded. "I remember our conversation on the road back from Perugia well, Sir John. I know what you need." When we returned from my incarceration, we had discussed various plans in case Pisa was held against us. One plan had been to use San Miniato which, until recent reverses, had been Pisan.

"We have a battle to fight. Robin, use your best scouts to head to Florence and find the Florentine army." He nodded. "Chamberlain Griffo, I will need some of the Pisan army."

"Not all?"

"Recent events have shown me that Pisa is not safe at the moment. I need good soldiers to defend its walls and keep our homes safe." My words were laden with threat. Had I not been ransomed so quickly then all might have been lost. I needed the chamberlain to protect what was ours.

"I will keep good men here, my lord, I would not like the doge to lose the city a second time." I heard the determination in his voice, he would do as he promised.

I turned to my officers, "We have no time to sit and count our treasure. Dai, your little sojourn is over and you will need to lead your men once more."

I saw the old Dai in his resolute face. "My father-in-law is a good man but from now on my wife is mine to protect. My family will be protected when this is over. I shall do all that I can."

"Good. Then all but William leave us and be ready to march as soon as we discover whence come the Florentines."

I waved to Michael to take my sons to their room and I was left with my treasurer. I was blunt, "This is not the safe haven we thought, William. I think that your relationship with the doge has coloured your judgement." He bowed his head and flushed. "We need to have somewhere else that we can use as a base. Lucca seems to me to be the best place. When Pisa closed its doors, Lucca did not. While we battle the Florentines, go to Lucca and speak with the leaders there. You have the authority to speak for me. Tell them that the White Company will defend the independence of Lucca in return for a safe place where we can store our treasure. We will need to employ more guards. You fund them and I will find them." Again he nodded. "This is your last chance, William. Do not let me down."

"I swear I have learned my lesson, Sir John. The company shall come first. My wife knows that better than any."

"I have repaid the men what they spent on the ransom. I would have you divide the spoils equally amongst me, my leaders and my men. We cannot afford to have any in the company who harbour grudges. This aberration has shown me that the only ones I can truly rely on are the warriors of the White Company."

The nobles who came with their men to fight for us were largely known to me and Chamberlain Griffo had chosen, so far as I could tell, well. "None of you will fight with the mounted element of my army. I want the men of Pisa to be a

Tuscan Warlord

block of iron before my archers. You will use glaives, halberds and pikes. Your job is to keep the Florentines from getting close to my archers."

Francesco Pagano was the most competent of the nobles and he had excelled during the retreat from Perugia when we had suffered our defeat, "And you have a plan, my lord, even though you know not the force that comes nor the place we shall fight?"

I smiled, "If they are coming from Florence there is but one place to halt them and that is San Minato."

Another of the nobles protested, "But it is now Florentine and with the mighty tower erected by Emperor Frederick, it is almost unassailable. I would not throw away the lives of the men I brought with me unnecessarily."

"And you will not. We will fight with San Miniato at our back. It is the Florentines who might need to fear the tower and the walls." I knew I was relying heavily upon Giovanni but he had never let me down and he was very persuasive. Dai and Sir Andrew did not have the Italian language to help them and Robin would be too blunt. I needed the weapon of the surgeon, Giovanni's tongue.

"Will you tell us your plan?" Pagano had flashed an irritated look at the complainant.

I smiled, "If I thought my hair would tell what my head thought I would shave every hair from it. Fear not when you need to know then you shall. What I need is for you to be ready to march as soon as you can. The White Company marches at dusk. The spies will find it hard to count the numbers."

I left with my men and I took my sons with me. I trusted my bodyguards and the White Company but Pisa was no longer safe. Doge delle Agnello had shown that he did not have the support of the Pisans. It was my company that propped him up. We had been loyal to Pisa for many years. It was time now for us to spread our wings. We needed to look out for ourselves. I took Remus merely because Ajax had endured a hard campaign in Faenza and Cesena. I knew how to husband animals and this might be a good opportunity to blood Remus properly. We rode cocooned by a wall of plate and mail. My men did not wish to lose me a second time. When we neared San Miniato, we stopped. We halted at the via Francigena, the main road between Rome and Europe. With the pope trying to re-establish Rome as the home of the pope, holding this vital junction hurt the pope. I had plans for the future.

Giovanni must have been watching for us for he rode out from behind a farm where they had sheltered themselves from view, with the men he had taken with him. "Well?"

"The people are unhappy with the Florentine rule, Sir John. They do not enjoy as much trade as they would like. They will not bar our progress but suggest we pass their town under cover of darkness so that they cannot be associated with us."

I nodded, "They are sitting on the fence until they see the outcome of this battle?"

"Do you blame them?"

"No, and it is the best we could hope for. As I have no intentions of losing, we will soon have San Miniato as an ally." I turned in my saddle, "Dai, move them out. We will make camp a mile or two to the east of the town at the bridge over the Esla."

I was one of the first to arrive and even though it was dark I walked along the road the Florentines would use when they approached us. By the time I got back the camp that Dai had begun was almost complete. There were fires to cook food and the men had made hovels. The Pisan nobility had their men erecting tents. I shook my head for it was a waste of time. By the time they were up and the nobles asleep, it would be time to wake. A delegation came to see me as pegs were hammered into the hard ground. Francesco Pagano was not one of them, "My lord your dispositions will result in disaster. We cannot fight with a river at our back."

My eyes narrowed, "I did not know that we had so many expert generals in Pisa. Perhaps you do not need me, eh?"

My tone told them my mood and most lowered their eyes but one, the clear leader, Bartolomeo D'Agostino said, "If we held the other side of the river, my lord, then they would have an obstacle before them."

"Which, if we were to defeat them, we would have to cross. Your plan, my lord, avoids defeat and that is all. My plan is to hold and then trounce them. The archers will be at the rear and your Pisans will form three lines before the river. All you have to do is to hold. The White Company will do the rest."

Robin rode in the next day during the early afternoon. He dismounted and then pointed east. "There are two and a half thousand warriors heading down the road."

"Mercenaries?"

He smiled, "No, my lord, not really. There is a company of Genoese crossbowmen and a handful of Hungarian knights but the bulk of them are the Florentines. We managed to get close to their camp and overhear them. They are confident that they can defeat you. They believe you have lost confidence and that your men are deserting you. That is clear for they have no scouts out and assume that San Miniato is still loyal to them. They have two trebuchets and two bombards with them."

"Have they indeed?"

John said, "What difference does that make, father?"

I was aware that I was teaching my sons, "It means, John, that they expect to have to break down Pisa's walls. They are not expecting," I spread my arms out on either side of me, "this." He nodded his understanding and I turned to Robin, "Have some food and then have your archers embed stakes for three hundred paces across our centre. The Pisans are a little nervous."

He laughed, "And we will be behind them. Our foot soldiers?"

"Will be two tempting targets. There will be two thin lines on either side of the Pisans."

"You are tempting them to try to outflank us."

I smiled, "Here the river has a bridge and is thirty paces wide. Upstream, more than a mile from here, there is a place where it is just twenty-five paces wide. I intend to send Giovanni and Dai to that crossing point on this side of the river. They will not use the crossing point for they can travel down this side of the river but it will provide an escape route in case I have been outwitted. They can wait until signalled and then launch an attack. When the Florentines are committed then they will launch their attack. The outflanker will become outflanked himself."

"And where will you be, Sir John?"

"On the weaker side. It is our left flank that will have to bear the brunt of the enemy attack. I intend to use a wagon there as an anchor. It will allow me to see the progress of Dai and Giovanni. When do you estimate they will reach us?"

"Late tomorrow would be my guess. I think, from their pace that they intend to stay in San Miniato and enjoy rooves over their heads and hot food in their bellies."

"Then we can expect their scouts from noon." I waved over to Dai and Giovanni. "Tomorrow morning, at dawn, head down the north bank of the Elsa. I want you to wait a mile from here. There is, I believe, a wood there which you can use for shelter. Have scouts out. If you are seen then the whole plan fails. You listen for my horn that will sound three times. When you hear it then form three lines and sweep into the Florentine flank. I will time the horn so that they have committed all their men to the attack and their attention is on us."

With my plans in place, I walked the camp with my sons and Michael. I exuded confidence and I shared jokes and banter with some of the archers. Francesco Pagano had brought wine and I shared a beaker or two with him. Inside I was worrying about all the things that might go wrong but to the army, there was no doubt, from my demeanour, that we would win. My sons were silent as we walked although Michael joined in with the banter. He had been brought up with the archers and whilst he was not one himself they admired and respected his courage.

When the three of us sat on the logs Robin had found to eat our food Thomas spoke. He and his brother had been silent during our walk but now, with no one close by they felt that they could talk. "And what do we do when the fighting starts, father?"

"The two of you will be with my bodyguards and Michael on the wagon." I nodded to the wagon we had taken from a nearby farm. You will wear our helmets and hauberks as well as your swords but you will use these." Michael had risen when I began to talk and brought out two eight feet long ash spears. "You will need time to get used to them. That will be your task on the morrow. Michael can advise you until I need him. It is a simple weapon. You can only thrust with it for the edge of the spearhead is not particularly sharp. When you are bigger and older, we might try a poleaxe or halberd but these are a good introduction. Michael will stand, in the battle, on the driver's seat. There he will be seen and that will draw heroic-minded enemies to attack him. He will wear his plate and helmet and that means he will be unsighted. Your task is to keep enemies from him and these long spears, used from above will be the perfect weapon. It may be you just deflect a lance with your spear. That is good. I need Michael to sound the horn at the perfect moment in the battle. You need to keep him alive so that he can do so. You need not worry about me for I have four bodyguards who will defend me with their lives."

I had spoken to Michael about this and it seemed to us that, risky though it was, it was the best way we could employ my sons. They would not feel as though they were doing nothing and would not necessarily be targets. Michael would. He would wear a thick padded gambeson topped with a mail hauberk. There would be plates on his arms, thighs and calves. He would not need sabatons but he would wear a breast and backplate. He would wear his arming cap and coif and that would be finished off by his bascinet with the visor.

I knew that I would attract bolts and blades more than any other men on the battlefield. My padding, mail and plate armour were the best in Italy and had been made in Milan. I had spent my florins well. My helmet, whilst not full-faced had a visor that I could raise or lower. I intended to fight with it raised.

When we rose it was a half-empty camp for my horsemen had slipped away in the dark. Dai and Giovanni had walked their men upstream while it was still dark. They were the key to victory and they knew it. Even the Pisans had not heard them leave such had been their stealth. Robin and the archers had embedded stakes. They were to stop horses and organised lines of men. Individuals could make their way through but, if they did, they would be greeted by three Pisans with pole weapons. Even the best Florentine warrior would struggle to defeat three men. As was their wont my archers had emptied bowels and bladders both before and within the stakes. Unwary soldiers might slip. We would endure the stench. After we had breakfasted, we waited.

    The Florentine scouts arrived at noon and reined in sharply when they saw our standards, stakes and camp. Leaving two to watch us the other eight rode back to their main army. I did not have the army stand to. There was no need. Men lounged and some diced and gambled. I nibbled on the ham a farmer's wife, grateful that we had left her farm alone, brought us. The plated knights who arrived were clearly the leaders. They stopped well out of arrow range and so I could not see their faces. I recognised the livery of a couple of them. They had with them their bodyguards. It would take time for the army to arrive and I was interested in what they would do.

    The first company were the Genoese crossbowmen. They had an equal number of pavesiers, the young men who carried their pavise, the man-sized shield that would protect them. Armed with just a sword their job was to protect the expensive crossbowmen. If a crossbowman fell then they would take up the weapon but as they were apprentices they would not be as effective. The lances arrived next. As this was an army of nobles, they had adopted fancier garb both for themselves and their animals. Some of the horses had mail trappers while many had mail or plate shaffrons. A large number also had caparisons. Their lances were also less standardised. Dai and Giovanni led men with identical weapons. If a man fell his weapons could easily be used by another. The light horsemen arrived next. Some would be the squires but most were men riding hackneys and protected by a metal helmet and leather armour. We did not bother with them. Their main use was in pursuit or a chevauchée. I used my archers for that. The bulk of the army was on foot. Some wore the livery of the mounted nobles but more than half were the levy from Florence. Their range of weapons was as varied as their lords. Some held a simple bill hook. I saw a few wicked-looking scythes too. Finally, the wagons carrying the war machines hove into view. I doubted that they would be used against us as the mighty stones hurled by the trebuchets could be easily avoided. They were for the walls. The bombards were more of a threat but I doubted that they would waste powder and ball on the Pisan levy.

The Florentine army formed up. A bishop came to bless them and then, as the sun began to dip behind us, they started to make a camp. It was something of an anti-climax.

"Robin, set traps and sentries. I do not think they will have the wit to send a night attack but you never know."

"Yes, my lord." He pointed to the bombards, "When we win, we can sell those bombards to Pisa."

"You are reading my mind, old friend."

There was no night attack and as dawn broke we heard the horns as the Florentine camp was woken. The Florentine army went through its usual pre-battle rituals. The men were shriven and they were exhorted to drive the hired foreigners from their soil. My men had heard it before but I saw some of the Pisans looking over their shoulders at me. I was being portrayed as the devil. We waited patiently. It was clear that they realised that they would have to use their horsemen on the two flanks and the nobles gathered there. That suited me. Nobles were always competitive and sought, not to arrive in one solid line but to reach it first and garner all the glory. It was why I had placed my foot soldiers there. They had the resolve and the skill to deal with such an attack. More importantly, they could fall back steadily rather than making it appear as though they were fleeing.

When the pavesiers moved forward we knew the attack was about to begin. It was only then that Robin ordered the bows to be strung. Only a professional company could leave that until the last moment. It meant the bows would have the maximum power. The pavesiers placed their huge shields two hundred paces from the stakes. They intended to punch a hole in our lines. The Pisans in our front rank had their own shields. The disadvantage of the crossbow was that it used a horizontal flight. The stakes before our men, whilst not particularly thick, were numerous and they were offset. Some of the bolts would hit them while others would be deflected. I looked over to Robin. He turned and smiled. I could leave the order to release to him. Behind the Genoese crossbows the mass of men on foot formed up. The Florentines had suffered at the hands of my archers before now and they had every man in the front two ranks armed with a shield. The horses of the nobles snorted and stamped as the powerful destriers and coursers were as eager to get into battle as their confident riders.

The horn sounded once and as the main lines moved up behind the Genoese crossbows, the crossbowmen stood up and sent their first bolts in our direction. There were more than one hundred and fifty crossbowmen as there were some Florentines with them. The snap and crack of the crossbows made some Pisans start and all of them ducked behind their shields. Some bolts hit the stakes and while some embedded themselves others flew off at a tangent. Less than half reached the waiting shields. The heads disappeared as the crossbows were reloaded. My archers did nothing. In fact, the crossbows were allowed to send four bolts without reply. It was clear to both sides that the crossbows were not working at such an extreme range. The Genoese general who commanded the crossbows ordered them to be moved forward. That was the moment Robin used our archers. He waited until they were on the move. The slightly uneven ground, the weight of the pavise and the weight of the crossbows meant that the crossbows and their protectors were not as well protected as they might have been. Six hundred arrows descended as they moved and more than half of the Genoese were hit. The second flight was in the air even while the survivors of the first arrow storm tried to raise their crossbows. They were forced to halt just forty paces closer to us. Behind them, the ground was littered with bodies, pavise and crossbows. The slightly closer range meant that when the crossbows sent their next bolts two Pisans were hit but when Robin's next flight descended to harvest more men the Genoese commander decided he had endured enough and led his survivors back across a battlefield covered with half of their company. The Genoese were finished and would have to return to Genoa to recruit more men.

The Florentine horn sounded twice when the survivors had passed through their lines. Dai and Giovanni would not be confused by the horn. Mine had a distinctive sound. Banging their shields to give them rhythm the Florentine foot moved forward. They were steady but their nobles were not. The plated nobles and the light cavalry went into an immediate charge. I heard Robin as he gave his orders. The horsemen would be in range first and his archers, already divided, simply aimed their bows obliquely at the charging horses. The charge was slowed as the arrows winnowed the horsemen. A horse is a bigger target than a man and more horses were hit. Not all fell but enough did to bring down others. The ones that did not fall often veered into the path of another horse. I had seen the same thing happen at both Crécy and Poitiers, it meant that the already loose line became even more fragmented. I heard the commanders of the two waiting blocks of men shout the order to brace. The front rank would plant the hafts of their pole weapons into the ground while the second rank would hold theirs over the shoulders of the front rank. The second rank would also lean their bodies into the backs of their comrades. Even a mail shaffron or trapper could not protect against a spear, halberd, glaive or poleaxe that jutted up from the ground.

Robin was a master of his craft and he switched the target for his archers once the horsemen were just twenty paces from our waiting line of steel. The foot soldiers had enjoyed an arrow-free march of more than two hundred paces and were confidently striding towards us. Robin knew that once they reached the Genoese bodies and the stakes then all cohesion would vanish. His arrows fell amongst both those with shields and those without. The ones who had no shields were in the fourth and fifth ranks. Many of them fell but the ones in the front ranks, protected by plate, mail, helmet and shields, suffered fewer casualties and that gave them confidence. As they passed through the stakes more of them died as they slipped or were felled by arrows sent at less than one hundred paces range.

When the horses struck our line, it sounded like a dozen blacksmiths all banging their hammers on their anvils at the same time. The screams of felled horses and men echoed across the middle. The foot soldiers in the centre could not see their flanks and I assume they thought that the sound meant they were winning. They surged forward and struck the Pisans. For me, this was the crucial time in the battle. I could rely on my archers and my own foot warriors but the Pisans were an unpredictable force. Francesco Pagano held the centre. I had allowed the Pisans to choose their own position. His men were like a rock and I watched the Florentines hit the line of shields and pole weapons and then reel.

Unfortunately, not all the Pisans were made of the same metal. Bartolomeo D'Agostino and his men were struck by the same number as Pagano but the effect was not the same. I heard his fearful voice cry out, "We are undone, flee!" He led his men and the company next to him to try to get through my archers.

It was a disaster. Robin's men who were close to the Pisan flight could not use their bows while the Pisans were heading for the bridge and the slackening of arrows encouraged the Florentines. I heard the Florentine horn as the leader sent in the reserves. The Pisan rout would have been seen and the Florentines saw their chance of victory. Their horsemen, whilst they had been previously stopped, were now pressing my two flanks closer to our centre. The gap left by the Pisans had allowed a company of Florentines to seize their opportunity and head for my wagon. Things were not going to plan but there was no need, yet, to panic. "Michael, sound the horn. Boys protect my squire." Holding my poleaxe before me I lunged at the Florentine warrior who, encased in plate, ran to try to climb the wagon. It was brave but foolish. He should have used his spear to try to ram it under my plate. He paid with his life as the spike on the poleaxe drove through his eyehole and into his head. He fell backwards and I swung the axe head in an arc as the three strident notes on the horn echoed across the field. My axe head hit metal and flesh but, more importantly, it halted the advance. Michael sounded a second call as my bodyguards stepped before and beside me. Our fate now lay in the hands of my horsemen.

The Pisan flight was now over for the rest had held and Robin's archers now sent their flights into the advancing Florentines. Francesco Pagano, angered no doubt by the flight of his countrymen, was exhorting the rest of the Pisans to do their duty. The wagon was now the focus of the attack and a narrow column of men, attacked on two sides by more resolute Pisans, made their way to get Giovanni Acuto and his handful of defenders.

Michael had dropped the horn to hang from his neck and the standard was embedded in the wagon. He used his glaive to sweep across the faces of those attempting to climb. The Florentines realised our weakness and they swung their weapons at our calves. Michael and my sons were lithe enough to jump up. My bodyguards and I were encased in plate and had to endure the cracks of spears and glaives upon the plate protecting our legs. We all had good plate but, even so, Walter, just before me, was felled when a war hammer broke his leg and he fell backwards. I brought the hammer of my own poleaxe down on the Florentine before me and such was the power of the blow that it smashed into the helmet as though it was parchment and crushed the skull. The spears wielded by John and Thomas were not the most powerful of weapons but they were accurate. They plunged them into the open faces of men who wore a simple bascinet.

"Well done, boys!" Michael's shout of encouragement was just what they needed.

Above the cacophony of battle, I heard a most welcome sound, the thundering of hooves. My horsemen were coming but the flight of D'Agostino and his cowards had created a weakness in our left flank and the men there were now pressed hard against my wagon. More horsemen saw their chance to get Sir John Hawkwood and they urged their animals on. It was then that the genius of Robin came into play. He switched all of his archers to send their arrows into

Tuscan Warlord

the Florentines trying to close with me. It was genius because I could see Dai and Giovanni already slaughtering the Florentines attacking our right. The six hundred arrows, many of them bodkins, slammed into the horsemen and emptied saddles. When Dai and Giovanni were at the stakes, the Florentines broke. It was the flight of D'Agostino magnified. Robin and his archers had no mercy in their hearts as they sent their arrows into the backs of the fleeing Florentines. By late afternoon the battle was over and only the dead and the dying remained on the battlefield.

Chapter 9

There would be recriminations when we returned to Pisa but that night there was only celebration. We had lost men, true, but not as many as we might have, given the perfidy of D'Agostino. As usual, we profited from both the horses we took, as well as the prisoners we could ransom and, finally, there were the purses of the dead. While the battlefield was cleared and the bodies that were not collected, burned, I went with Giovanni to San Miniato. We had completely defeated the Florentines and they accepted the overlordship of Pisa quite happily. What they did not agree to was a Pisan garrison. Perhaps the sight of some of the Pisan army fleeing back to Pisa had made them fear that a Pisan garrison might not be as resolute as they might wish. We compromised. Some of those who had first joined the White Company with Giovanni, Italians in the main, were now at the end of their working life. They had made money and wished to enjoy it. The council of San Miniato happily accepted the old warriors as a de facto garrison and a reminder that the White Company ruled this land. It suited me too and I agreed to pay the garrison from White Company funds for the first three months as a gesture of good will. It would not be at the same rate as fighting men but everyone was happy with the arrangement. We had the captured bombards and I knew that Pisa would happily pay for the weapons. We had burned the trebuchets but the bombards were a bonus. We could not use them but Pisa could.

With the arrangements made, we headed back down the road to Pisa. The Pisans had left before us having enjoyed the pillaging of the field. I spoke with Francesco before he left to thank him for his service.

"Unlike many of my peers, Sir John, I am grateful that, hitherto, you have borne the brunt of the fighting. Too many nobles have grown lazy and do not realise that they have a duty to protect Pisa. I shall raise the matter at the next meeting of the council." He lowered his voice, "I like the doge, he is a good man but he needs to be stronger. A stronger man would not have been ousted so easily."

Riding back to Pisa surrounded by my leaders, we debated our position. I was blunt, as ever, "I no longer feel safe in Pisa and I wish the move to Lucca to be sooner rather than later." Even Dai did not disagree with that. "And there is more. We are a company that votes on matters but it is in my mind to seek other employers than the Visconti family and Pisa. We have been loyal to both but in my hour of need neither offered any help. It has shown me much. When this contract runs out, we will find another employer."

Dai was the only one who questioned me, "My lord, we have homes in Pisa. The bank that contains our coin is there. We cannot simply abandon the city for fear of the retribution that might follow."

Robin laughed in his usual blunt manner. He cared not who he offended and he had known Dai since he had been my squire, "Retribution against the White Company? We could take the city with just my archers. Without us, they would be Florentine already. They need us more than we need them Dai. Your mansion, wife and family will be safe."

I covered my smile. Once Robin spoke then no one would argue with him but from their faces, none, save Dai, wished to.

The ones lining the streets as we triumphantly entered Pisa were the men alongside whom we had fought. The notable absence was D'Agostino and the companies that had fled alongside him. I wondered if he had been the spy. His actions had almost led to disaster. I would deal with him at my leisure and I would do so in a way that would tell me if he was the spy or not. I visited with the doge and told him what we planned. I wanted him to become a more active ruler. My words, telling him that we wished to move to Lucca did not have the effect I hoped. I was counting on a resolution to act more like a leader. Instead, he looked fearful and said, "Who will protect me and my family if you are not here, Sir John? I am surrounded by vipers and those who would stab me in the back."

"Giovanni, surround yourself with strong men, nobles like Francesco Pagano. Isolate those, like D'Agostino, who are your enemies. Make money for Pisa." He shook his head and I tired of my efforts to persuade him. I stood, "In spring when our contract with Pisa is over then you will need to make arrangements for another company to fight for Pisa."

His bony, veined hand darted out to grab mine, "Do one thing more for me before you leave."

"If I can then I will."

"Livorno is now Florentine and I fear that they will take the last of our trade from us. Take your company and raid Livorno. There will be a great profit for you and I would be in your debt."

I laughed, "Having saved you twice already you are more than in our debt but I will do as you ask."

When I left, I realised that the prospect of raiding Livorno was an attractive one. It had once been Pisan and we knew the port well. It was rich and the profit we would make would be equal to a year's wages from Pisa. There was no garrison to speak of and having defeated the Florentines already, the port could expect no help from its parent city. I became quite excited as I headed back to my home. I did not tell my leaders what I intended. It would be better if they had time to enjoy both the victory and the coins they had accrued as a result of San Minato. What I did do was speak to William. That was partly because he was our treasurer but also, he was the son-in-law of the doge and he would discover what had been asked of us sooner rather than later. The old doge was loose-lipped.

I began with the news of the raid and he nodded so quickly that I knew the doge had spoken of such a raid while we were in San Miniato. "Now, the finances. Have you arranged for a bank in Lucca and houses for us?"

"I have and our costs will be cheaper there than in Pisa. We will still keep our bank and properties in Pisa but by spreading the load we minimise the risk of losses. We are having a bank built as we speak and I have bought a house for you. Dai and I will look around for homes that will suit families." I knew what he meant. Robin, Giovanni, Sir

Andrew and my other leaders could make do with my home but men with wives and families needed to involve their spouses in such decisions."

"Good, now I have spoken to the others. This is our last contract with Pisa. She is tottering on the brink of extinction already and is only propped up by our presence." He did not argue. "You can begin to earn your stipend once more, William. Do what you do best. Negotiate with any who might wish to hire our company. We will consider any master so long as they pay."

He nodded, "Bernabò is often tardy with his payments and sometimes there is a shortfall. When his contract is up do you wish to renew?"

"Only if he puts gold in our hands first."

Although we had a voting system in the company most seemed happy for me, advised by William, to make the strategic decisions.

"When will you attack Livorno?"

"We will give the men a month off and then make a sudden raid. I will only tell the men a week before we leave. My leaders, I will tell when I have finalised my plans."

I knew, as I headed back to my home that I was becoming a tyrant and using the company for my own ends. However, I did so knowing that my company would never suffer. I was a warlord and so long as I was successful then all would be well. It gave us a month to lick our wounds and to enjoy the fruits of our labours.

Before we left, I decided to deal with Bartolomeo D'Agostino. Had he come to me since our return and apologised for deserting us I might not have bothered with the desertion but, since our return, he had actively campaigned against our presence in Pisa and, in the council meetings, had demanded that we pay reparations for the losses in battle. It irritated me and as one of my bodyguards now had a permanent limp and could no longer function as an active member of my company as a result of his flight, I decided to beard him. Francesco aided me, albeit unwittingly. I was invited to receive honours from the city council for my victory at San Minato. I had been offered such honours before now, they were normally some sort of weapon or trophy that had been made to honour me. I had not accepted one in person before but this time I chose to.

I went with Michael and my sons and we were dressed appropriately. When we entered the chamber, we were applauded by most of the nobles there but one section, centred around D'Agostino, remained seated and silent. I estimated them to be a third of the assembly. He had support but clearly not enough to make a difference. I was a realist and knew that if we suffered a defeat then the support for my enemy would grow. We had to endure the speeches of, first of all, Francesco who was a better warrior than an orator and then the doge. It was he who presented me with the engraved sword. It was too fine to use but I knew that it would impress at court. I anticipated such events in the future.

"Would you say a few words, Sir John?" The doge invited me to speak but I do not think he knew the dam he was bursting.

I smiled, "Thank you, doge, Signior Pagano. It has been an honour to serve Pisa for all these years and I am happy that you, doge, have been restored to the position you deserve. Those backstabbers in the council who sought to undermine you should be ashamed." I was staring at my foe when I spoke and I heard the sharp intake of breath from the whole assembly for I did nothing to disguise my look. . They had not expected this. "I would like to take this opportunity to thank Signior Pagano and all those brave men who defended the road from Florence at the recent battle of San Miniato." That brought applause from most and I sensed relief. "There were however some craven cowards who chose to flee. That the flight caused unnecessary deaths is inexcusable." There was silence so palpable that it could have been cut by a knife. I paused and stared at Bartolomeo D'Agostino. When I spoke my next words it was clear that the words were aimed directly at him for I used his name, "The nobles who fought for Pisa alongside the White Company deserve the appellation, noble. Bartolomeo D'Agostino does not."

He leapt to his feet, "I demand an apology. My name has been sullied. Withdraw your words, Sir John!"

I smiled, "I will not. I was given my spurs, Signior D'Agostino, by King Edward of England for bravery on the battlefield of Poitiers. What have you done to earn yours? Did you inherit them? I will not apologise but instead, demand that you apologise."

"I will not for you are a foreigner and have no rights in this assembly." His face was red and he was ranting.

I was calm when I spoke, "I have been invited here by the doge and the assembly. I say again, apologise or…" I allowed another pause, "let us take our matter to a higher court and have a trial by combat."

He was like a ship when the wind drops. He seemed to shrink into his seat. I had every right to demand a trial by combat and even though he was a good fifteen years my junior there was not a man in the chamber who thought he might win.

I allowed the silence to become unbearably uncomfortable and when I spoke, even though my words were quietly spoken I saw some of the nobles jump, "It is a quite simple choice. Either apologise or fetch your weapons and meet me to allow God to decide who speaks the truth."

I saw him looking for support. Those who were seated close to him had pointedly moved away. It was clear that no one was willing to help. I saw him scowl and then say, quietly, "Perhaps I was hasty and…"

"Apologise or fight."

He took a deep breath, "I am sorry."

He was not going to get away as easily as that, "For what?"

"For deserting."

"And?"

"And for the losses suffered as a result."

"Say it as one speech and not dragged out of you like a schoolboy caught stealing cherries from an orchard."

"I apologise Sir John for deserting you at the battle and for the losses that were incurred."

I smiled, "Then I am content. Thank you for this gift, my lords."

There was an audible sigh as though everyone had been holding their breath. After we had left the building Michael asked, "My lord I am still learning and I know some of the reasons why you did what you did but what was the real purpose?"

"Partly to see who was the spy that betrayed us and now I know it was he. Mainly, however, it was to prop up the doge. I humiliated one man to ensure that he would be isolated. The doge and the loyal nobles now have the chance to win over those who sat close to D'Agostino. I can do no more."

John said, "Would you have fought him had he agreed?"

I stopped and put my hand on John's shoulders, "Here is a valuable lesson for you both. Never threaten to do something if you are not willing to carry it out. My word is my bond. I would have fought him."

Thomas asked, in a hushed voice, "And would you have won?"

Michael could not hold his laughter, "Had it taken your father more than two passes to kill him then I would have been surprised. I have seen your father fight in such combats. He always wins."

D'Agostino left Pisa that day. He had been shamed. I did not discover where he had gone but I knew that I had many enemies and he would find a home with them. The result was that the doge was more secure and Francesco was able to wrest power from the dissenters. I had done all that I could for Pisa.

I was able to give my full attention to the raid on Livorno. My leaders and I spent a week planning the attack and then we briefed our men. It was an innovative attack. The day before we attacked the city proper, we took a ship travelling from Florence along the river to the port. These were not sea-going ships but barges. They sailed downriver using the current and a simple sail and then upriver dragged by horses. By the simple expedient of placing a chain across the river, we halted one. We put aboard Giovanni and some Italian speakers dressed in sailor's gear. They would be our Trojan horse. Once inside the port they would open the gates and allow us in. We planned for a dawn attack. Every man at arms was mounted. Robin and his archers were on foot. We waited outside the port in the suburbs that had sprung up in the last few years. Robin had archers within fifty paces of the gates and when Giovanni opened them his archers raced in and secured the port. It was our easiest victory for with more than fifteen hundred mercenaries in the port there was no resistance. We plundered at will. The warehouses were emptied and convoys of wagons took the loot the fifteen miles to Pisa. We emptied the treasury for the port charged fees for its use and then systematically destroyed the harbour. Cranes were wrecked and thrown into the sea. Florentine ships were burnt and the rest were sent away. By the time we left after four days, Livorno was no longer a functional port. The Florentines would be able to rebuild it but it would take time.

 The raid had a number of effects. Firstly, it made us incredibly rich and the new bank in Lucca was filled with the proceeds of the sale of goods and the gold we had taken. Secondly, the doge was now in a really strong position for Pisa had returned to its place as the pre-eminent port on this coast and every merchant was richer as a result. The third result was that, in the new year, Florence sued for peace. She had endured enough. She could not afford to hire another company and rebuild Livorno. It did not mean that Florence had given up on her ambitions, she still wished to rule Pisa, but I had bought the doge the time to make her stronger. I had not betrayed my first employer. When we left, I could hold my head high knowing that I had done all that I could for the doge and for Pisa.

Chapter 10

Lucca 1370
As soon as the contract ended, we left Pisa. William had done well and our new bank and homes were ready for us. The fortunes we had made also ensured that we were popular in Lucca for my men spent their money there. On a simple level, the innkeepers and whores had constant trade for warriors who needed such comforts and that made them richer. My men also paid for weaponsmiths and tailors to make them armour, weapons and clothes. Bootmakers prospered. Pisa's loss was Lucca's gain.

I spent some time in my new home and then travelled to Milan. I needed to know if Bernabò was still funding us and if not what that meant to us. Once more he tried to fit me up with a wife. I smiled and declined. That done he was all business.

"You and your company have done well this past year, Sir John. You seem to have profited from your incarceration."

"The White Company secured my release and it was they who profited alongside me. I reward loyalty."

He was thick-skinned and ignored the insult.

"What I need to know, Bernabò, is are you still our paymaster? We have not been paid by Milan since Borgoforte."

"Where you profited greatly."

"As a result of our own endeavours. By my reckoning, we are owed fifty thousand florins by Milan."

He adopted an innocent look, "But you did nothing to earn it."

"Was I not asked by you to fight for Perugia? Did you not request that I fight the Florentines?"

He had a silky smile, "You did not actually fight against the pope and I believe that Pisa rewarded you for fighting for Florence."

We were alone in his chamber although I knew that there would be men at the listening holes hidden behind the walls,

"Then I have to say that I will be seeking a new employer. You should know that we will listen to offers from anyone. Even your enemies."

For the first time, the mask slipped, "We are old friends, Sir John. You will not abandon an old friend, surely."

"We are business partners and if the business does not pay then I find another paymaster."

"Money is tight at the moment. I will send what we owe by Christmas."

"That does not buy us as allies."

"And we will pay you fifty thousand florins a year, beginning next year, not to fight against us and to accept no commissions to fight for Milan."

"Agreed but if we draw our weapons then we double our fee." I saw him suck in his cheeks. "It is not open for debate."

"Then I agree."

I stood, "Then have your men draw up the papers and bring them to Lucca. I am assuming that your listeners have heard enough to include all the details."

He smiled, "You, Giovanni Acuto, have become an Italian."

I am not sure if William was happy with his lack of involvement in the negotiation but he accepted it as did the others when we held our first meeting in Lucca. We would not be going to war that year for it was not necessary. We were no longer employed by Pisa and having received most of our back pay from Bernabò we had no need to fight. Our raid on Livorno had brought us riches and we spent the first half of the year settling into our new homes. I took the opportunity to take my sons hunting in the forests to the northeast of Lucca. Pisa had not been well endowed with hunting grounds. Hunting made for better warriors.

In light of our abduction by the Germans, Robin insisted upon four archers accompanying us. Tall Tom was one of them. He had begun the training of the boys and still took a keen interest in them. There were wild boar in the forests but we would hunt deer and use bows. It had been some years since I had enjoyed a hunt and I found myself more than a little excited at the prospect. The boys and I, along with Michael and the others, all wore a leather jack. Our breeks and smocks were either green or dun-coloured and would help us to blend into the woods. A local forester, for a fee, agreed to be our guide. Eventually, my archers would be able to find the game themselves but this first foray needed local expertise. He told us where to tether our horses and with strung bows and arrows in an arrow bag about our backs we headed along the game trails. The forester was armed only with a boar spear as was Michael, who was no archer. We were not hunting wild boar but if we were attacked then their spears would be our best defence.

As we tethered our horses I said to the boys, "Today will give you a lesson in war. This is not for amusement but to give you the skills that will make you a better warrior. Regard the deer as an enemy whom you wish to surprise. Watch where you place every step and use your nose, ears and eyes to alert you to the prey. When you loose your arrows you do so to kill. My archers and I will allow you two the opportunity to make the kill. That is a great burden you bear for you do not wish to make the animal suffer, do you?"

"No, father. I hope we will not let you down."

I gave them a rare smile, "Every lesson involves the possibility of failure. It is how you deal with failure that men judge you by. Trust your skill and your instincts. My blood courses through your veins and Tall Tom here has taught you well."

I looked at Tom who nodded and added, "Remember my little lordlings, you are not yet fully grown and the bows you use are not as powerful as ours. You will have to release your arrow when you are closer than you might like. Keep your arrow loosely nocked and when you are ready draw and release in one smooth motion."

They nodded seriously. He had been a good teacher and such men are rare in my experience.

If the boys thought we were going in a roundabout way they were right for the forester was taking us to get upwind of the herd he was stalking. As with all such men he knew the trails well and understood how the herd moved. It took two hours to get into position. I was feeling my age but I would not ask for a rest. My body needed to be as hard as my mind.

When the forester held up his hand and stepped aside I knew we were close. Tall Tom and I stepped forward while Michael took one flank and the forester the other. They would take no part in the hunt. Their sole task was to protect us from disturbed pigs. I had chosen my hunting arrow when we had left the horses and I nocked it. I held the bow and missile in my left hand and I sniffed. The slight breeze brought the musky smell of deer to me. I tapped my nose and John and Thomas also sniffed. Their eyes widened and they nodded. Tall Tom and I stepped to the side to allow them to occupy the game trail and Tom gestured for them to lead. The other archers followed but it would be Tom and I who would flank my sons.

It was as we walked down the trail that I realised how close they had grown. I remembered when Roger and Elizabeth had complained of their fighting. I had intervened for I knew that it would make them stronger and now I saw that it had made them closer. John was the elder and he naturally led but Thomas was close by. He was not so close as to interfere with John's draw but he would be able to react quickly if John found game. Tom and I spied the herd before the boys. Not only were we taller but we had done this before and knew what to look for. The path was descending to water. The herd was grazing but making its way to drink.

When Tom and I stopped the two boys took a step forward and then realised that we had stopped. They both halted and I was pleased with their precautions. They sniffed and listened and then carefully peered into the foliage. I saw them stiffen when they saw the deer just sixty paces from us. The hunt was on and much would depend on how close they could get to the animals before they released. It delighted me when they set off but did so slowly. Each foot was raised and lowered as though there was a pit before them. We moved painstakingly slowly but we still moved faster than the grazing herd. Tom and I were well within range but the boys still moved closer. They had heeded Tall Tom's words well and seemed to be trying to move in slow motion.

That they were close in every way became clear when seemingly without any sign they both stopped. I had not seen it for I was watching the herd but I guessed that they had exchanged a subtle look. I saw them both draw and I instinctively drew too. They did as Tom had said and the two draws and releases were almost simultaneous. Tom and I also drew. The arrows from the boys were well struck but they hit the rump of the large doe they had chosen. She sprang away. Tom had the quicker reactions than I did and his arrow slammed into the side of the skull, killing the doe instantly. I was on a full draw and my arms burned. I tracked a smaller doe and sent my arrow to hit it in the neck. It was a quick kill.

The herd bounded off and we hurried to the two dead animals. Tall Tom was proud of the boys and it showed in his praise, "Good hits, my little lordlings."

"But you had to finish it off." Thomas was not happy about that.

He laughed, "The first time I went hunting with my father my arrow hit fresh air. I was punished by being sent to find all the spent arrows. I did not miss a second time. When next you hunt you will do as your father and I did and go for the head." He gave a slight bow to me, "A fine hit, my lord and on the fly."

I shrugged for I had been lucky. I could not have held the bow much longer and it was only the close range and the fact that the deer had danced into view that had made it look so spectacular. "We have done what we came for." I reached into my purse and took out a small gold coin. I flicked it at the forester who deftly caught it, "Thank you forester." Turning to the other archers I said, "If you wish to hunt more then do so. We will remain here and we will blood the boys."

Happy to be able to hunt and knowing that the herd would still be close enough to track they left us. Tom went to the large doe and took out his hunting knife. It was razor sharp and he ripped open the belly of the deer. He reached inside and pulled out the heart. He proffered it to John first.

I said, "It is a custom but you need not if you do not wish to."

Tom said, "If you bite a piece of the animal's heart it is said it makes you a better warrior." He bit a large chunk from it. Blood covered his mouth and teeth.

John took the heart and he bit into it. I saw him struggling not to gag but when Thomas, eager to emulate his brother, took it and also bit then John swallowed. It was not as bad as he had expected. Michael and the forester grinned.

Michael said, "Now you are blooded and have done that which I have not. You have hunted and eaten the first beast you have killed."

Tom was ever practical, "And now we have to gut the animal and then cut a stave to carry it home."

The forester said, "I can do that."

I shook my head, "Thank you, forester, but it was their kill and they should do it. Michael and I will gut my kill."

I also had a sharp hunting knife and after slicing it open, I took out the guts including the bowels and the stomach. It stank. Michael went to cut a stave as I laid the offal on the ground. Carrion would feast on the bounty and nothing would be wasted. The boys did as I had done but it took them longer. They managed to do it and having watched Michael knew where to source the stave. Michael and I rammed the stave into the animal. We pushed it through its mouth and out of its rear. Tom had to help the boys but when it was done, they hefted the beast so that they could carry it. My animal was smaller and I was proud of my sons for even though they struggled they sought no help and we made our way back to the horses.

The horses neighed and stamped at the smell of death. We left the carcasses close to them so that they could get used to the smell and then, after washing the blood from our hands with water from our skins, we ate the food we had brought. The boys relived every footfall of the hunt and I was pleased that they were self-critical. Their arrows had hit almost the same spot and they knew that they should have discussed where they would aim before the hunt. A valuable lesson had been learned and I knew that the next hunt, or fight, would see my sons acting in unison. It was what made my White Company so successful. We acted in unison. The lances knew what the archers would do and vice versa. It was the mutual trust that made us stronger than any other company.

Our archers had slain three deer. Strong men, they came with the animals slung over their shoulders. After they had eaten, we headed back to Lucca. Although the boys were keen to eat their kill they learned another valuable lesson, patience. The animals would need to be hung to let the flavour develop. Tall Tom was pleased that they threw themselves into their training. They were now desperate to be better archers. They had killed for the first time. One day they would kill men, the hunt had made that a more likely possibility.

We still recruited and while William dealt with the detail it was Giovanni, Robin and me who had the final say. We rarely took on Germans or Hungarians. That was largely because few applied but the ones who did were, generally, not as good as the English and Italians who sought to join us. That suited me because it meant we had fewer language problems than some companies. As the summer passed and the new men were trained and embedded into lances William did as I had asked and sent men to seek new employers.

It was in September when we heard the news that Pope Urban had died having recently returned to Avignon from Rome. The Roman venture had been a failure and the death of the pope who had waged war on us seemed a fitting sign. For us and every other company and city-state in Italy, this had huge ramifications. It would take time to elect a new pope and when one was elected would he have the same policies as his predecessor?

As the year drew to a close and we awaited the news from Avignon, the debate when we ate was often heated. My sons, who now attended our feasts, listened to every word.

"But surely, we cannot fight for a pope. Do you not remember, Sir John, that it was on the pope's orders that you and your sons were taken?"

"Dai, it was Pope Urban who did that. The new pope will be a different man. Do not confuse the office with the man. We have fought against other companies and then with them. We fight for money and you must remember that."

William had thrown himself into his role as a spymaster, "The rumour is that the favourite to be the new pope is also a Frenchman, Pierre Roger de Beaufort."

"And that is no surprise given that the pope lives in Avignon but I have heard that Urban's attempt to relocate to Rome, whilst a failure, might pave the way for a future move."

I smiled at William. This was what he did best. He listened and evaluated every scrap of information. He sifted the wheat from the chaff so that he could present us with golden nuggets.

It was in the new year when we were asked to intervene in the Emilia-Romagna region. It was Bernabò Visconti himself who came to ask us to help. William sat with us for the meeting. I was no longer beholden to the Lord of Milan and spoke to him now as an equal. This was the first time that William had seen me in this manner and I saw the surprise on his face.

"Sir John, I wish you to go to Emilia-Romagna. Manno Donati and Lutz Von Landau are raiding my lands there. They are fortifying some of the villages and towns making it impossible for me to collect my taxes. The men of Bologna are assisting them."

"But who is paying them?"

"Your old employer, the Marquis of Montferrat."

I had made the marquis more ambitious thanks to our campaigns in Savoy. I nodded, "This will cost you. One hundred thousand florins." He frowned. I shook my head, "My lord, remember our agreement. You have paid for us to be available to fight for you but when we draw a sword then you will also pay. If we do nothing you will lose more than one hundred thousand florins, will you not?"

He was defeated, "Agreed."

I turned to William, "Make a note of that." He scribbled on the wax tablet. "And how many men do we face?"

"That I do not know. Landau has his own company of a thousand men but he also has Donati's men. They number more than a thousand. Bologna is paying their wages as well as the marquis."

I knew what he was saying. The mercenaries would have full purses.

"And I am free to act as I wish?"

"So long as Donati and von Landau are stopped do as you will."

"And our money?"

"Will be sent as soon as the threat is over."

"Then we have a contract." I held out my hand and, somewhat reluctantly, the Lord of Milan shook it. The White Company would fight once more for the Visconti family.

Chapter 11

Rubiera

We headed first for Reggio for we had friends there. It was a Visconti town. It was as neutral as it could be and we had never had to fight against them. Giovanni had discovered that von Landau had been pillaging the land thereabouts. It gave us somewhere we could use as a base. We also learned that von Landau had raided Pisa with four hundred horsemen. He had done little damage and Francesco Pagano had led the stout defence against the Swabian. We were welcomed but only after I had sent Giovanni ahead to let them know as we came as saviours rather than scavengers. They chose not to let my company enter the city but allowed us to camp close to its walls. We were supplied with food for they knew that with the White Company outside its walls, they would be safe from attack.

Giovanni's scouts soon discovered that on our approach the mercenaries had taken refuge in Bologna. I had no intention of allowing us to lose men fighting professionals behind walls. That was not what we did. I gathered my leaders. "If Bologna protects them then Bologna can pay the price. We will divide it into five columns. I will lead one, and Robin, Dai, Giovanni and Sir Andrew the others. They will be made up equally of archers and men at arms. I want every animal, bean and piece of grain taken from the towns, villages and manors that supply Bologna. I would draw them from behind their walls and then we can do battle with them. Tomorrow all five columns will raid but after that one column will remain here to guard our camp." I saw Robin and Giovanni nod their approval. They were the only ones who had realised the need for such caution.

This was the land of the Emilia-Romagna. It had been rich farmland since the time of the Romans and the Etruscans before them. Thus far it had avoided the ravages of war and the people were totally unprepared for our sudden raid. The raids were remarkably violence-free. Five columns meant that the towns, villages and manors were completely overwhelmed and had no opportunity to defend themselves. The citizens complained and they moaned but neither a villager nor a soldier was hurt.

We gathered back at Reggio and celebrated our easy first day by slaughtering an old bull. We would eat well. "I will stay here tomorrow. The rest of you use the points of the compass so that we gather as much as we can."

I had two hundred men left to me and that would be more than enough to defend our camp especially as half of them were archers. When one of the sentries shouted that horsemen were approaching, I had the camp stand to but I was not worried especially when I saw that there was just one knight with twenty retainers. They came to talk and not to fight. I waved them through and the knight dismounted. I vaguely recognised his coat of arms and when he introduced himself it became clear who he was, he was the Lord of Modena.

"I am Azzo d'Esti, and from your livery, you must be Sir John Hawkwood."

"I am, my lord. What brings you here this day?"

He gave me a wry smile, "My people reported mercenaries raiding the lands of Bologna yesterday and came to me for protection."

"We have not raided Modena, my lord, nor its lands."

"And will you?"

I shook my head, "We fight to free this land from the Germans and Swabians led by von Landau. As they now squat behind Bologna's walls, we are forced to raid Bolognese land to encourage them to fight us."

He frowned, "I have heard that von Landau and Donati are good leaders with a fine army. You are that confident that you can win?"

I waved over Tall Tom, "Tom, string your bow and select a good arrow." I scanned the sky and saw a pigeon. It was high overhead. I pointed to it and Tom drew back the bow. It looked like a difficult strike for the bird was moving and was in the air but I knew that pigeons usually flew in a straight line and I had confidence in Tom's ability. The bird was struck and John ran to retrieve it. "Now the army of von

Tuscan Warlord

Landau may have good warriors but they do not have English archers and a man is a much bigger target than a bird." John gave the bird to Tom and I smiled and said, "Thank you, Tom."

Tom and my boys left, the boys quizzing him about the hit.

"We only fight, my lord, our enemies. Are you an enemy?"

He shook his head, "The pestilence that struck Modena twenty years since left us weaker than many. We have strong walls and since the wars between Emperor Frederick and Pope Gregory we have not had to fight." He lowered his voice and leaned in, "It may be, Sir John, that if we are threatened, we might have to hire the White Company."

"We fight for pay."

"I thought you were the men who served the Lord of Milan and the Visconti are greedy predators."

"We have fought for him but we are our own men. Besides, my lord, it might be that you would not need the whole company. A couple of hundred archers on your walls would ensure that no one could get close."

He smiled, "I am glad I came to speak to you in person. I was warned that Giovanni Acuto was a terrifying man and I might not return."

I laughed, "I am not the devil even though I am portrayed that way. I am a soldier and that is all."

After he had gone, I wondered how many more cities there were like Modena. Perhaps William might visit the smaller cities and find out if they wished to be protected by the White Company. It was a thought.

We raided for three days and I wondered if von Landau would ever leave the safety of Bologna's walls. Giovanni had left men watching the city and it was they who galloped in one morning as the sun was rising in the east. "Sir John, they have decamped from Bologna. They left at the third hour."

"And where did they head?"

"They are coming here."

I could not be annoyed with my watchers for von Landau had done all that he could to avoid detection. Knowing he would be watched, he had left in the dark and it was only the fast horses of my men that gave us a chance. "Change your horses." Cupping my hands I shouted, "We march to war."

I went to my tent and Michael was already close by with my armour. As he dressed me, I said, "I want forty men to stay here and guard our camp. Make it the older men."

"Yes, my lord."

My leaders entered the tent as my breastplate was being buckled, "We march towards Modena. It may be that we can stop him there. We shall see. He has a longer march to reach us than we have to reach him. We will not make this a race. I want our horses as fresh as they can be and his to be tired. Robin, your archers will be the vanguard. If you spy some ground where you think we have an advantage then let me know." He nodded and I knew that I could rely on him.

Michael asked, "Will you need the wagon?"

I shook my head, "I do not wish to race nor do I wish to travel at the speed of a snail. We will ride to war and I will fight amongst my horsemen. John and Thomas, take your bows for today you will fight with Robin and the archers." My words were to ease the disappointment that they would not be at my side.

One advantage held by von Landau would be that he had travelled in the dark for some of his journey. We had to endure the noonday heat and I determined that we would take it easy even if that meant meeting our enemy closer to Reggio than I might have wished. In the end, we did not have to travel far. Robin himself rode back.

"Sir John, I have found where we can hold them."

Even I was surprised, "That is fast."

He nodded, "I passed this way yesterday and Rubiera seemed a good place. I did not wish to make a hasty judgement. It is just a mile ahead of us. The river is fordable and if we hold the west bank they will be encouraged to cross. My archers can make it a killing ground. I sent four archers down the road to spy out the enemy when they approach."

"Good." It seemed like a good place from his description, but I needed somewhere I could guarantee victory.

The town of Rubiera was little more than a village. Belonging to Modena we had not raided it, but I could see that there was little to take. The Lord of Modena had been right. The devastation of the plague had decimated the population. I saw unworked fields as we passed through. There would have been little point in raiding. We used the houses to disguise our horses. Robin and his archers dismounted and tethered their animals. I handed out some coins to the boys from the town to watch them. I rode to the river. The Secchia was wide just north of the town because it became very shallow. There was a bridge to the south of the town and I sent men to guard it but von Landau would have a wide front and be able to bring his whole company to battle if he chose. He did not have to fight. Had it been me I might have declined battle but his master, the Marquis of Montferrat, wanted a victory. My parting from the marquis had been acrimonious. While the Lord of Montferrat was in his mountain lair, he would have told his commander to hurt us if he could.

"Robin, I want your archers in a double line along the river. Have the polemen before you." He nodded and went off to give his orders. The road to Reggio would be guarded. Von Landau would not pass us but that did not give me the victory that I needed. "Michael, find a wagon and have it placed behind Robin."

"You intend to command from the wagon again, Sir John?"

I shook my head, "No, but I shall give the illusion that I do so. I want von Landau to make every effort to get to me." I added, "When that is done have Sir Richard of Telford come to me."

I waved over Sir Andrew, Giovanni and Dai. I found a piece of dusty earth and took out my dagger. I used the tip to illustrate my words. "Here is the river and here are our archers. Giovanni and Dai, I want you to gather three quarters of the lances and be ready to charge across the river when von Landau approaches. Sir Andrew, choose one hundred good men and they will come with me. We will cross the river upstream and make a flank attack. Giovanni, you will attack only when you hear my horn. Until then you hold."

If they were unhappy with the risk I was taking they wisely said nothing. I was counting on the news of my victory over the Florentines at San Miniato being at the forefront of von Landau and Donati's minds. They would see what I hoped they would see, me on the wagon and the bulk of my horsemen facing him.

Sir Richard arrived with Michael and the wagon. He had shown since he had joined my company, that he was a good warrior. He had embraced the concept of the White Company. He had used his treasure well and had just bought plate armour that looked like mine. The only difference was my distinctive helmet with three white feathers. I tossed it to him, "Today, Sir Richard, you and your men will fight on the wagon. You will have my standard and wear my helmet. I want you to be the honeypot that the enemy seeks. You should be safe behind Robin and our foot soldiers. There will be no Pisan weakness."

He grinned as he donned the helmet, "I am honoured, Sir John." His squire gave me his open-faced bascinet.

"I promise that you will share in any treasure that I take."

He nodded, "I know and since I have joined your company, I have learned why the White Company retains so many good men. They are loyal to you, Sir John. They know that you are fair."

"I have done this long enough now to know that you have to look after all the members of the company for it is the strength of the company that brings victory."

Michael had brought Ajax and he tied him to the wagon. I would ride him when I went to battle but for the moment I rode my third horse, a chestnut called Copper. He was a new horse and I had yet to blood him. I was just getting to know him.

The archers who had been shadowing the enemy column rode in an hour before dusk. "They are a mile behind us, Sir John. There are more than two thousand well-armed and mailed warriors." Jack was Robin's right-hand man and a reliable archer.

Ned, another centenar laughed, "Aye, but they have no archers. There are two hundred crossbowmen."

Jack nodded, "And they have some handguns too."

"Good, the archers' horses are in the town. Get yourselves some food. I do not think we will be stringing bows this evening." Sir Richard was in the wagon and he shouted, "Do you wish to swap places, my lord?"

"No, don the helmet and when they stop to view our lines, wave your arms as though directing men."

The metal snake arrived as the last rays of the sun were disappearing behind us. They halted at the river and I saw the leaders gather. I had never met either Donati or von Landau and so I could not work out which of the six men was which. However, it became clear who von Landau was, for he was the one in the centre. He had a yellow livery with three creatures upon it. I could not make out what they were but they were distinctive enough for me to be able to mark his position. I was amongst my own lances and as my whole company wore white livery, I was indistinguishable from the rest. I was hidden in plain sight. I saw von Landau pointing at the wagon. Sir Richard was playing his part well and enjoying himself as he shouted at men that he knew who turned and raised their hands in acknowledgement. The Swabians would have no idea what he was doing but would, I hoped, confirm the mistaken identity. It became clear that they would not fight but they made a defensive camp. Von Landau was clearly a cautious commander.

I walked Copper back to the wagon as the sun dipped in the west and we were plunged into darkness. "Robin and Giovanni take command here. Keep a good watch on our enemy. Sir Andrew, we will sleep but we will wake at the third hour of the day and walk our horses to our position."

Dai asked, "What if he does not attack?"

"He will attack. A condottiere does not march more than forty miles just to sit. The Bolognese wish us to be gone and for their lands not to be raided. He has to fight. All you need to do is hold until you hear Michael sound the horn three times and then you attack. Your attack will draw their attention to you." They all seemed happy. I turned to John and Thomas, "And when I return, I expect Robin to report that you obeyed every order instantly."

"We will father but you take care."

"Of course, John."

I would not say that I was worried about my action for I had every confidence that we would succeed but I was excited. This was like my first battles when I had been just one small part of a larger plan. That I was crucial to the success meant that I was aware of the pressure I was putting on myself. The result was that I did not sleep well. I rose before the appointed hour and went to make water. By the time I returned to the house we were using Michael was up. My sons were sleeping with the archers and it was Michael who dressed me and then himself. I ate as he fetched our horses. Ajax had been well rested and I could see that he was eager for war. I fed him an apple as Michael ate and then we walked through the sleeping camp and the sentries to Sir Andrew's camp on the extreme right of the main camp. He was awake and he and his men were breakfasting. My arrival hastened them, They finished their breakfast and joined us as we walked our horses along the road that led to the bridge.

We could have crossed the river using the bridge but I knew that we were close enough for the Swabians to have sentries and the sound of hooves on the bridge would alert them. We walked another mile and then we forded the river. It was only in the middle where we had to swim. Once on the other side, we allowed the water to drain from mail and plate and tightened the girths. There was no need to ride for we had plenty of time and we walked half a mile north of the river and awaited the dawn. It was not long in coming. The enemy camp was hidden but the tendrils of smoke rising in the sky marked its position. We began to walk towards it. Our helmets hung from our cantles and with our coifs about our shoulders, we could hear everything. The birdsong stopped as we neared and then, in the distance, we heard the sound of the Swabian camp coming to life. To those who are not warriors, there is no difference in the sounds of any military camp but to us, there was and I recognised that this was a camp preparing to go to war. Even at a distance of more than a mile, we could hear the sound of neighing horses as they were saddled. The jingle of armour carried over to us. Von Landau was preparing for his attack. I could not see it but my mind could envision what was happening. His hand gunners and crossbows, behind their pavise, would be lining the riverbank. The foot soldiers who would make the initial attack would be moving to their positions. The horsemen would not be mounted, that would be a last-minute action. They would be eating, some would be making confessions, whilst others would be bantering with their comrades. It was the warriors' way.

We stopped for I estimated that we were a mile away and there was a farmhouse behind which we could hide. Once the farmer and his family saw that we meant them no harm they relaxed and offered our horses water. I sent Michael up to the roof. He covered his armour in a cloak so that the light would not reflect and give away our position. Michael was thorough and he ensured he had seen all before he returned. "They are preparing for battle. There are three groups of horsemen, one on each flank and a smaller group at the rear. Von Landau is with them. I saw his banner."

I nodded, "They will be the reserve. Are there any watchers looking in our direction?"

He grinned and shook his head, "There is nothing between us and their reserves."

It was perfect. "Then let us mount."

We pulled up coifs and donned helmets before hauling ourselves into the saddle. He handed me a lance and then mounted his own horse. The horn around his neck was vital as was he and he rode behind me and Sir Andrew. We rode our horses slowly. I heard the crack of handguns and saw the smoke spiralling in the air. The sound of crossbows could also be heard and then I first saw and then heard the flight of six hundred arrows as they shadowed across the sky, looking and sounding like a murmuration of starlings. We still had plenty of time as we neared to within half a mile and then halted in a field which, obligingly, had a slight hollow. The missile duel was a preliminary to the main event, the Swabian charge, We could not see the enemy but by the same measure, we were invisible. It allowed us to form a treble line. The first two were men at arms and knights while the longer third line was composed of the squires, Michael excepted. We knew then the attack began for the handguns had stopped. We could still see the fall of arrows. It was time and I led my men up the slope and out of the field. The wall meant we had to reform after we had crossed it but as all the attention of the Swabians was on the attack we had time. The Swabian horn sounded and as we rose to within four hundred paces, I saw that the first two bodies of Swabian cavalry were charging.

"Now, Michael."

Even as the first note sounded, I waved my lance and we trotted forward. We had time. The first hundred or so paces would be slow. Then we would canter for a hundred and then the gallop and the charge. The three blasts on the horn had confused the Swabians. The cacophony of battle hid its origin but my men knew what it meant. I knew that Dai and Giovanni would be charging one body of horsemen and I hoped that the Swabians would think the three blasts came from them or were a command for them. The attention of von Landau and his reserve was still firmly fixed on their front. There were forty or so camp guards on foot but we and their horsemen would be evenly matched. The difference would be that we had lances and were charging. The Swabians were standing still and had, as yet, to don their helmets. Michael dropped back for his task would be to lead the squires. They would take out the sentries and capture the camp.

I had to haul back on Ajax's reins. He was the best warhorse in the company and he was competitive. He wanted to get to the enemy first and I had to fight him to hold the integrity of the line. It was the thundering of our hooves that warned the Swabians. When we were two hundred paces from them the shouts and cries from the sentries made the horsemen turn. Von Landau, in his bright yellow livery, shouted something and his horsemen tried to wheel to face us. It was a battle he could not win for we were now galloping. Even if they tried to countercharge us, they would only be able to muster a walk. I pulled my hand back and rammed my lance at the brave Swabian who rode directly at me to buy time for his comrades. His lance was not yet lowered as my lance struck him squarely in the chest. The metal head drove through the plate and into his body. He fell to one side as his horse veered to the other. His dying body slipped from my lance. I barely had time to raise it again as a second Swabian, following the man I had killed, rammed his lance at my head. It was a courageous strike. He would either kill me or miss me. My open bascinet allowed me to move my head to the side as I struck his horse in the chest with my lance. He missed me and my lance was lost but as his horse fell, he was thrown over his mount's head.

    I drew my sword and made for von Landau. I might not have been wearing my distinctive helmet but I was riding the best horse and he came for me, recognising that I was the leader. He had a lance and I just had my sword. He too wore an open helmet and I saw the wolfish grin as he pulled back his arm. This would be about timing. As we neared, I gauged the moment to perfection. He had aimed at my chest and I angled my shield to deflect it along my side. At the same time, I swung my sword horizontally across his chest. I did not use the edge for that would have blunted my weapon. It was as though I had struck him with an iron bar. He rolled backwards over his cantle and I wheeled Ajax around. As I did so I took in the battle. Dai and Giovanni had routed one group of horsemen and they were engaged in a mêlée with the others. Robin must have given the orders for a general advance for I saw a battle raging on the riverbank. When Ajax had stopped, I was able to see that my attack had destroyed the reserves and Michael and the squires held the camp and baggage train. Jumping from the back of Ajax who bit and snorted at any horse who came too close, I put my sword at the Swabian's neck. I had stunned him when he had fallen and his eyes were closed. As they opened, I said, "You are Lutz von Landau and you are now my prisoner. Do you yield?" I pressed hard enough with my sword for him to know my intent.

"I yield. May I know the name of my captor?"

His eyes widened as I said, "Sir John Hawkwood."

He laughed, wryly, "Outwitted by an old man!"

I am not sure he meant to insult me but he had and I shouted, "Michael, come and take my prisoner." I remounted Ajax as Michael came to guard the man who would bring me as much in ransom as we were due to be paid by the Lord of Milan.

With their leader captured the rest of the reserve surrendered. They were a professional company and understood such things. It signalled the defeat of the enemy. The horsemen at the rear seeing that their leader and camp were taken, wisely disengaged and fled. It was like the breaking of a dam. At first a trickle, it became a torrent as the horsemen fled. The Swabian army was largely on foot and seeing the horsemen flee created the rout. As a company of mercenaries, the Swabians were rendered ineffective. We had won and I was still whole. I had shown my company and the rest of Italy that I was not a spent force. I was still a man to be reckoned with.

Sir Richard was disappointed that he had not needed to use his sword, for although the Swabians tried to get to him the arrows of our archers kept them in the shallow river. I thanked him for the use of his helmet and gave him von Landau's sword. All were happy.

Chapter 12

We kept von Landau with us while we awaited his ransom. He was not Sir John Hawkwood and we only asked fifty thousand florins for him. We also ransomed some of the lesser leaders. It took four months to gather the ransom and for it to be delivered. During that time we ensured that the cities we had been sent to defend were strengthened and when winter approached headed back to Lucca. Our journey was slower than normal as we had captured wagons full of loot. There was a cloud in the sky and that cloud was the lack of pay from Bernabò Visconti. During our sojourn in Emilia-Romagna, I had sent many messages asking for pay but the riders came back empty handed. Before we left for our new home, I paid my soldiers from my own purse. My leaders all refused payment but I insisted that every lance and archer be paid. It was not their fault that Visconti had reneged on his payment. I was angry with the Lord of Milan for we had defeated his enemy. We had suffered losses. I paid my men as I wanted no desertions and I did not need the money. My English estates not to mention the manor in Bordeaux all brought the money I needed. It was not as though I had a family to support.

As we rode home, however, I brooded. I took it as an insult that I had not been paid. It was Michael, now grown into a man, who acted as a sage counsellor. "Sir John, we both know that Bernabò Visconti is not a man to be trusted." I turned and looked at him as though seeing him for the first time. "Oh come, my lord, when you joined him you knew that he was untrustworthy and all that he has done hitherto has been to use you." I reflected and saw that he was right. He went on, "How many times did he send the company to war for him and used not a single Milanese warrior? The fact that we won and profited is immaterial for had we lost Visconti would have lost not a moment of sleep."

"How did you see this and I did not?"

He smiled, "Because you enjoy the praise after victories." Was I being insulted? He hurriedly carried on, "I speak to you now as someone who sees you as a father figure, my lord, and there is no slur intended. You are what you are. We all know that you are a great leader and your men and leaders would follow you into the fires of hell knowing that you would have a plan to defeat the devil. Giovanni is a great leader but he is happy to serve you. He is well-read and has spoken of you in the same breath as he talks of Caesar and Alexander the Great. Those men had flaws in their character but they were warlords who led their armies to carve out huge empires. You are greater than the Visconti family and your reputation will last long after theirs is forgotten."

It was as though he had pricked me with a poniard, "But will I be remembered, Michael? I am a condottiere like others who have gone before. Who remembers Sterz or Paer?"

"No one but they are not Sir John Hawkwood who leads the White Company. Be happy in who you are, my lord, and forget Visconti. We have coins in our wagons and whilst you have not made as much as you might, thanks to the tight-fisted Visconti, we are far from poor and William will already be seeking a new employer."

He was right, of course. When it became clear that our pay would not be coming, I had sent word to my treasurer to actively seek a new paymaster. I smiled more for the rest of the journey. John and Thomas approached more often and less nervously. We enjoyed the ride and I was happy that Michael had felt courageous enough to beard me. Few, other than Robin or Giovanni, would have said what he said.

When we reached Lucca, it felt like home. Pisa had been my home for many years but Lucca was a smaller place. It felt safer for it was in the mountains. The only city which took an interest in Lucca was Pisa and with my company there the city was safe from any predators. As they did not have to pay us and, indeed, we brought an income into the city, we were seen as an ally. In Pisa, we had been used. I could only see that now but as I had learned hindsight was always perfect. My house in Pisa had been sold and those who had looked after me there now made my Luccan one as cosy. Jack White, who ran my home said, quietly, as he served us food, "You should know, Sir John, that there is a papal envoy staying at the home of William Turner."

"Do you know why?"

"No, Sir John, but he has a strong escort of papal mercenaries."

I nodded. The new pope had done what all the other popes had done and employed non-Italians as soldiers. They had allegiance only to the pope. I suppose coming from France, rather than Rome, gave the popes a mistrust of Italians. I was not worried about the visit. I had been excommunicated once and if it happened a second time I would live with it. I was, however, preoccupied for the rest of the meal.

William brought the cardinal the next day. He was younger than I expected. He looked to be in his early thirties. He spoke English well. "Sir John Hawkwood, may I introduce the papal envoy sent by Pope Gregory."

"I am, Sir John, Robert de Genève, the Archbishop of Cambrai, Bishop of Thérouanne and," he smiled self-deprecatingly, "rector of Bishopwearmouth in County Durham." The man was silky smooth, "I always use my last title even though it is the one that raises eyebrows for I was happy there in the north of England." I knew what he was doing, he was trying to ingratiate me with his mention of an English home. I was not fooled.

"You have done well to be both archbishop and bishop at such a young age."

"Pope Urban was kind and Pope Gregory has seen fit to elevate me higher. My title of cardinal is so new that it is not yet ratified. When it is then I shall be happy to be greeted as cardinal."

I waved them both to seats and Jack brought us wine and food. I waited for it was clear that William and the cardinal had enjoyed a conversation already and I had to trust William. He looked at ease and he would not do so if there was a threat to me. The cardinal nibbled at the bread and ham and washed the mouthful down with wine. After dabbing his mouth with his napkin he began, "Sir John, Pope

Gregory intends to return to Rome. There is opposition to that move from Florence. The doge of Florence does not wish to see their power diminished and he has found an ally in the Visconti family."

So it began, now that we had divorced from Visconti then both of us might be used. I looked over to William who smiled and shrugged. Had Visconti known of this offer and was that why he had not paid me? If so, he had made a mistake.

"Pope Gregory would like to hire the White Company to fight for him against Milan and Florence." He cut a slice of ham, "This is well-cured ham. I like the piquancy." Jack had remained to serve us and he nodded his thanks.

I was well aware that the cardinal was giving me the time to reflect on his words and I knew what his next ones would be.

"You will lead the papal forces in this campaign. It is you, Sir John, who will command the pope's soldiers. I will remain with you as an adviser as well as the paymaster and I will bring papal troops to aid you. I will ensure that you are paid what is due."

I knew that he would be more than an adviser. He would be the one who held my reins. He must have known about Visconti's refusal to pay me. He either had good spies or William had spoken to him. I looked directly at William, "Will I be happy with the pay, William?"

"You will, my lord. The pope will pay us fifty thousand florins a year. The initial contract is for three years but can be extended if there is mutual agreement."

It was my turn to play for time and I also ate the bread and ham. Unlike the papal envoy, I took a large mouthful and washed it down with half a goblet of wine. I saw the bemusement on the face of the cardinal. He was young but he knew what I was doing. I could not see an argument against this contract. True the Avignon papacy was influenced by France but Pope Gregory's decision to return to Rome made sense. That Milan and Florence were opposed was also clear. The question was, could the White Company defeat Florence and Milan? Michael had been right, I did

Tuscan Warlord

have arrogance and self-belief, but I was also a realist. I would not be able to defeat both of them alone. I would need men upon whom I could rely. Nor could I beat a combined Milanese and Florentine army. I would have to defeat them piecemeal.

"If I agree then when would you have us take the field?" I leaned forward before he could answer, "By that, I mean when can you bring the first payment for the company and the men who will serve alongside my company?"

He replied, "The New Year; that will allow you to recruit more men as well as give me the time to bring men here." He frowned, "Pisa strikes me as the port we should use but that city is an ally of Visconti, is it not?"

"If you use the ships of Genoa to bring your men then the Pisans, who fear Genoa, will not oppose you. They have no standing army and they are a chicken waiting to be plucked. Since we left their service, I have been waiting for a move from Florence to take the prize they seek."

"Then all is well. I will return when they least expect us, in the depths of winter, and we will land at Pisa." The cardinal was a man of action.

He returned to William's home and I sent for my leaders. They were all pleased to have a contract and a lucrative one but they mistrusted the pope. Robin shook his head, "Visconti could have been a pope for they are as cunning as he is. My fear is that we are used and then abandoned."

Giovanni d'Azzo smiled, "He needs us more than we need him. We know that we can defeat Florence any time we wish and as for Milan? Bernabò has used us more times than I care to count. He has underpaid us and I, for one, relish the opportunity to fight and defeat him."

That made Robin smile, "You are right Giovanni. We do not have to loose an arrow until we are paid and when we do fight, I pray that you choose Milan to be the enemy, Sir John, for I would enjoy taking the ransom from their fat carcasses."

My two most trusted advisers were the ones who convinced the others and we joined the pope.

Knowing that we would need more men we actively sought recruits. The lances were not a problem. We employed some who had fought for von Landau and Donati but archers were as rare as hen's teeth. The trickle that came from Gascony would not be enough. In the end, we had to send Tall Tom back to England. He would be away for up to six months but Robin and I agreed that England was the best place to hire the finest of archers. With Sir Richard of Telford, who went as a guard and also to visit his home, they left for a hazardous voyage first to Narbonne and thence across Toulouse to take ship from Bordeaux. Sir Richard was keen to visit his old manor for he had personal scores to settle and he wished to see if the maid he had courted was still single. He would hire us English lances and billmen. I also gave him a letter to take to parliament, I was still an English noble and one day I wanted to return to England. I asked for a pardon for any crimes I might have committed whilst leading the White Company. I knew that I was not getting any younger and that one day I would no longer be able to wield a weapon. I wanted to return to England safe in the knowledge that any crimes I had committed in Europe would not follow me. The presence of my sons had made me sentimental about both them and my daughter. I had not been a proper parent and now I was preparing to be one.

Tall Tom spoke to me the night before he left, "Would you have me visit Mistress Elizabeth and Master Roger?"

"No, Tom, neither is worth the time it would take. As soon as you reach Bordeaux take ship."

The small chest of gold nobles they carried would be enough to encourage archers, billmen and men at arms to join us. I hoped it would not encourage bandits but Tall Tom and Sir Richard were seasoned warriors. I had confidence in them.

I had less confidence in Dai and William. Although they both had homes in Lucca, their families lived in Pisa and the two men divided their time between the two. In William's case, there was some justification for he used the merchants he knew in Pisa as well as the Agnello family to gather intelligence that would aid us. Dai, on the other hand, needed to be with us in Lucca. A month after the envoy had left, I brought matters to a head. He had been away for a week in Pisa and we were practising on foot. I had realised that using our cavalry charges was making us predictable and I knew that the Milanese when we fought them, would have studied our methods. Dai had missed the previous week of training and when I gave the order for men in the second ranks to switch with those in the front the only section which fell into disarray was Dai's. It was not just the embarrassment, men were hurt. Leaving Giovanni to continue the session I took Dai away. He was one of my senior leaders and I would not belittle him in front of the men. My bodyguards came with us and they made a circle so that we would be neither seen nor overheard.

"Dai, that mistake was inexcusable. The men we lead are valuable and the four who were hurt we can ill afford to lose."

"I am sorry, Sir John, but that manoeuvre was a new one. I will get it right next time."

"Unless you agree to live here in Lucca while we prepare for this coming campaign there will be no next time." He looked at me with hurt eyes. "If you wish to live in Pisa with your family then you can do so but you will not be a member of the White Company. I will give you the command of the bank."

If I had slapped him in the face, I could not have shocked him more, "The garrison of the bank are old men and I am still a young warrior."

"Then either bring your family to Lucca or tell them that you will see them in a year when we have defeated Milan."

"I cannot leave my family,"

"I did."

"Caterina is close to her father."

I shook my head, "Dai, the days of Caterina's father as doge are numbered. He has enemies and we are no longer there to protect him. It is a matter of time before he is ousted and has to flee again. Who is head of your family, you or Caterina?"

I let the words sink in. Dai was still the loyal warrior who had been my squire but he had allowed his heart to sway his head. It had happened to Sir Andrew too. Robin and Giovanni were more like me, they were in control of their heads and their loins. He nodded, "There will be tears."

I could not understand how tears would sway anyone. Elizabeth had tried to use tears all the time to get her own way and she had failed. Antiochia had never cried, even when I had left. I think that if my first wife had not died then she might be with me in Lucca. It had not been meant to be.

"Then give your wife a handkerchief to dry them." I strode off.

I went back to the training ground. Robin was grinning. He and his men were not needed for the tactic we practised and he grinned, "Is he sorted then, Sir John?"

"I hope so. I can do without these distractions. We have hard times ahead of us." I walked over to Giovanni. The men had paused, "How are the injured men?"

"Embarrassed more than anything. Dai confused them and they were torn between doing what they knew was right and what he ordered them to do."

"And that is my fault." I cupped my hands and waved Michael over. "Fetch me a horse. I would be seen."

The men took some time to gather. The practice ground was not as big as it might have been and was of an odd shape. I climbed on the back of Remus. I saw Dai approaching, his head was hung. I shouted, "Men of the White Company, know that we practice new tactics for we will be fighting against those who know our methods well. We may have to fight another company, perhaps even the Company of St George. If we are to win then we need to surprise them. This new tactic, switching lines, is not only for when we fight on foot but for when we fight on horseback too. When we have mastered it on foot then we risk our horses. Let me go through it again." I took out my sword to demonstrate. It was the one given to me by Pisa. It was too fine to use in war but this was a time to wear it as a reminder to my company of the honour it brought. "We know that when we fight men who are armed as we are then the battle will often be even. The Romans knew that and they were able to switch their first and second ranks. When the command is given: 'Switch' then you all turn to the right and the man behind steps into the line. Not all of you will have a shield but enough of you will have to enable you to have some protection. We can always, if the battle is hard, change the second and third ranks. This must be a seamless movement. The second rank needs to strike as soon as the man before them moves. Remember, move to the right. Now form three lines. Robin, come with me and we will watch how they do this time."

I had not mentioned Dai but everyone knew what he had done. My leaders, men like Sir Andrew, Sir John Thornbury and Andrew Gold would all strive to get it right. Sir John and Andrew Gold had both performed well in the battle against von Landau and had done all that was asked of them. As a reward, they were given command of one hundred lances each. Sir Andrew and Dai each commanded two hundred and fifty. We had the scope to use complicated systems when we went to war. Giovanni was the one who would give the command. It did not take long to form the lines and I shouted, "Now wield your weapons as though there is an enemy before you."

Robin and I looked down the line. This was our chance to look for weaknesses in the men. Just swinging a sword or pole axe was tiring and we sought those who slowed before others. I swept down my sword and Giovanni bellowed, "Switch!"

This time even Dai got it right. Robin and I kept the front rank longer than the others and then I swept down my sword again. "Switch." This time it was as good as the first.

"Good." I looked at the sky. It was getting on for the late afternoon. "That is enough for today. Tomorrow, I want the horsemen to come mounted. We will try cavalry and infantry together." As they departed, I said, "Robin, our archers are our strength. I would have you employ horseholders. It strikes me that if the horses can be kept closer to the archers, then we have the chance to react more quickly."

Tuscan Warlord

He nodded, "Aye, Visconti knows better than any how we use our archers. If I was fighting the White Company I would have my light horsemen get around the flanks. If they did that then we might be compromised. It will be an expense. One man to four horses would be a minimum and the men would need both arms and protection."

I calculated in my head, "That would be a hundred men or so. We can afford that. If you cannot get all that you need here in Lucca then go to Pisa. We need young men whom we can train. Who knows, there may be enough talent to make them into billmen or halberdiers."

That night I dined with Michael and my sons, "Michael, today showed me that I need you not as my squire but as a leader."

"But who will carry your standard and pass on your orders, Sir John?"

"You are not afraid of the responsibility are you, Michael?"

"No, but I hate the thought of leaving you."

"And you would not but Dai's mistake today made me realise that you would not have made that mistake. The men know and trust you and I would not be alone. I have two sons and while one holds the standard the other can take messages."

I had not mentioned it before and the reaction on my sons' faces made both Michael and I smile. Michael nodded, "Then I will do so."

"And I will knight you too."

"You need not, Sir John."

"It is my gift to give so do not spoil it for me."

Men make plans and they hope that all goes well. While the appointment of Michael as commander of one hundred lances met with approval from the majority of my company, Sir John Thornbury objected. It did not manifest itself for a week or two. Robin was away or else he would have noticed and Giovani was preoccupied. It was when we were, once more, practising, this time the switching of horsemen, that matters came to a head.

Michael's lances had more of the new men than any other company. The trickle of new horsemen was given to him. It was as we switched that one of them, Ned Longshanks, fell from his horse. He had turned the wrong way.

Sir John could have done as all the others did and remained silent at the mistake but he did not, "And that shows why striplings who are promoted before their time should be left to hold a banner and not be given responsibility."

Michael flushed and I saw the anger on the faces of Dai and Giovanni. In Giovanni's case that was a rare occurrence and showed me the unfairness of the comment. I had merely been an observer but I rode over to the men as Ned hauled himself back into the saddle, "I am sorry, Sir John, I got my right and left mixed up. It will not happen again."

I nodded, "Mistakes happen Ned and that is why we go through this so often. Better a mistake here than in the heat of battle." Sir John made the mistake of snorting. I whirled around, "Sir John, you are relatively new to the White Company and whilst you did well in our last battle you have not yet earned the right to criticise fellow officers."

The whole of the White Company was watching the interchange. The vast majority knew that Sir John was digging a hole for himself.

"Officers? I had heard that the White Company was well-ordered and managed but if you appoint boys to be officers then I have my doubts."

I nodded and turned to Giovanni, "Sir John no longer commands a hundred. Divide his men amongst the other companies." I turned back to the stunned Englishman, "I can promote and I can demote." He rode up to me and his face was effused with anger. His hands were bunched into fists and I knew he would next go for his weapons. My bodyguards were behind me and I almost felt their hands go to their swords. I held up my own hand, "Hold for Sir John will withdraw. He does not wish to test me further, do you, Sir John?" My tone and the threat were enough to make him unclench his fists.

He tore his tabard from his armour, "I want nothing more to do with you or this company. My lance and I will leave this day and I will seek employment elsewhere."

"And that is your choice."

As he and his men rode away Michael said, "I am sorry, Sir John. Perhaps he is right and my promotion was a mistake."

I affected outrage, "You are saying that Sir John Hawkwood made a mistake?" I smiled, "My mistake was promoting that man. He has left us and we will be stronger for it."

Although Sir John was a good leader he had not been right for the White Company and although his leaving left us short of men, it made us stronger. What I did not know was that he would run to serve the Visconti family. I had made another enemy.

Chapter 13

The Battle of the Panaro River.

While we waited for the arrival of the papal army, I sent Giovanni and our Italians to find the Milanese. It was not the time for war but, like us, they would have men in place ready to obey the orders of the Lord of Milan. We knew the targets that they would seek. Although the papacy resided in Avignon, various popes had appointed the heads of the noble families to be vicars and to rule the cities on their behalf. It was an uneasy relationship and explained why the new pope had hired the White Company. He wanted all the states under his jurisdiction. Rome was too far away for us to be concerned about. The Orsini and the Colonna families fought over Rome and the Lord of Milan would not interfere there. Queen Joanna of Naples was the one who manipulated the lands around Rome and she was the enemy that the pope might have to deal with. I knew that the queen and the Hungarians had a blood feud but that was as far as William's information went. The other papal states were more likely targets. The Pepoli family held Bologna, the Ordelaffi in Forlì, the Manfredi in Faenza, and the Malatesta in Rimini. Ferrara was ruled by the Este brothers. Having already spoken to the Lord of Modena I guessed that Bologna and the Panaro River would be their first target. When, on their return, that was confirmed by Giovanni, it gave us the chance to plan in a little more detail. The result was that by the time Robert de Genève arrived, we had plans in place and I knew what we would do. We had made enough friends in Parma and Modena for us to be secure knowing that Bologna would not be an enemy and we had the best chance of halting the Milanese. There was some worry that, in our absence, the Florentines might take Pisa.

It was Dai who brought the matter up and I shrugged, "Dai, Pisa is no longer our paymaster nor is Visconti. We have left enough men to defend Lucca and I think our new home is too big a mouthful for Florence. She wants Pisa and one day she will get it. I feel sorry for the men like Pagano but what can we do? Our business is war but only when we are paid. The pope pays us and so we fight his enemies."

I knew in my head that Florence would not risk antagonising the White Company. If they took over Pisa then they would leave alone that which belonged to us.

Our allies arrived in the middle of December. The voyage they had endured must have been terrible but the cardinal had heard that the Milanese were mustering. Robert de Genève came dressed not like a cardinal but as a warrior. He was plated and helmed. He had with him French mercenaries. In the main, they were, like us, men at arms but he had some Breton horsemen and crossbowmen. The crossbowmen might be a hindrance unless we defended a town but the Bretons were useful. They could ride and guard my archers. It would give us a greater range and security.

This time the cardinal stayed with me and so we were able to discuss our strategy. I allowed him an opinion but made it quite clear that I commanded. As he had brought fewer men than I had he did not argue. "I thought to head to Emilia-Romagna. That is where, when the Milanese come, we can stop them. The Panaro river is not the Po and we can use it to defend against his horsemen and yet it will not be an obstacle when we choose to cross."

"You have thought all of this out and yet the Milanese are not even here, yet. We know that they are mustering their army but the last reports I had was that they were still in Milan."

"I know Visconti. He is penny-pinching and he will leave it to the last moment to send his men and when they come it will be lightning quick. He will use horsemen and that is why we will meet him on foot. The Bretons you brought might be the edge he does not expect. He knows my company well and whilst I do not think that he will actually lead, he will have advised whoever it is well. I just hope that it is not Ambrogio."

"Why, Sir John, do you fear him?"

I laughed, "I fear no man but he is a friend and I would prefer not to fight a friend. I think that Ambrogio is too clever to risk a battle with me. He will make some excuse to his father and fight elsewhere."

He nodded and then said, "I heard, before I met you, that you had a good mind. I can now see it is true. It is a pity that Pope Urban was so pig-headed. Pope Gregory is a more pragmatic man. If he is to keep away the poachers then what better gamekeeper than the master poacher?"

We did not leave straightaway for I wished us to practise together for a couple of days. I made certain that the French leaders knew exactly what we were doing. I confess that the language skills of Robert de Genève would be vital. I was used to Italian and English. My French had deteriorated since the Battle of Poitiers. It would come back but while the cardinal was with us then there would be no misunderstanding.

We left Lucca on a cold winter's day and used our normal practice of seeking back roads and masking our movements with light horsemen and archer scouts to reach the Romagna. The roads were atrocious at that time of year but the weather aided us and we saw few men on the road. We reached Reggio safely but it was there that we encountered a problem. Since Giovanni had scouted, the town had accepted the overlordship of the Lord of Milan. Bernabò was a clever man. He had not needed soldiers to take the town he had offered them money. It was probably the money that was owed to us. We were lucky that we arrived when we did for there were no Milanese in the city and as we arrived at dawn we were in their city before they could bar their doors. They protested, of course, but between us, the cardinal and I persuaded them that they would not be harmed and that Bernabò Visconti was unlikely to take it out on them as we had managed to occupy the town quickly. To ensure that there was no treachery the leading nobles were placed under house arrest and guarded by papal guards. I was not foolish enough to rely purely on my instincts and I sent detachments of archers and Breton horsemen to Parma, Ferrara and Mantua. It was as well that I did. Ettore Visconti, one of Bernabò's many illegitimate children, led the army and they came by Mantua. We had to decamp quickly. We lost

Reggio and with Parma now also Milanese our options were diminishing. Holding a town with belligerents within was asking for trouble. I realised that the plan I had devised in Lucca would have to be the one we used. The Panaro River would be our battleground. We rode to Spilamberto, just twenty-eight miles away and waited there. We had the Panaro River before us but the bridge there and the direction the Milanese were taking meant we would have to fight at the bridge.

As we surveyed the ground on a wickedly cold evening where our breath vaporised before us, I summoned my leaders. "Robin, I want fifty archers and the same number of Bretons to the north of us close to the river near Modena. I think that the Lord of Modena will bar his gates to the Milanese as he is neutral in this but as Parma and Reggio have both taken Visconti's promises we cannot be sure and I do not wish to be surprised on our right flank." He nodded. "The rest of us will form up on the east bank of the river. I intend to fill the bridge with men at arms. We will deny him the crossing. He may force the river but at this time of year that will hurt him."

Robert de Genève asked, "I can see how your plan will stop him but will it defeat him?"

"First, we stop him and then I decide how best to beat him. We have rough numbers only and Ettore may use some of his erstwhile allies. Until we see how the enemy battles form up, we are in the dark. What I know is that the river will stop a mass charge of cavalry and with our superiority in archers we can hurt him while he funnels men across a narrow bridge. After the first clash, I will have a better idea of how to defeat the Milanese."

The cardinal showed he possessed a harder side than I expected. He ousted those from the best houses and took them for us. I suppose it was the difference between us. My company were a professional body of men who expected to endure hardship during the campaign. The pope's men expected comfort.

I slept with my men in barns, stables and in the open. It was a cold night but I know that I was respected for suffering the same conditions as they had. My resourceful men and night guards had found and cooked food that was offered to me as I headed to the bridge.

Dai approached me with a mug of heated ale infused with butter. As I drank it, he said, "Sir John, allow me to lead the defence of the bridge."

"You think I cannot choose the best man for the task?"

He shook his head, "I feel I have to prove myself to you. My marriage to Caterina and the doge's soft life changed me, temporarily. I am still the man who was your squire and this battle is my chance to show you that."

"You have nothing to prove to me but I need a good man at the bridge who can obey orders. The command is yours. Choose your men."

In such a situation I always let my leaders choose the men alongside whom they fought. The bridge would hold just one hundred men and Dai and his squire headed through the camp assigning men. That allowed me the freedom to use Sir Andrew, Giovanni, Andrew Gold, and Michael as I saw fit. Sir Andrew and Andrew Gold were both horsemen at heart and I gave them two hundred horsemen each to guard the flanks. "Your task is to attack any large body of soldiers that breach our lines and to guard our flanks. Listen for the commands given by my horn. If I sound the charge then do so on their flanks." Thomas had spent the last months learning to play the horn. It had been decided that John would carry my standard but Thomas would blow the horn.

"Aye, my lord."

"Go, choose your men." I turned to Robin, Giovanni and Michael, "I do not think that either of those men or their lances will be needed this day. I want the rest of our men in a solid line close to the bridge. Robin, your archers will be in a double line behind them. Our task is to hold the Milanese at the river and let Dai and the men at arms on the bridge blunt their attack."

"And the pope's men?"

Even as Giovanni spoke, I heard footsteps behind me and the cardinal said, "Aye, Sir John, what of the men I brought? I was not invited to this briefing."

I smiled, "I spoke with those who were up and about, Cardinal. I thought you still abed."

His eyes narrowed, "Next time wake me."

I nodded, "I need your crossbows on the flanks of my archers. Make it even numbers. Your horsemen will be the reserve. If I order the charge then they join my men and attack the flanks. The Bretons can attach themselves to Sir Andrew and Andrew Gold. No one crosses the river without an order from me. Is that understood?"

Robert de Genève shrugged, "This will be the first time I have seen you command and so I will watch and learn, but I confess that your battle plan seems a little timid. I had expected more from Giovanni Acuto."

"That is a word men rarely use when describing the actions of the White Company. When this day is over we shall discuss it again."

I ended the conversation for the battle horns of the enemy sounded. They were forming up in the distance. We could not see them for the houses but we had spoken enough. "To arms."

My bodyguards had dragged a wagon and it was placed a few paces from the bridge. There was enough space for us to reinforce Dai and his men but I was close enough to have a good view along the river. The sound from the west meant that they had not tried a flank attack. The archers and Breton horsemen I had left to the north might well be idle during the battle. It could not be helped. I clambered onto the wagon. This time I wore a simple bascinet but the three white feathers still identified me. I had brought a poleaxe with me as well as my shield. Thomas and John laid them in the well of the wagon. My bodyguards formed a wall before me. They had placed a wooden chest in the wagon and standing on that gave me a good view over them. I would be targeted but that was a risk I would have to take. It would take a very lucky bolt to hit my face for even though open-faced, my coif covered all but my eyes, nose and mouth. Once they had committed their men I would heft my shield into place. Thomas and John were encased in plate and mail. They, too, had open helmets but they were not standing on the chest and they were shielded by the four bodyguards. I hoped this would be enough protection

John planted the standard in the bottom of the wagon and ensured that it would fly freely. The wind obligingly came from the west and that meant it would flutter behind us and not interfere with my vision. "Thomas, have a good drink and then listen to my commands. Bolts will come for your brother but you are the one who will pass on my commands."

"Aye, father." His voice was filled with the nervous excitement I would have expected.

Dai and his men were already in position. I saw that Dai was in the second rank. He had placed his men halfway across the bridge. It was sensible as it would encourage the Milanese to charge and try to use their weight against Dai. It would be in vain. We had often practised bolstering men at arms from behind. They would not move and would be like a rock. Robin and the archers were spreading out behind Giovanni and Michael's men. Further along, I saw the crossbows and heard as they pulled back the strings. Some had a winding mechanism whilst some retained the traditional spanning hook. Their initial shower of bolts would be the most effective as they would all strike together. After that, it would rely on the individual crossbowman. Robin's archers could keep up solid showers of arrows for much longer.

It took time for the Milanese to form up and filter through the small town. I saw their leader, Ettore, look at the river. I had seen him in Milan but had never spoken to him. The livery with the serpent upon it marked him as a Visconti. It was an appropriate symbol. He must have known, as I did, that it was easily fordable but he had to balance an attack across its icy waters with the chance to drive us from the bridge. He had a line of dismounted spearmen as well as crossbows and pavesiers. His horsemen were close but I could not see them. I heard them and as the breeze blew it brought their smell across the river. He would use them once he had breached our line.

Robin was close enough to me for me to communicate with him, "Robin, the honour of the first strike is yours. Choose your moment well."

"Aye, Sir John." Cupping his hands he shouted, "Sunday arrows!"

I smiled. He was ordering his men to use war arrows. The Milanese on the other side would know the words war arrows and bodkins. Robin's simple code would be enough to confuse them. The men nocked their arrows but held their bows loosely in their left hands. They were patient men.

Giovanni and Michael shouted, "Shields." The line of soldiers at the riverbank hefted their shields and ducked their heads behind them. Each of them wore greaves and when the bolts came, they would slam into metal or leather-covered wood.

The Milanese had brought a few handguns too and it was those weapons that began the battle. It was laughable. The cold and the damp made half of them fizzle and misfire. The others sent their lead balls to fly across the river. There was little force behind them and it sounded like hailstones on a roof. I had my shield ready when I saw Ettore's sword swing down. The crossbows cracked and their bolts flew across the river. Even as one hit my shield I heard Robin shout, "Draw!" The reassuring creak of longbows being drawn lasted but a moment before Robin shouted, "Loose!" The men would now draw and release until ordered to stop. They would be regular as though Robin was using a metronome. Unlike the attack of the bolts, the arrow attack brought cries and screams as arrows plunged down to hit both spearmen and men at arms. An arrow falling vertically, even a war arrow, had enough force to penetrate and with shields to the fore and not above, men were hit and they fell.

The Milanese horn sounded and the men who had been waiting to attack Dai began to move across to the bridge. Robin had been waiting and his order was clearly heard, "Bodkins at the bridge!"

This time the needle-sharp arrows would pierce plate and mail. The cracks and cries were louder. I saw men at arms fall and trip others. Tardy arrows pinned fallen men to the ground and the line of men that struck Dai was piecemeal. The first ones who reached his line were killed to a man. I watched as the second wave took the time to form up. This time the second and third ranks held shields above their heads and the arrow storm had less effect. The second wave of Milanese men struck Dai's men as one and we heard the clash of steel on steel. Such a mêlée was a brutal form of war. Those fighting were similarly armed and armoured. Men would be hurt but they would continue to batter each other until there was a weakness. It was when Dai shouted, "Switch!" that the battle of the bridge swung in our direction. The Milanese were confused and the second rank of men, led by Dai himself, were fresh and their blows brought death. The Milanese fell back. Our practice had paid off and as Dai shouted his commands, so the Milanese were driven back.

The stout defence of the bridge forced Ettore Visconti's hand. He sounded the attack across the river. This time the French crossbows brought by the cardinal came into play and, along with my archers, harvested the Milanese who waded across an icy river which, whilst fordable sapped energy from legs and slowed progress to a crawl. Those who reached the eastern bank were met by a wall of spears, halberds, poleaxes and billhooks. It was as I stood on the chest perched above my bodyguards that I saw all before me. The Milanese were committed and the river was filled with their army, mounted and on foot as they struggled with the cold and the torrent of missiles.

"Thomas, sound the cavalry charge!"

I had three groups of horsemen who were fresh and armed with lances. There would be a delay as they obeyed my orders. They would have to ride beyond my line of foot soldiers and then launch their attack down the river. Horses would not be affected as badly by the icy waters. My wagon afforded me the opportunity denied to Ettore Visconti. He could not see beyond the swaying battle of the bridge. He did not know my commands and perhaps thought that I intended Dai to cross to the other shore. He was mistaken and I smiled when he brought his reserves to bolster the beleaguered attack on the bridge. There were no reserves for the mass of men in the river. The battle seemed to be a stalemate. The Milanese were fighting along the eastern bank and we held the bridge. When our horsemen struck both flanks simultaneously it came as a complete shock to the Milanese in the river. Robin's arrows were still harvesting men who were slow to raise a shield and my pole weapons were preventing penetration on the eastern shore. When the lances of Sir Andrew Belmonte, Andrew Gold and the papal horsemen struck disordered men in the river then the battle was, effectively, over. The Milanese horn sounded the retreat but the men in the river had made the decision to flee already. It was then that the Bretons came in to their own. They pursued the fleeing Milanese soldiers who were forced to abandon their weapons and baggage as they fled back towards Palma. We had won and Milan was denied the Emilia-Romagna. I had fought just one battle against a greater force than mine and we had not only routed them but suffered far fewer casualties than might have been expected.

Chapter 14

The cardinal had the good grace to praise me after the battle, "You have a well-deserved reputation, Sir John. You handled the battle well."

I nodded, "Our losses were light and the Milanese lost five hundred men." A greater loss to the Milanese was the horses, weapons and equipment. The Bretons who had followed them reaped a rich reward.

"And what next?"

"We have done that which the Pope wished and defeated the Milanese. We are too few to prosecute this war in winter. I propose to spend the next months in Bologna while our archers and the Bretons probe for weaknesses. The land around Parma, Ferrara and Reggio can be plundered to encourage them to return to the papal fold. Thanks to our victory we can eat Milanese supplies for a month." I smiled, "I look forward to our first pay from the pope."

The sharp look from the cardinal told me that he did not appreciate the comment and was also a warning that the pope might prove to be another Bernabò.

I do not think that the Bolognese appreciated my decision but it was a papal town and I had the cardinal with me. Once more we camped outside the walls while the pope's men enjoyed warm beds. My men, however, were the ones who benefitted from the raids and, along with the Bretons who became firm friends, my men's purses bulged.

Much to the annoyance of the cardinal I often accompanied the raiders. It was not simply to seek thrills but to gauge the enemy and his plans. I also visited with the Lord of Modena. He was, in theory, neutral but he was, in reality, opposed to the greed of the Lord of Milan. He did not wish to be gobbled up. He gave me information about the Milanese movements and, not long before Easter, he told me of the arrival of reinforcements at Parma. I had been waiting for such information and I held a council of war back in Bologna.

The cardinal had become increasingly anxious about our lack of belligerence. He saw our raids as pinpricks and wished us to earn our pay. All my leaders, as well as the papal ones, were present. "Cardinal, thus far we have had no pay at all. When can we expect some?"

He smiled, "I have sent to Avignon and a ship will arrive at Rimini. You will be paid by the end of the month."

"I hope so for my men are becoming impatient. They can endure a cold camp but not if their pay is withheld."

"That is easily solved, Sir John, take the field and defeat the Milanese."

"Cardinal, they have been reinforced and until we know the true numbers we wait. They are safe behind Parma's walls. They hold Reggio. We do not have enough men for a siege. My plan is to have a mounted column, led by Giovanni d'Azzo. He will lead two hundred men at arms, one hundred archers and a hundred of your Bretons. He will watch Parma so that we have early warning of any movement." The cardinal looked sceptical, "Trust me, Robert, Giovanni has more skill than any other man in my company. He will lose no men and learn their intention."

Of course, before he left Giovanni and I spent many hours together. We were of one mind and our discussion was fruitful.

When the men arrived from Rimini it was just papal reinforcements. There was no gold. I was angry. This was Visconti all over again. I bearded the cardinal who, annoyingly just smiled at my complaints. "Sir John, you will be paid. It just takes time."

"That is not the agreement we made."

"If you leave now and head back to Lucca then you will have no pay at all." He shrugged. "I now have equal numbers with the White Company, Sir John. I think I have the beating of the Visconti family."

I left knowing I had been outwitted and cheated by the pope and his man. It was clear to me that we would not be paid. That night I sat with Robin, Dai and Michael. I explained to them what we would do. "Michael, pay the men from my chests."

"My lord, the men do not need that."

"They do. I want their loyalty. From now on we let the pope's men take the risks. If we are not paid by summer then we will take the war to Milan and raid every Milanese town. I will take the payment from them. If the pope treats me like a warlord, then I shall act as one. Robin, find good, rich targets for us."

Unlike Michael, he was not appalled at my decision and he grinned, "Aye, my lord."

Giovanni brought the news that the Milanese, now reinforced were moving to the Enza river. I told that to a puzzled cardinal, "But why, Sir John? Why not simply come down the road through Reggio?"

"Because that would mean a repeat of his failed attack in January. He will come towards Montechiarugolo and that will give him options in his approach."

He looked pleased, "Then this time I will lead the attack. We head for Montechiarugolo."

I was not happy about that decision. It had been too many years since I had followed the command of another and it had rarely ended well. The Black Prince was the last leader who had made good decisions and Poitiers was a lifetime ago.

It was the papal troops who led and we followed in their dusty wake. It was now May and the roads were beginning to bake. Surprisingly my men did not complain. If anything they were enthusiastic but I knew that was because I had paid them and they knew it. Albert Sterz and Heinrich Paer would not have done so and my men realised that.

Ettore Visconti was no fool and he had learned from our first encounter. He saw that the scouts who approached were not the White Company and he put into place a plan which almost succeeded. He had a lightly armoured body of men waiting for the cardinal and his army. We were a mile behind. Robert de Genève was using his Breton horsemen as a screen but they did not have Robin and his archers for guidance. I later learned what had happened but all that we heard was the sound of horns signalling the attack. When I heard the clash of steel and the cries then I ordered Robin to form two lines of archers on either side of the road.

"Giovanni, take command here and hold the line. Dai and Michael, bring your men with me. John and Thomas stay with Robin." My mind was working so quickly that I am still unsure how I thought of what I did but I knew that the cardinal was not supposed to attack until I arrived. Either he had attacked prematurely or he had been ambushed. Either way, I needed to prepare to defend against an attack on my men. I could not, in all good conscience, simply abandon the cardinal and so leading half of my men at arms I rode up the road to see what had happened.

The lie of the land, the houses, farms and trees all obscured the fighting unit we crested a small rise and looked down at the river and the valley. My experienced eye took it all in quickly. The cardinal and his men had been drawn into a trap. I saw bodies of men and horses floating down the river. The suburbs had been filled with crossbowmen and soldiers on foot. The papal troops were surrounded. Fleeing in every direction were the foot soldiers who had followed the men at arms and Bretons. Visconti had allowed them to escape the trap so that he could destroy the cardinal and his elite troops.

I shouted, "Form two lines. We will break through those at the rear and help to extricate the cardinal."

It sounded like an easy command but we had obstacles in our way. There were houses, bushes, trees and small outbuildings. The training at Lucca had been vital and I had enough leaders to take command and lead small groups of men to do as I had commanded. I had not taken a lance, neither had most of my men and we drew swords and hefted shields. Without a horn, it was the signal of the sword that initiated the attack. I rode Ajax, not at a gallop but at a steady ground-eating canter. The slight slope aided us. The sound of battle ahead would mask the sound of our hooves until it was too late for the Milanese. I swerved to avoid a shield dropped by a fleeing soldier and then aimed Ajax at the knot of men on foot, armed with glaives and other pole weapons who were hacking at the papal rearguard.

Inevitably the thunder of hooves alerted them and they turned. As the pressure on them decreased the cardinal's rearguard hacked and chopped at the fewer men who faced them. A Milanese halberd was swung at Ajax's head but I had anticipated such a blow and jerking the reins back my war horse stood on his hind legs, which slid along the cobbles and his front hooves smashed first into the halberd and then the Milanese warrior. There was a sickening crunch as the hooves landed and crushed the man's ribs. It was fortunate that he was dead already. The warhorse had cleared a path and my sword swept into the side of the next Milanese helmet. The bodyguards with me quickly slew the others and as the Milanese attack on the rearguard disintegrated, I yelled, "Cardinal, withdraw up the road!"

Such was the press of men and the confusion so much that it took me some time to see the beleaguered banner, I saw a man speak to the cardinal and then a horn sounded.

I then shouted orders to my men. They knew the orders were for them for they were in English, "Hold on both sides of the road. On my command, we turn to the right and head back to the archers." I had realised that Ettore Visconti had used dismounted men with pole weapons to ambush the cardinal and his men. All we had to do was enable the papal horsemen to flee and then follow. It sounded easy but only a well-trained company like ours could achieve it.

There was a slight hiatus for we had cleared the men before us but, on our flanks, the Milanese were rallying and trying to get at my men. The papal horsemen gratefully galloped along the road, now clear of attackers and headed up the road. That the Milanese would follow was clear. I did not doubt that Ettore had a reserve of horsemen. A fleeing army that had been demoralised was perfect for pursuit.

"Make four lines!" My command meant that the flanks pulled in and made our wall of horsemen shorter but stronger. As the papal troops passed so more men attacked our fore. Pole weapons are very effective against horsemen but unless they have a langet to protect the head they are vulnerable and can break. The majority of the men who came at us were armed with swords. Had the Milanese utilised archers then we would have been in trouble but their crossbows did not have a clear line of sight and we were safe on the backs of our horses. After the cardinal and his bodyguard passed me, I knew that there would be few survivors from the advance guard. Once more I used my warhorse to clear a space. I stood in the stirrups and pulled back on the reins. His mighty hooves, allied to his snapping teeth cleared a space and when he landed, I shouted, "Fall back!"

Every rider turned to the right and it was a flawless manoeuvre. The hours on the gyrus had paid off and no rider crashed into another. As we funnelled down the road there was a hiatus as the Milanese waited for their orders. Men on foot do not pursue horsemen. I let most of my men pass me and when I was at the rear with Dai and Michael I risked turning. I saw men riding up the road, through the press of men. Many of the Milanese foot soldiers were already stripping the bodies of the papal dead. That would delay pursuit but I also saw squires fetching horses for the men at arms who had fought dismounted. They would hurry down the road to seal their victory. Everything now depended upon the skills of Dai and Giovanni and I was confident that this defeat would not be as disastrous as it might have been.

We crested the rise and I saw a line of dismounted men at arms, pole weapons brandished, backed by archers. The road was clear but I knew that once I had passed down it then it would be closed and the Milanese would face a wall of steel. The cardinal and his bodyguards had not stopped. They were heading back to our camp. Routed men are hard to rally. I wheeled Ajax around and saw John and Thomas with my standard. The relief on their faces was clear. The gap in the line was filled and we heard the thunder of horses. Robin had ordered bodkins. He knew that mailed men would follow us. He waited until they were just one hundred and fifty paces from us and had begun to spread out before he ordered the arrows to fly. The horsemen had just scaled a small slope and they were not travelling fast. Robin's arrows emptied saddles and slew horses. The survivors stopped eighty paces from us and then, as bodkins slammed through plate the order to retreat was given. Ettore had his victory. It had not been against the White Company but he could return to his father having defeated the pope's men.

We did not follow the cardinal immediately, I had men ride to discover the Milanese intent. They were taking their victory and not risking another miserable attempt to pass my archers. By the time we reached our home, the healers were dealing with the wounded. Even the cardinal had suffered a slight wound. Leaving my sons to see to my horse I went to speak to the cardinal. I did not make a judgement but listened as he ranted and railed.

"The Milanese have no honour. They feigned a retreat and when I sent the Bretons and French men at arms after them, they sprang an ambush. The Bretons were all lost."

I nodded, "You were keen to force the bridge and to seize a victory."

His eyes narrowed and he nodded, "I thought we could end this campaign quickly."

"And that is always the surest way to ensure that you do not. They have hurt us but not the White Company. We still have the edge. I now command the largest number of men and it is I who will make the strategic decisions."

He looked angry and then subsided, "I have had a lesson in pride. Your victory at the Panaro river seemed so easy I..."

I nodded, "I will send a messenger to Visconti."

"You would sue for peace?"

"Will there be more men coming from France?" He shook his head. "Then we have to rely on the White Company and that is not enough to defeat the Milanese. I will negotiate."

"Very well."

"And our pay?"

"I will send to Avignon."

I was not convinced that the pope had any intention of paying us but at least I was fighting for a cause that was slightly more noble than that of Bernabò Visconti.

It took a week to arrange but a parley took place at Modena. The cardinal remained silent as I had requested. I knew Ettore, having met him in Milan and I knew that he admired me. I used that to my advantage. I greeted him almost as an uncle he occasionally met.

"Ettore, it is good to see you. I can see that you have skills as a leader. That was a cunning ambush."

He nodded, "Yet, once again, you win. Your grey hairs belie your skill, Sir John."

"They are evidence of experience. So, Ettore, do you wish to continue this campaign against the papal lands?" He said nothing but he did not seem confident and I offered him a way out. "As you can see the pope is still in Avignon. Your father's fears that he will return any time soon to Rome are unfounded. It costs money to pay for men in the field." I glanced at the cardinal who quickly looked down. "Both the Milanese and the Pope have lost men. What say you we have a truce?"

"How long for?"

I shrugged, "Let us say a year."

He smiled and held out his hand. I shook it. "I will have the treaty drawn up and the Lord of Modena can witness the arrangement."

We had not once referred to the cardinal. I care not if he was upset for we had yet to be paid. A week later when all was signed and sealed the cardinal and his men left for Rimini and a ship back to France and we headed down the road to Lucca. We had made a small profit but we had not been paid and as we headed through Tuscany, passing many tempting targets Giovanni and Robin voiced the thoughts that were in many of the leaders' heads.

"We could raid here, Sir John. We have not been paid and there are many ripe plums we could take."

"Not yet, Robin. The men have been paid by me and I will get the arrears from the pope. For once we fight for a nobler cause than is usual. Fighting for the pope can only help our heavenly aspirations."

Robin laughed, "I think it will take more than a papal blessing to get us into heaven. You and I, Sir John, are what we are."

I smiled, "You may be right but let us have a winter in Lucca and see what Tall Tom and Sir Richard have found for us. Who knows, William may have another employer for us."

Lucca 1374

We had good news when we returned to Lucca. Although William had not found another employer and no arrears had reached Lucca, Tall Tom had fifty archers and Sir Richard Telford had brought back more than forty lances. We had more than made up for the losses we had suffered. Sir Richard had presented my petition for a pardon and found a great deal of support from those who had fought alongside me at Poitiers. I now had a way to find a home in England.

Sir Richard also brought back the maid he had sought. She had waited for him and they had married in England. He had shown his commitment to the White Company by bringing her to Italy and they took a house close to mine. Mary was with child when they arrived and both Caterina and Bianca, now both the mothers of a clutch of children took her under their wing.

Dai asked, "Does this not make you wish for a wife, Sir John? You could have a family."

"I have a family. There is John and there is Thomas not to mention a daughter, Antiochia. If I want to lie with a woman, I can pay for one. That is cheaper than being wed to a harpy who rules my home. I am content."

It was that winter when John and Thomas spoke to me about their future. They were now sixteen and fifteen. Their training had broadened them out and they now looked like young warriors. It was John, always the leader, who spoke, "Father, Thomas and I have enjoyed our time as your squires."

I nodded, "And you have acquitted yourselves well."

"We are not archers. We have not trained every day since Tall Tom went to England and while we can draw a bow neither of us sees ourselves as archers."

"You would be men at arms."

It was John who answered, "We would be knights. Holding the standard and blowing the horn are no longer enough for us. Help us to become as you are, a knight." He took a breath, "Serving the pope made me think that I might like to be a knight in a military order. The knights of St John still hold Malta. Serving God is a greater calling than being a mercenary."

I felt a little hurt by his words although he meant nothing by them. "I had thought that the two of you would be White Company and, in the fullness of time become leaders like Dai and Michael."

John nodded, "And we might well be but I also wish to serve God. Until I am knighted then I will not consider leaving." He laughed, "Who knows I may never be good enough to be a knight and I would not be a sergeant of the knights of St John. One step at a time. We will train with your men at arms and learn skills to help us become knights. With the influx of new men brought by Sir Richard, this is a perfect time, is it not?"

I nodded for I could find no fault with his logic. "Very well but you know that means daily training. I no longer need to train for I am the leader of this company but you will be up at dawn each day. If we do this thing then I give you to Giovanni and he will use you as any other aspirant knights. It would be as though you were no longer my sons."

Thomas liked his food, "We would still live here with you?"

"Of course, you are my sons and will enjoy that privilege. That will be the only one."

John nodded, "Very well. We are happy with that." Thomas grinned his agreement; the two brothers were of one mind. John's plan to serve God was the only difference between them.

And so, although we were living in the same house, I saw little of my sons, save at mealtimes. Often, I was away and did not see them then. I was busy. William had received messages from emissaries who wished to speak to the two of us. We had envoys sent from Milan, Florence and Venice. All had the same message. They wished to hire my company.

Tuscan Warlord

The defeat on the Enza river was seen as the cardinal's and not mine. If anything my reputation had been enhanced by the battles fought against Ettore Visconti. What convinced us to stay with the pope, who had still to pay us, was that there was no guarantee that any of the three city-states would give us gold. It was the possibility of an Italy ruled by the pope that kept us in papal service. Milan was the keenest to employ me. I spent a long time with the envoy, more than the Florentine or Venetian ambassadors. The Milanese noble was a friend of Ambrogio and I knew that Bernabò had sent him for that reason. It did not persuade me for I had a hard mind that ignored the calls of friendship.

"Bernabò still owes me for the service I did him last time. Tell him that I might, and I stress the word might agree to serve him if all unpaid debts are paid."

"I will speak with him, my lord. You should know that he still speaks highly of you as do his sons Ambrogio and Ettore."

I shrugged, "Praise merely makes my head grow bigger. I prefer my purse to see similar growth."

My men made the decision to cease training and become warriors again. As spring approached Robin and Giovanni invited me to the mansion that they shared. It was, ostensibly, to enjoy boar that had been hunted and a gift of wine sent from Modena. It soon became clear that while I had been engaged in negotiations with three city-states they had been speaking with the men. Since Michael had been knighted and led men, I no longer had my ear to the mood of my company.

"The men are restless, Sir John. Had we been victorious in our last battle it might have been different but we merely held the field and saved the cardinal. There was little loot and no ransom. They need to be paid or they need treasure."

I was loath to pay them a third time. I had paid from my own purse when we had returned to Lucca and my funds, whilst not low, were not as healthy as they might have been. Roger's last payment from Bordeaux had been less than I had expected.

"What do you suggest?"

Tuscan Warlord

"We raid. Parma, Ferrara and Mantua are all rich targets. They are not papal states and we have yet to raid them. Parma is Milanese and the other two are isolated from liaisons and alliances. We plunder the land and bring back treasure. It will keep the men happy and their skills honed. Perhaps it might encourage the pope to pay us."

Giovanni had hit the nail on the head. We needed to make the pope realise that we were a dangerous enemy. By raiding beyond Bologna we were showing that we could threaten the very papal cities that we had once protected. I did not take much convincing.

I was, however, a practical man and saw an opportunity to see how the new men worked out. Andrew Gold had proved so effective that I had knighted him and he was now, along with Sir Michael and Sir Andrew Belmonte one of my ablest sub-commanders. My organisation used Robin, Dai and Giovanni to command larger bodies of men but the three subcommanders were able to make smaller raids and that was what was needed. All three cities were too large a nut for my company to take but we could make life so hard for them that they would be forced to pay us off. We headed to Parma first as we had recently campaigned there and my archer scouts knew the land well. We hit in July when they were preparing to harvest and there was no defence against the seven columns that struck. I led one composed of the new men, including my sons. I made it clear as we raided that when we fought Milan or Florence then we could expect stiffer opposition. The Milanese army was back in the north and could not respond quickly. The result was that within three weeks envoys from Parma brought fifty thousand florins to send us elsewhere.

We headed for Ferrara having first sent our profits to Lucca. We also knew Ferrara well and while we would not dream of trying to take its walls, the countryside was another matter. Here the harvest was even more advanced and it took just a fortnight to bring the usual payment from the city, seventy thousand florins. As we neared Mantua, a city less well known to us, we did not get as far as raiding. It was the middle of August and Mantua did not want to lose anything.

They paid eighty thousand florins to send us to another city and we never even drew a sword.

We had done all that we intended and headed south, laden with treasure and booty towards Pistoia. The city was an ally and they feted us as we rested there. It was while we were there that senior leaders from Florence rode in. Although they came with an armed escort, I was not worried. I had a whole company with me.

"Sir John, we have come from Florence with an offer for you."

I shook my head, "I have told your envoys before that I have no intention of deserting the pope, at the moment." I added the caveat in case the Florentines had papal spies. It would be a warning to the pope that I could desert him if the price was right.

"No, Sir John, we understand. We wish to make an annual payment to you and the White Company. We will pay you ten thousand florins a year so long as you do not attack Florence."

I frowned, "You had a similar arrangement with me when I served Pisa. That stopped some time ago."

The envoy, a merchant rather than a soldier shifted uncomfortably. I had heard of Giovanni Dini. He was a successful spice merchant and a leading figure in the Florentine council of guilds, "You are right, my lord, and that was a mistake, an error of judgement. This payment is from the merchants of Florence and will continue even if the warmongers of the city rail against you."

"Under those terms I accept."

The raids had been even more successful than I might have hoped and after we returned to Lucca, I spent a long time working out how we might use the same tactic again.

William now had full coffers and, after discussing it with the senior leaders, began to invest in various enterprises. It would give us financial security. Our raid had shown all of us the possibilities presented by using the company as a warband.

It was close to Christmas when Robert de Genève returned. He was not a happy man and he wasted no time,

Tuscan Warlord

once the pleasantries of his arrival had been dealt with, in letting me know the extent of his anger. "His Holiness is less than pleased with the actions of your company. They seem more fitting to a bandit warband led by a warlord than the actions of a papal company."

I held up my hand, "Let me stop you there, cardinal, and clear up this mistaken statement. We are not a papal company. We fight for the pope because he pays us. As he has not paid us this year then legally, we have no master and can do as we see fit."

"You signed a contract, Sir John."

I smiled, "Then fetch your lawyers and they can argue the case. The fact is we have not been paid and that could if we chose, render the contract null and void. When we raided, we did not touch any papal lands. We could next time."

"Next time?"

"We have received many offers of work: Florence, Milan and Venice. I still hold to the spirit of the contract but if we are not paid then my hands are tied. How do I pay my men? Feed them?"

I could see that he had a dilemma. The pope would have known of his envoy's mistake at the Enza. He would have not been happy with the cardinal.

"I will return to Avignon and speak again with his holiness. Until then do I have your word that you will not attack any city-state?"

I smiled and spread my arms, "Of course not. Send payment soon or my men and I will raid when and where we choose. That raiding will include papal cities." I had no intention of fighting in winter again. The January battle, whilst a victory, had taught me that winter was not the time for war but the cardinal did not know that. When we had fought at the Panaro river it had been in the depths of winter.

Ten thousand florins were delivered by Easter of the next year. It was a fraction of the amount owed but I suppose it showed goodwill. More importantly, it stopped us from raiding papal cities. That had pleased John who had become increasingly religious since his first talk with me. He had thrown himself into training but he was now different to his brother. Thomas saw his future with the White Company and, increasingly, John did not. They were both far from ready for spurs but it was a nagging doubt in my mind.

Chapter 15

Romagna 1375

My old nemesis, Perugia was the fuze that lit the revolt against the pope. To be fair to the city it had been assailed on all sides thanks to its loyalty to the pope. After it had been captured by the Germans, the city had allied itself to the pope and its neighbours had shown their displeasure with disputes and border raids. They had had enough and revolted. This time it was one of the pope's French mercenaries, Charles de Apremont who brought the papal missive. He waited until I had read it and given him my answer before he left. As soon as he had departed, I summoned my leaders. Jack had a good feast prepared and I told them what we had been asked to do.

"The pope wishes us to go to Romagna and ensure that it is safe before we head to Perugia and bring it back into the papal fold."

Giovanni shook his head, "The walls are strong and a siege is always costly on many levels."

I nodded, "And that is why we will not go directly to Perugia. There are enemies of the pope in Romagna. They are the lords who support Milan, Venice and Naples. All those are enemies of the pope. I intend to raid the Romagna and make it secure. We have still to be paid and by raiding smaller towns and taking them we earn the gold to pay our men and yet do not risk them in a costly siege against a well-built town and castle. We will be doing as the pope wishes as well as giving ourselves a more secure base."

Robin asked, "And who has revolted, just Perugia?"

I shook my head and waved the parchment, "According to this Cesena, Faenza and Forli have all declared that they own no allegiance to the pope. Bologna stands alone in that area and we will go there first to secure that city. If Bologna joins the revolt then Rimini and Ravenna will both be threatened."

Dai said, "It seems to me sensible if we send soldiers there."

Tuscan Warlord

There was a general agreement. Sir Andrew Gold nodded, "I can take my one hundred men there if you like and hold it. It will be enough and it will afford me the opportunity to show you, Sir John, that I am worthy of greater command." Since Sir John Thornbury had abandoned me to join with Milan Sir Andrew had been keen for promotion. He saw himself as a leader like Sir Andrew Belmonte. I was not yet sure.

It seemed a good idea to allow him an independent command. "You can hold it with one hundred men?"

He laughed, "Do not forget that I have the sons of Sir John Hawkwood in my company. Bologna will enjoy the honour of our presence."

"How are my sons progressing?"

"They have great sword skills and that is down to you, Sir Michael, but they are also incredibly strong. It is a powerful combination."

Robin nodded, "Archer training will do that. You will need to keep a close eye on them, Andrew. The sooner they can be knighted the better."

I shook my head, "I waited a long time for that honour, Robin. They will have to earn their spurs. They are my sons but they get no favours. Sir Andrew, hold Bologna and we will raid Romagna and that will encourage the other rebels to reconsider their position. It will be like Mantua all over again."

We left in late spring and ensured that we passed through friendly or at least neutral cities. Keen to avoid being raided we were feted and fed by towns and villages. We reached Bologna and I left Sir Andrew and his one hundred men there. I felt relief that while we fought my sons would be safe behind Bologna's walls. Ravenna was papal but Cortignola was not and we headed for the castle-dominated city. They barred their gates and manned their walls. Although I had no intention of a lengthy siege, I surrounded the town. I had chosen it because it was ill-maintained and I intended to use that to our advantage.

We lit fires and the men made hovels whilst I outlined my plans. "The men in the town and the castle will be busy even now repairing the castle. Listen." We could hear the banging as they tried to make their walls more defensible. "They will continue long after dark. As soon as the sun sets, we attack. I want every man except for the squires, who will guard our camp, to ascend the walls and take the town while they work. The sounds of their labours will mask our approach."

Dai asked, "They have the odd sentry, they will see us."

"They will only do so at the last moment and if Robin has one in four of his archers with a nocked arrow, then as soon as the alarm is given the sentries can be taken." I saw the others all nod. There was clearly risk involved but the reward would be we would have property in the Romagna. Cortignola was not papal and independent of other city-states. It was a small castle and demesne but it would furnish an income. If the pope was going to be tardy in payment, then we would find other ways to augment our income.

We did not wear helmets; coifs would suffice and we all wore cloaks that we would discard once we ascended the walls. They would disguise our approach. We left our camps just after the sun had set and crept like shadows across the ground. The banging and noise from within were deafening even outside the walls and must have made sleep impossible for those not toiling at the walls. I did not see the sentry who stood to shout a warning but one of Robin's archers did and the man fell from the town walls. There appeared to be little reaction to his fall and perhaps they thought he had simply slipped whilst working on the walls. We were just ten paces from the masonry when the alarm proper was given. Someone in the castle's tallest tower must have spied the movements and rang the town bell. By then it was too late for arrows flew and guards fell. I was boosted up over the walls by my men and, along with my bodyguards, ran the few paces to the gate. We were plated and well-armed. The men there were labouring and had no mail and were armed with tools. They dropped their weapons and we opened the gates. It was an easy victory.

We discovered the next day that the lord of the town was away and it was the townsfolk themselves who had tried to prevent our taking of the town. That had made our victory

Tuscan Warlord

easy and also made the townsfolk resentful that they had been abandoned by their lord. My leaders and I met with the council and I explained that we came not as conquerors but as guardians. I pointed out that a garrison of the White Company would keep their town safe and that we would only take the same income as the absent lord. They saw the wisdom in that and agreed. They owed nothing to their lord and the White Company was the most powerful company of mercenaries in Italy. They had protection. We now had a town. Should Lucca decide to abandon us we had a bolt hole.

If the pope expected us to go to Faenza and the other rebel towns he was in for a surprise. We decided to take more castles. Our success at Cortignola and our unique approach to the management of the towns and castles meant that four more towns with castles fell to us without even a siege or an armed camp. As we approached, they simply opened their gates and allowed us in. They ejected the two lords who were still in situ and like Cortignola agreed to become White Company castles.

I sent a rider back to tell William that we needed him in Romagna. We had taken the castles but they needed to be managed and that was William's work. That done we set about making the five castles defensible and we toiled along with the townsfolk to do that which the lords of the manors should have done themselves. I was able to pay my company, not from what we took from the townsfolk but what we took from the treasuries in the castles. It was not exactly what we were due from the pope but it would do.

In the New Year Cardinal Robert de Genève arrived with a thousand men not long after William and some reinforcements did. The cardinal was not a happy man. I sat in the castle at Cortignola with him, Giovanni and William and allowed the papal prelate to rant and rave about my warlord-like activities while I ate some of the local ham and sipped the wine they made in the manor.

"This is not what we paid you for, Sir John. You were sent to retake the cities that rebelled and not carve yourself a fiefdom. That is the action of a bandit warlord. The pope demands that you take measures to reimpose papal authority in this part of the world."

I waited until I was sure that he had vented his spleen. I wiped my mouth and looked at him. His red face showed his anger. Then I turned to William, "Whilst we have been here, William, was a payment sent from the pope to Lucca?"

He covered his smile well, "No, Sir John."

I looked at Giovanni, "Since we came to the Romagna?"

He kept a straight face as he said, "Not a single florin, Sir John."

"So, Cardinal, despite the promises that were made by you on the pope's behalf, we have still to be paid. Why should I risk my men when there is no payment?"

"They fight for the pope and for God."

"Ah, this is a holy crusade then? The men of Faenza, Forli and Cesena have become heretics and deny the word of God."

"No, that is not true and you twist my words. They defy the pope and he is God's representative on earth."

"An elected man and one who was not unanimously chosen. He is what they call a French pope, some even call him the anti-pope. I hear that there are moves to appoint an Italian pope in Rome."

I saw the cardinal colour, "He is the elected pope and you will obey his commands."

I allowed the hint of a threat to come into my tone, "Or else what?"

The emptiness of his threats became clear and he looked helplessly from William to me and back, "I will send to Avignon and have your arrears sent."

I smiled, "Good. When it arrives, we will take the field."

"But I have promised…"

"And you promised before. You have used up your goodwill, cardinal."

"You know, Sir John, that there are forces at work that clearly illustrate that God approves of the pope." I raised my eyebrows in question. "Have you heard of Catherine of Siena?"

"I cannot say I have."

"She was visited by God and has become a bride of Jesus."

I smiled, "Cardinal if you visit any of the nunneries that proliferate in Italy you will find many women married to God."

"This one is different. When God came to her, he told her that the pope had to return to Rome. There is a strong movement for the pope to be returned to the Holy City."

I smiled, "Then, if God supports the pope, I need do nothing but I hear that Rome does not want a French pope."

The cardinal sent a man to take a ship back to Avignon. We had called his bluff.

In the end, it was events in Bologna that changed things. A month after the cardinal arrived Sir Andrew Gold and the men I had left at Bologna arrived. My sons were not with him. The English knight looked unhappy.

My leaders were present for we had been warned of his approach and met him in the inner bailey of the small castle. "Your arrival is unexpected, Sir Andrew."

He nodded and shifted uncomfortably from foot to foot, "Bologna has rebelled against the pope. We were duped, my lord. We were invited to a feast to celebrate your recent victories and the capture of so many castles. When we entered the great hall, we were surrounded and disarmed. We had no chance to fight."

Sir Andrew would no longer be one of my leaders. Such a failure was inexcusable but now was not the time for dissension. "And my sons?"

"They are held hostage for surety of the city's safety. If the city is attacked then they will both be hanged from the city walls."

I was angry and I felt my fists clenching. I wanted to hit, to hurt, even to kill but I was now Sir John Hawkwood and I could not be allowed to show my true feelings. My head was reeling that I had put my sons in danger. I had made the mistake of trusting another. I should have placed them with Michael, Giovanni or even Dai. I had wanted to give them a different kind of leader and it had ended in disaster. "Thank you, Sir Andrew. You and your men need food. I will speak to you in due course. I want a council of war now."

My leaders followed as did Sir Andrew Gold. I shook my head, "Sir Andrew go with your men and get food. I will speak with you at a later time." The anger was in my eyes and the threat in my voice. Sir Andrew nodded and, hanging his head, left.

Once in the hall, I had the gates barred. I wanted no eavesdroppers. The cardinal had come with my leaders and I wanted to hit him most of all for he had a smug look on his face. I knew not how but I suspected him of some involvement in this event. My inner core of leaders were as upset as I was. They were as fond of my sons as I was. All were silent.

"We cannot attack Bologna but I would have them release my sons."

The cardinal had regained his confidence since the arrival of Sir Andrew Gold, "A neat trick if you can pull it off, Sir John. How will you manage it?"

I gave him a cold stare, "I have learned much from my dealings with the church, Cardinal. I have learned that simply because you say you will do something does not mean that event will come to fruition. Bologna thinks I will not attack her because of my sons. I want the word to be spread that I am so angry that I intend to send for more men and to wipe Bologna from the face of the earth."

"You cannot do that, Sir John." The cardinal showed fear for he believed my words.

Robin shook his head, "What is it about churchmen Sir Robert? Do you not listen to Sir John? He said he would not necessarily do that which was promised. Carry on, Sir John, and ignore the crowing of this cackling cardinal."

My other leaders all smiled as the cardinal flushed.

"The nearest rebel town is Faenza. It is also the closest rebel town to Bologna. We ride into Faenza and destroy the town. Does that meet with your approval, Cardinal?"

"Apart from its destruction, aye. The people are rebels and should be punished but the town is papal and the pope will need its income."

Ignoring his words I continued. "We leave in a week. I want the rumours that we are going to attack Bologna to be widespread. I shall act my part too. William, I want you to return to Lucca and take with you the treasure we have collected. Sir Andrew Gold and his men can be your escort. When you reach Lucca send back to me any recruits who have come to join us."

"And Sir Andrew?"

"He can guard Lucca." I stood, "I will go to speak to him now. I will ask no man to carry my words. He will hear my displeasure from my lips so that there can be no doubts."

Sir Andrew and his men were eating in the hall used by the warriors. It was a cosy place and they were seated cheek-by-jowl. Many of the lances had been with me for a couple of years and I saw the shame on their faces. I walked up to Sir Andrew, "You and these men will be the escort tomorrow for William when he returns to Lucca."

Sir Andrew said, "Is this punishment for Bologna, my lord? If so, it is unfair. We could do nothing."

I turned and snapped in his face. Spittle flew and he recoiled at my words, "Could do nothing? Were you sent there to feast and fete or were you asked to hold the town for me, the company and the pope?" His head dropped. "You have not only jeopardised the lives of my sons, who were left in your charge, but you have also lost a city we were charged to keep. Think yourself lucky you still have a head." I whirled around, "Some of you may gain my trust again but you will have to earn that trust." Many of them nodded. "For the rest of us, we now have to assault Bologna."

"But my lord, your sons."

"My sons are now in danger but I have a greater responsibility to the men of the White Company. Pray, Sir Andrew, that Bologna does not carry out their threat for I will make no threat, I will just act. Do you understand?"

"Yes, my lord." I saw the terror on his face. The men he had led would do all that they could do to regain my favour. Sir Andrew now realised his mistake.

My whole plan to take Faenza depended upon the belief that I intended to attack Bologna. It was a risk but I did not

Tuscan Warlord

think that my sons would be harmed until I marched up to the gates of Bologna with my company and that would not happen.

William and his escort left the next day. Their progress would spread the word of an imminent and dreadful attack on Bologna. I deliberately kept apart to fuel the rumours that I was incandescently angry. The reality was that I was planning the details of the attack on Faenza. When we attacked it would be ferocious. I wanted Bologna to be terrified of me and sue for peace.

Chapter 16

The mood amongst my men was one of anger. The taking of my sons had made it personal. Despite the title, the White Company, the reality was that this was Sir John Hawkwood's company and they all felt a close bond between them and my family. We had been to Faenza before and knew the town and the castle. The last time we had been welcomed but this time, forewarned perhaps, when we left Cortignola their walls were fully manned. My ruse about attacking Bologna had worked but they were not willing to risk falling easily, for the papal banners flew above the men led by the cardinal.

We surrounded the walls. The two weeks we had waited to attack had been necessary so that we could build the trebuchet, called '**The Minotaur**', and four rams that would be filled with men and attack the four gates. We surrounded the city and assembled the trebuchet. Our lengthy preparations were for a purpose. Bologna would have spies in the hills watching us and I wanted them under no illusions about what we intended. The building of siege weapons clearly signalled our intent. When Faenza had fallen then we would head to Bologna. We had to be patient and thorough. It was hard for me as I knew that while John and Thomas would be well treated, they had a Bolognese blade hanging over their heads. I knew I had not been the best of fathers but that did not mean that I had no affection for my three children. I had bad dreams just thinking about what my sons would be enduring.

I wanted Faenza terrified and the ring of campfires around their walls was an early warning. While the trebuchet was assembled, I had my men take every animal from within a mile of the walls and we feasted on their flesh, allowing the smell of Bolognese animals being cooked to drift over to them. I had every soldier ready on the morning of the attack well before dawn. We ate at the third hour and the cardinal's priests blessed us. We had absolution for any sins we might commit for we were fighting for the pope and God. The rams were each three hundred paces from the four gates. Their hides had been soaked overnight in water and as the ram crews waited to attack, they poured more water on them. The smoke rising from the four gatehouses told us that they had fire and that meant boiling water, heated sand, or pig fat. I did not want the men in the rams burnt alive. As dawn broke the inhabitants saw a sea of white around their walls. They had seen my men and the pope's on the previous days but we had been occupied. Now we stood in serried ranks, mailed, plated and armed in silence. The only splashes of colour were the red shields and tunics of the papal troops. Most were in the second rank but I had the pavesiers and crossbowmen spread amongst my archers.

    We had taken forty drums from the castles we had taken and I had Robin's horse holders ready to beat them. Silence, like my army, surrounded Faenza and when I dropped my sword arm and the drums began to sound it was as though a thunderstorm of Biblical proportions had descended on the city. The men manning the walls recoiled as they anticipated the start of our attack. It did not materialise. In my head, I was counting the beats. When we reached a thousand. I raised my sword and the drums all stopped. The sound did not and it echoed for a moment or two before silence fell once more. The next time I lowered my sword it was the signal for the trebuchet to begin hurling the rocks we had gathered. In a perfect world, we would have had one on each gate but they took time to build and needed skilled engineers to build and man them. One would have to do. They were slow to load but as the first rock arced towards the gates of the city, I saw every eye in Faenza watching its flight. Men moved out of the way but as it struck the crenulations, shards of stone flew off in every direction. I saw one man whose eye was pierced by a dagger-like piece of stone tumble over the walls.

    The stone had been sent too high and the engineer adjusted the machine for the second stone. More shields appeared on the walls and that made me smile. A shield might stop or slow an arrow or a bolt but if the stone struck the shield would have no effect at all and both man and shield would be mashed to a pulp. The second one was better aimed and hit the wall just six feet below the fighting platform. There was a cheer from the walls as there appeared to be little damage. I smiled for I could see what they could not. The mortar surrounding the stone, as well as the stones themselves, had moved. By the time three more stones had struck almost the same place the damage was clear to us. The Italian engineer adjusted the trebuchet and moved a little to the left. I knew what he was doing but the defenders appeared to be mystified. He was weakening the wall.

It took until noon for the stones to have the desired effect but when they did it was dramatic as the battlements close to the fighting platform simply collapsed as one lucky stone took out the key stone. The gate stood but it would not last long against a determined attack. The engineer began to batter the gate with stones and I had my horn sounded three times. It was a signal for the rams to move forward and for the archers and crossbows to begin to pick off the defenders. Robin's archers had the advantage that they could hit men that they could not see by loosing their arrows high into the air. The spent arrows could be collected after the battle. The movement of the rams meant that men had to expose themselves to throw rocks and hurl spears at the machines. All the time '***The Minotaur***' continued to batter the gate and gateposts. When they and more stones dropped into the ditch, it exposed the interior of the city. The other three gates still held but the main gate was now open. The trebuchet shifted targets to allow the ram to close with the gate. It would not be needed to break down the gate but the men inside would have protection until they were close enough to the broken gate to leave the safety of the ram and flood in. Behind the ram marched Giovanni and a hundred picked men. With shields above them and protection from Robin's archers, they would reach the city largely intact. We had, as the saying goes, over-egged the pudding. In reality, we had not needed four rams but the use of all four had spread out the defenders and, more importantly, was a message for the larger city of Bologna. The ram emptied and with a roar, the men at arms raced to the gate and clambered over rocks and fallen masonry. In theory, they were in danger once they entered the city but Giovanni and his men were so close to them that they became one body. There were no mercenaries in Faenza and my professional warriors took the first gate.

It was I who raised my sword and shouted, "For God, the White Company and the pope." I led the archers and papal troops to follow Giovanni into the city. The townsfolk outnumbered us, or at least they would until all the other gates were taken but our entry drew defenders from the other three gates and that discrepancy would soon disappear. I had given clear orders. Any who opposed us was to die, regardless of age or sex but those who laid down their weapons would be spared. More fought on than I wished and more than three hundred perished but, by the end of the day the city was ours and we began, systematically, to empty it of its treasures. Every merchant and noble we could find was evicted from their homes and sent towards Bologna with just the clothes they carried on their backs. We occupied and ransacked their homes. The poor we left alone. Some fled but most stayed as their existence was no different under our rule than it had been.

We ate in the palace of Faenza and we dined well. With sentries set, especially on the broken gate and the trebuchet disassembled and brought inside we were secure. The cardinal was impressed with the speed of our victory but not my apparent mercy, "Sir John, why did you let the merchants and nobles go? We could have ransomed them."

I laughed, "We took what they had. Who would ransom them? You do not understand war, cardinal. The majority will flee to Bologna as it is the largest city. Others will go to Forli or Cesena. What do you think they will say?" He said nothing. "They will speak of terrible war machines that reduce walls. They will tell of arrows descending from the sky and terrifying men in white who slaughtered all who stood before them."

"You make it sound as though my men did nothing."

"And what did they do? Go and count the bodies with bolts in them. You will only need your two hands and then find those bodies with arrows in them. For that, you will need a company of men and all their limbs."

"We did all that we were asked."

I leaned over, "If the pope had warriors that he could trust to get the job done, then he would not need to hire mercenaries," I paused, "and then not pay them." It was the start of a deterioration in the relations between the pope's man and me.

It took another three days to be ready to march. We could have done it sooner but I wanted Bologna sweating. Robin's archers had, effectively, sealed it off from any help and the waiting would make them fear our attack even more. We made regal progress down the road and went at the speed of the trebuchet and rams. When we arrived, in the late afternoon, we made a camp and I set the engineers to assemble '***The Minotaur***' for I wanted them to hear the hammering as a sign of their doom.

I wanted everything done the way I had before and so my White Company faced the wall. Some of the white surcoats were splashed with blood from the battle of Faenza. There was blackened evidence of burning. It showed the Bolognese that we meant business. The drums began to bang and then they stopped, at my command, and after the echoes had ceased the silence was broken by a voice from the walls.

"Sir John, hold your attack. Here are your sons." He had my sons brought and two men stood behind them with bared daggers at their throats. "Leave our city or they die."

Robin was next to me and I simply said, "Robin."

He and Tall Tom raised their bows and drew in unison. The two arrows whizzed through the air and slammed into the skulls of the two men with knives. Their lifeless hands dropped their knives and the two bodies fell to the cobbles in the city.

"Let my sons go and we will not assault. If we have to come and take them then not a stone of Bologna's walls will be left standing. Your women will be sold to the Turks and the head of every man placed on the walls."

"You swear that you will not assault us if we do this?"

"I swear that I will not attack your walls this day, nor for a month hence. Forli and Cesena will have no such period of grace."

"We need an hour to talk."

"Then talk but leave my sons where I can see them."

"Very well." The numbers on the walls thinned as the city leaders left. The two men left to guard my sons pointedly stood well away from them. I saw Thomas look over at John and smile. He said something but I heard not the words. John looked terrified and I felt the anger in me swell and grow.

I turned to Robin and Tall Tom, "Thank you. They were well-aimed arrows."

Tom nodded, "The boys minded their lessons, Sir John. They saw us aim and stood stock still. They have courage."

Robin spat, "We could clear the walls, my lord. None would get close to them."

Shaking my head I said, "We will wait for their decision."

The cardinal sidled up to me, "The pope will want Bologna brought back into the fold, Sir John."

I turned and glared at him, "And I want my sons back. I did not grant Bologna immunity; I gave them a period of grace. Besides, we have yet to be paid, Cardinal, we may choose, when my sons are returned, to head back to Lucca and seek an employer who actually pays us."

Any further debate was ended when the helmeted leader who had spoken to us returned, "We agree. Cardinal, you are God's witness to Sir John's words. He will not attack for a month."

"I hear, doge, but know that I have not made any such promise. I will leave with Sir John but the pope wants his city back and that means we will return."

The doge shook his head, "We chose to ally with the pope and now we have left him. Is there no free will?"

"There is God's will. Think on that, doge."

The boys disappeared and a short while later the gates opened and two servants fetched the boys and their animals. The speed with which it was done told me that they had acted swiftly to be rid of us. I dismounted and the boys ran to me. Not quite men grown I put my arms around them and they hugged me.

Thomas said, "I knew you would come and that you would save us." John was ominously silent.

I led them from the walls and headed for my tent. I left the dismantling of the trebuchet to others. It was not important to me. Michael came with us and when we entered, he closed the flap and stood guard. Michael might be a knight but he was also a friend. I sat them on my camp bed and poured them wine.

"Did they treat you well?"

Thomas nodded, "We were guarded and kept at the top of a tower from which there was no escape. There were guards who liked to mock us and they tried to humiliate us but we never showed fear. The Bolognese fear you, father. They are terrified of the White Company."

All this time John had said nothing. He just stared at the cross in his hands. He kept turning it over and over. Both boys had been given a cross to wear around their necks by their mother when they had left Bordeaux. Only John held his.

"What is the matter, John?"

Thomas said, hurriedly, "He will be fine, father. He just needs time to get over our incarceration."

"I thought you said you were not mistreated."

"We were not but…tell him, brother. Our father needs to know your mind and the serpents that lie within."

Silence filled the tent. The distant noises from the walls of Bologna felt like another world. Inside the darkened tent were just the three of us. Michael ensured that we were secure from any who would listen to us.

"John, you are my eldest son and can tell me anything. I know that what you endured was terrifying. I was abducted, too."

He nodded and then looked me in the eyes, "But God did not come to you in the night, did he father?"

Of all the words that I had expected to hear those were not the ones. I looked at Thomas who simply nodded. "God came to you?" He sighed. "Tell me all and I will not interrupt until you are done."

He drank some of the wine but his hands never relinquished their hold on the crucifix. "When we were taken, I was as defiant as Thomas here." He smiled at his little brother, "He is the warrior, father. It was the night when I felt fear and pain. Each night we did as we had been taught and said our prayers but unlike Thomas, I could not sleep and in the darkness, I saw the devil and his followers. When I woke Thomas they were gone. I did not sleep for three nights and on the fourth, I prayed that God would come to our aid and he did, or at least I think it was him. It might have been his son or an angel but it was a presence and his voice was soothing. The voice told me that I had to give up the sword and take the cross. I was to become a priest and in doing so I would be protected. I slept and when I woke, I felt peace. The evil spirits never returned and I have enjoyed sleep. Father, I must leave the White Company and do as I was commanded. I am sorry. I cannot wield a sword nor draw a bow. I must obey God." He shook his head, "I had thought to be a knight of God but he has chosen another calling for me."

I believed in God, we all did, but this was so unexpected. I looked at Thomas who simply nodded, "I worried about my brother for he did not sleep. He told me about the visitations." He shrugged, "I confess I did not see or hear anything but I did sleep. I do not doubt my brother's words, father."

"You are sure about this, John?"

"I am. I regret letting you down but..."

I swashed a hand before me, "You are not letting me down. You never could. You are my son and I am proud of you but there will be no coming back from this. I will speak to the cardinal if you wish, I am sure that the pope can arrange something, but it would mean you would leave your family. Not just Thomas and me but Michael and the rest of the White Company."

"God has called me and I cannot deny him. I know not what kind of priest I shall be but you and the others have trained my mind and body well. If we still held the Holy Land, I would take the cross and fight the Turk but that land is lost. I will be a priest."

I was in shock. I could fight Bologna for my son but I could not fight God. The three of us spoke for a while and then I said, "I will go to speak to Robert de Genève. I will have food sent to you."

Michael had been there to stop others from listening in but he had heard all. He saw my face and said, "Sir John, I love John as though he was my own brother but you can do nothing about this. It is clear from his words, which even through the tent wall were filled with sincerity, that he believes and you cannot fight such faith."

"I know, Michael, but I did not see this coming. It is like losing a son."

"Not so. If anything becoming a priest gives him more chance of a longer life. Thomas will be the warrior and John the priest. It is meant to be."

My leaders and the cardinal were at the trebuchet which was being disassembled. It was Giovanni who saw my face first and knew that something was amiss, "Sir John, were your sons…"

I shook my head. There was no easy way to say this and I blurted it all out without a preamble. Giovanni, Robin and Dai were as close to my sons as was Michael and they were silent as they took in what the words meant.

Sir Andrew Belmonte was more philosophical, "This is a good thing, Sir John. We are soldiers and any voice that can speak to God on our behalf cannot hurt."

He was not a father and could not know. Robert de Genève, for once, looked at me as a man and not a mercenary. His voice was gentle, "Sir John, if there is anything that I can do, then just ask." I smiled and nodded. "Suddenly his face beamed, "I am a fool, Sir John, I can do more than offer empty words. I can offer him a place at my rectory in Bishopwearmouth. It is in England and the people there are kind. He can train to be a priest in the land of the Prince Bishop."

"And if you do this, Robert, then I am in your debt."

Tuscan Warlord

"No, Sir John, I do this as a friend. You and I may disagree on matters military but I know that you are a good man and I have seen how you have cared for your sons. Added to the way you watch over your men it tells me that Sir John Hawkwood is not the monster his enemies make out. It will take a few weeks to organise but he can take a ship from Ravenna and by the end of the year he will be safe in Durham."

It was good that my men knew our business for I was of little use as we packed up our weapons of war and headed for Forli. Knowing that I might not see John ever again or, if I did it would be many years hence, made me want to relish each and every moment with him. It made me think more about Antiochia. The last time I had seen her she had been a toddler. The letters from her grandfather and grandmother did little to give me a picture of her face. I knew her character but I was enough of a realist to know that doting grandparents who had no other relative would have a jaundiced view of her. I resolved to visit England and see her with my own eyes.

Forli wisely chose to take the olive branch offered by the cardinal and they surrendered before we had even unpacked **'The Minotaur'**. The cardinal was inordinately pleased and he sent a message to the pope telling him of our two successes. He also asked for payment but my view was that the pope would not be paying us. He also arranged for a ship to take John first to Marseille and thence to England. It was not totally altruistic. He was sending two of his priests to Cambrai and Thérouanne while a third servant, Walter, was going back to Bishopwearmouth. John would be safe and, in my view more importantly, not alone.

I left my company and went with Michael and my two sons to Ravenna. Giovanni was left in command of the soldiers as we prepared to march to Cesena. We expected the ship to dock in the afternoon and we reached the quay at noon. We were able to sit and enjoy the view whilst talking for what we thought might be the last time. Thomas was even more upset than I was. He had grown up trying to best his brother in all things. He had striven to be like him and now he was being left. He told me he felt abandoned. John was treading a path he would never take. I looked at my eldest son with new eyes. I saw the clay that was becoming a man. I know he looked like me, others had said that for I rarely looked in a mirror. I was not a vain man. I could not see him being a priest for he looked like a warrior. His broad shoulders had come from the archer training and his reflexes were like those of a cat. How would he adapt to becoming a priest?

Father Giorgio would watch over my son until they docked at Calais and thereafter Walter, returning to Durham and retiring from the cardinal's service, would watch him. As we saw the ship approach and while John and Thomas spoke privately, I went to Father Giorgio and Walter. I gave Walter a noble, "I trust that the two of you will see my son safely to his final destination. Neither of you has sons and you cannot know the pain I feel."

Walter shook his head, "Not true, my lord. I have two sons at home in Bishopwearmouth and when I left to follow the cardinal I knew not when I would see them again. You may trust your son to my care. Until I see my own boys then John Hawkwood shall be as my own son."

His words reassured me and made me feel that I was not quite the villain I thought I had become. With no tides to speak of in the Mediterranean, there was no need for a lengthy turnaround. The soldiers Robert had been waiting for disembarked and a parchment was handed to him. The captain was keen to take advantage of propitious winds and the passengers were quickly boarded. In one way it made life easier as there was no time to hug and unman ourselves. John boarded and waved and then the billowing sails hid him from view.

As we rode back and while the cardinal was engrossed in his missive I spoke to Thomas, "So, Thomas, do you still wish to become a warrior?"

"More so than ever, father. All that our capture did was to ensure that I will never be taken as easily again." He tapped his boot and I saw the pommel of a dagger. "I will go armed and any man that tries to take me had better enjoy the sight of his own blood."

I shook my head, "Use your mind, Thomas. When we were taken in Arezzo, I knew the futility of fighting. Fight the battles that you can win and accept that some battles may end in stalemate."

It was only a short ride but the cardinal was more than preoccupied. He read and reread the pope's parchment over and over. I only noticed because he never attempted to speak to us. I forgot about the pope once we reached Forli. The sooner we took Cesena the sooner we could capture Bologna and I could have my vengeance on that city. I resolved that when I was done with Bologna we would quit the service of the pope and return to Lucca. He had not paid us and there were others, like Florence and Venice who would.

Chapter 17

The delays in our assault meant that Cesena was better prepared than the other towns had been. Perhaps they were encouraged by the fact the Bologna remained free, albeit temporarily, but whatever the reason the walls bristled with helmeted men. Many warriors who had fled Faenza and Forli had joined them. We assembled the trebuchet and I sent my archers to raid the surrounding lands. They came back with fewer animals than on the other raids and that fact told us that the city was well-stocked and supplied. They had also embedded stakes in the ground before their gates. It would not stop a ram but it would slow one down and allow the defenders to hurt men at arms who left the safety of the ram to remove the obstacle.

The cardinal seemed agitated, "These people need to be crushed. We should attack sooner rather than later."

I shook my head, "You have more papal troops, Cardinal, but I still command. We will be methodical. They will expect us to attack as we did before. We keep the rams hidden. We have to reduce the main gate first in any case so let us keep them in the dark as to our battle plans. They are surrounded and whilst we did not capture as much food as before we have more than enough to keep the men well fed." I stared into the papal prelate's eyes, "Even though we are yet to be paid."

"I told you, Sir John, when the ship returns, she will have your pay aboard and by then Cesena will be ours."

I waited until the trebuchet had been checked by our engineer before I gave orders to begin the battering of the walls. We had learned from the first battle and Robin had his best archers close to the mighty war machine. When the stones hit the walls they took advantage of the sight of men suddenly exposed and the defenders of Cesena learned to keep shields before them even when protected by crenulations. Although we could not keep the trebuchet hurling non-stop, we had to replace ropes every few hours, we had enough archers and crossbows to ensure that in the odd lull, they would find it hard to repair their walls. We had made the gatehouse at Faenza fall within a day but the extra defences of Cesena meant that as darkness fell, the gates were still intact. I had anticipated such a stern defence and we had made preparations. The engineer had tightly packed balls of straw and hay soaked in oil brought forward. He was not happy about using fire for the mighty machine could be damaged but I knew that we could build another one if we needed to. This would be a lesson for Bologna. There they would be watching developments knowing that Cesena had prepared well for this attack.

We heard the hammering and the banging as the defenders scurried around repairing the damage from the attack. The oil-soaked ball was fitted and in one swift motion was ignited and let fly. It was dark but the engineer had the range and had made the ball of fire the same weight as the stones we had sent. When the ball exploded on the wall, sending the burning oil-covered shards of stone and straw to envelop the repairers, it came as a complete shock. The engineer sent burning fireball after burning fireball into the night. There must have been a cauldron of oil or pig fat waiting for the rams for the sixth fireball hit something inflammable that illuminated the whole of the wall and gatehouse. Great spikes of flames leapt into the air and the walls were filled with cries. The walls were stone but the fighting platform was wooden and when the burning oil spread it made the fighting platform untenable.

I said to the engineer, "Keep sending fireballs but do so over the walls to land in the city. I will lead men to attack the gates."

"Yes, Sir John."

I drew my sword and turned, "We attack! Are you with me?" The roar told me that they were. I saw that Thomas was with my men. He wished to be a warrior and this is what warriors did.

Not all of our men were ready for the assault, half were eating but I had enough men to do the job and holding my shield before me I waved them forward with a sword held aloft. The gates stood but many of my men had axes, halberds and poleaxes. With no defenders to hurt us as we hacked, we could destroy the gates. The flames would make the wall close to the gate impossible to defend. The hardest part was clambering, in the dark, over the fallen masonry. Robin and his archers were close behind us and the flames made the night like day. Their arrows would be there to guard us.

I stood with Dai, Giovanni, Michael and Sir Andrew. Our shields were there to protect the backs of the men at arms with axes and halberds but we were not needed. The fallen masonry and burning fighting platform meant that they could not use the murder holes and arrow slits at the side. The screams and shouts of the burning men inside were punctuated by the regular thuds and cracks as the gate was methodically destroyed by bladed, poled weapons.

"Switch!"

The metal studs and nails on the gate blunted weapons and men tired. Those who replaced the first wave had renewed energy and soon we saw through gaps in the gates, the effect of the engineer's burning balls of fire in the city. They had hit rooves and buildings were ablaze. We had to switch a third time before the strengthened gates fell and then I led my men, now reinforced with the cardinal's men and the rest of the White Company, into the city. It was like a scene from hell as flames licked above us and in the city before us. There were men being tended to while others ran at us to prevent our entry into their city. It was a forlorn hope. We hacked, chopped and slashed our way through Cesena's narrow streets. We had to secure every house and building as we went. The result was that it took until dawn for us to reach the town square and the citadel. It was there that we halted for we had won. There were still armed men before us but they were beaten. I only stopped because my men and I were weary. The smell of burning filled the air. Some buildings had been burnt with people inside and the stink of burning flesh was nauseating.

The Cardinal strode up and said, "This is not over, Sir John."

Tuscan Warlord

I had sheathed my sword and taken off my helmet. I nodded, "It is, cardinal. They are beaten. We have Cesena."

He leaned into me and said, quietly, "The letter from the pope told me to make an example of Cesena. He wants everyone dead as a lesson to others. He wants no more rebellions in his lands."

I could not believe what I was hearing, "Let me make it clear what you ask of me, cardinal. You wish my men to kill everyone in the city, even if they surrender?"

"I want everyone dead, is that clear enough?"

Giovanni, Michael and Robin had been close enough to hear the cardinal and I looked at them. I saw in their eyes that they would not do it and I had no intention of being involved in such an atrocity. "White Company, fall in and follow me."

Thomas said, "If my brother heard those words he might reconsider his idea to be a priest."

I turned and walked away with Thomas close by me. Even as we retraced our steps to the wrecked gates, I heard the sound of crossbow bolts slamming into defenceless citizens. Dai had been clearing another part of the city and he joined us, "What is amiss, my lord?"

Giovanni said, "The pope wishes Cesena slaughtered and Sir John will not do it."

We passed through the gates but could still hear the screams and shouts as people were killed. I had planned on going to our camp and eating but the sound still drifted over. I laid my helmet on the floor and sat on the camp chair I used. The rest of my leaders stood there and Michael said, "Sir John, we cannot sit by and do nothing. This is wrong."

Robin, normally a practical man who knew the realities of war nodded, "Aye Sir John, it is bad enough that we are not paid but to be ordered to kill innocents does not sit well with me."

Giovanni was our Italian and he said, "You have already decided that our contract is over, my lord. Let us stop this slaughter for if we do not then I for one will never sleep again."

They were all right and when I saw Thomas' eyes pleading with me, I nodded and rose, "Come with me but listen to my orders. Thomas, fetch my horn."

It was clear that the whole company felt as I did for none of them had begun to take off their plate and mail. With my coif hanging down my shoulders but with a drawn sword I marched back into the town. I pointed to the walls, "Robin, send half of the archers to the unburnt sections of the fighting platform." He detailed the centenars to carry out my orders. "Dai, take your men and get to the other side of the square. Use your shields to make a safe haven for the people of Cesena."

"Yes, Sir John."

It was clear that my men were warriors and not butchers. They were not afraid to fight but there were rules that we all adhered to and the pope, along with his prelate, had clearly broken them. The men of Cesena, having realised what the papal troops intended, now stood with shields and pavise to protect their families. The cardinal was using his crossbowmen to break them down while some of his French men at arms were using pole weapons to smash through shields on the flanks.

"Now, Thomas."

The horn's strident notes echoed from the buildings surrounding the square. I shouted, "Lay down your weapons, this is over."

A crossbowman deliberately picked up his crossbow and placed a bolt in it. Even as he raised it to aim at the man being helped to his feet an arrow slammed into him.

"Obey me or the only men who will die this day will be yours, cardinal."

"We are obeying the orders given to me by his holiness."

"That does not make them right. Obey me or you will be the first to die."

Robin was next to me and he slowly raised his bow and aimed it at the cardinal who was less than forty paces from us. I saw the fear in the eyes of Robert de Genève. He nodded and said, "Do as this mad Englishman says."

The weapons were lowered and Robin eased off from the half-pull. It was then that the leader of the French men at arms, Guy de Malmaison suddenly rushed at me. I was almost isolated for there was just Robin and Thomas close to me, the rest of my men and leaders were spread out in a semi-circle. I pushed Thomas behind me and drew my dagger. I barely managed to block the blow from his sword as it came for my unprotected head. He had a shield but I managed to stab under his right arm with my dagger. Had I struck perfectly then I would have severed tendons and he would have lost the use of his right arm. As it was, I just sliced through the flesh but it was enough to make him step back.

"Step away, Sir John, and he will die."

I knew Robin could kill him easily but all the pent-up anger of my sons' incarceration, the lack of pay and now the order to massacre innocents made my blood boil. As he stepped back, I brought my sword down towards his head. He thought he was stronger but he was wrong and he merely slowed down the sword which cracked his helmet. He took another step back and I lunged with my dagger. If a man is overbalancing, he has little control over his shield arm and he did not block the blow. The bodkin went into his cheek and blood spurted. He began to exaggerate his steps to get away from me and that merely accelerated his fall. As he began to tumble, he spread his arms wide and my sword struck his helmet and his skull squarely in the middle. I think that my archer's arm gave enough power to crack the helmet and fracture his skull but the edge also sliced through his nose and jaw. He lay and twitched and then lay still.

I turned to Robert de Genève, "Now it is over."

He nodded and was defeated.

Giovanni shouted, "Disarm the papal soldiers." My men hurried to obey and Giovanni walked over to the survivors of the massacre, "And does Cesena surrender to Sir John Hawkwood and the White Company?"

A plated knight walked over to Giovanni and handed him his sword, "We do and we thank Sir John and the White Company."

Tuscan Warlord

We could not simply leave for I knew that if we did then the cardinal would simply march back in and finish the job he had been given. The cardinal took the trebuchet and rams and marched his men back to Bologna. We helped Cesena repair her walls. We were seen as saviours and not attackers. We were fed and treated well. When Bologna surrendered then Cesena sent an envoy to the cardinal to let the pope know that Cesena would be a papal city once more. Of course, it was only a temporary state of affairs. Once we left then the cities we had taken would rebel again and Robert de Genève was not the man to take them without my help.

We retired to my newly captured castles and we spent a month repairing them. Cortignola was a particularly fine castle and I knew that the income from my Romagnan territory would make up for the loss of pay from the pope. We were a democratic company and I asked for volunteers to stay and garrison my new castles. The massacre of Cesena had sickened some of the men and we had enough. The castellans were natural leaders. One was a centenar who had taken up with a local woman and now wished for a family life. Some of my men had been with me for many years and I understood their reasons.

Instead of heading directly back to Lucca, we took a meandering route through Tuscany. Ostensibly the pope was still our employer and so we raided the lands of his enemies. We captured Città di Castello which had rebelled against the pope and spent a month there while we raided the land around Siena, Perugia and other Tuscan towns and cities. We were making money. I think we might have stayed there longer and made the castle another one of our conquests but Siena and Perugia paid us money to stop us from raiding and to leave their lands alone. It was Robert de Genève who put a stop to the raids. He arrived at the newly conquered castle, Città di Castello, with chests full of our back pay. I had not seen him since Cesena and it was clear that he viewed me as an enemy.

"Sir John, Pope Gregory wishes you to stop raiding these lands. He understands that your motivation is the lack of pay and you have now been paid in full for your services hitherto. You will vacate Città di Castello and then return to Lucca. The matter is not open for discussion. Failure to obey will result in excommunication for you and all your company. That may not bother you but I am sure it would many of your men."

I nodded. Indeed I was ready to return home but I was curious about what had brought this on, "Why the sudden change of heart, Robert?"

You have roused the pope's enemies and there is now a league against the papacy. Florence and Milan, Siena, Pisa, Lucca, Arezzo and Queen Joanna I of Naples have all formed the league. We now have a war."

"And does the pope still wish me to fight for him? After Cesena that would be difficult."

"I have advised him against paying for your services in the future. Whilst you are undoubtedly a good general you have shown that you cannot be trusted."

I laughed, "And the pope can be? We will take your money and head home."

We headed back to Lucca. The news of the massacre of Cesena preceded us and towns and villages hid behind doors as we passed and the journey home was not a pleasant one. Word would eventually reach them that it was not the White Company but the pope who had committed the atrocity.

Before we reached Lucca, laden as we were by wagons loaded with loot, we were stopped outside Pisa by a small army. It was led by Bartolomeo D'Agostino. Also present was Francesco Pagano but he was at the rear of the delegation.

"Sir John, the people of Pisa will not allow you to pass through Pisa."

My eyes narrowed. We could take the route around the city but I wanted to know why we were being barred from the city we had defended for so many years. "The people of Pisa have short memories. We have never fought against Pisa and my company still owns lands and property in the city. Why can we not enter?"

He was silent and the men around him glowered at me. Francisco Pagano forced his horse through the others and reined in next to me, "They fear you, Sir John, and do not trust you. They believe that you will try to reinstate Giovanni delle Agnello and his family to power."

"As I did not know that he had been ousted that comes as a surprise to me."

"Those of you with property in Pisa can enter but not the company."

I heard the rumble of Robin's voice behind me, "We are wasting time, Sir John. Let us sweep aside these peacocks and ride into the city that could be ours if we chose."

When more of my men murmured their agreement, I held up my hand, "Francesco, you know me and you know that I speak the truth."

Francisco Pagano looked more than uncomfortable, "Aye, Sir John, but there are others who rule Pisa now and I am in the minority."

I nodded and turned in the saddle, "Then you may be right, Robin. Giovanni, order the men to prepare for war."

D'Agostino almost squealed, "No! No! You cannot come through Pisa but we will pay you to detour around us."

"How much?"

"Forty thousand florins."

"Fifty."

He was eager to avoid another humiliation at my hands, "Fifty it is! Now, wait here while it is fetched."

The speed with which the chests were brought told me that they had anticipated buying us off. It had been unnecessary for we had no plans to attack Pisa but it showed me that we now had no friends in Italy. We would have to fight for whatever we needed.

It was almost winter when we reached Lucca and Thomas and I were glad when the door slammed behind us. Perhaps John had been right although his choice of the church, in light of Cesena, was not a path for us.

I had Jack bar my door for three days so that I could clear my thoughts. When William was eventually admitted he brought good news. "The pope did not send all our back pay but he sent enough to pay the men and we have had an influx of men from England. We have fifty archers and sixty lances."

"And any new employers?"

"As we had the papal contract, I sought none but there are many out there who would hire us. I will begin to seek a contract." He paused, "Given your isolation, I wondered if you are tired of it all."

I nodded, "I confess that I am thinking of returning to England. John's departure has made me think of Antiochia. Is there news of my pardon?"

"Not yet but perhaps some of the new lances might know more."

"I would like to meet them." I was thinking of Sir John Thornbury. I did not want to make a mistake like him again. The men were all young and I saw that as a good thing. They would be keen and malleable. The only news they could give to me about my pardon was second-hand. William Coggeshall was just twenty years old and the second son of a noble family. His elder brother had attended a recent parliament and William told me that he believed the pardon was going through all the procedures that were necessary to facilitate it. It was good news but it meant I delayed my return to England.

It was then that Bernabò Visconti came to visit me. It was one advantage of living in Lucca. Unlike Pisa which was an enemy of Florence and therefore not as neutral as the Lord of Milan would have liked, it was seen as being a place where we could meet without hidden messages emerging. He stayed with me. My house was large enough and I felt it gave me an edge in any discussions we might have. Although Thomas dined with us, he left as soon as the meal was ended for he knew that there would be discussions between the two of us.

Visconti was obviously keen to begin for as soon as Thomas had departed and the servants cleared the table he began, "Sir John, you have seen the perfidy of the pope. Those who oppose the pope speak of Cesena as clear evidence of what Pope Gregory is capable of." I said nothing. "And he did not pay you." He allowed himself a wry smile, "As I remember that was why you left my service."

"And yet, thanks to the efforts of my company, independently of any overlord, we have made money and now own castles in Romagna."

He nodded, "Very astute of you, I am sure. Yet if you join the league against the pope then you will be on the right side and make a profit. We will allow you to keep your castles. I have heard rumours that Pope Gregory sees those as his as you were in his service at the time."

"Unpaid service."

"Sir John, the opposition to the pope has now grown. There is a league against him. His papacy is an affront to God. Cesena showed the world that. Join us." He paused and, perhaps sensing that my resolve was weakening said, "Pope Gregory has appointed Sir John Thornbury as commander of his papal forces." My raised eyebrows asked the obvious question and he nodded, "It is confirmed and why should I lie when you could discover the truth yourself if you chose."

He was right of course. I nodded, "I will need to speak to my leaders."

"Of course. Come to Milan when you have decided. Bring William with you and I will have lawyers draw up the papers that shall be needed." He smiled, "I have missed having you at my side, Sir John. It felt wrong to be on opposing sides. Together we are a mighty force."

My leaders saw nothing wrong with changing sides. It was all business. Giovanni made the point that we could demand whatever fee we chose as they had come to us rather than us seeking the work. I took Michael and Thomas with William and me when we headed north through a snow-covered land. It felt like a new journey. Just before we had left Lucca, I had received a letter from John who was now in England and, from his words, quite content. Coincidentally Antiochia also sent a letter. Her grandmother had died and her grandfather was ill. She asked if she could visit me in Italy.

As we rode north, I was torn. I wanted to see my daughter of course I did, but the journey from England to Italy was fraught with danger. Travelling with those I thought of as family allowed me to speak openly and I asked their advice.

Thomas began, "If I have a sister then I should like to see her, father. It is good that she comes to visit."

William nodded, "You have often spoken of her and her mother. I am just surprised that you have not been home to visit her."

William's words made me angry for they were true and my vitriolic words were aimed more at myself than him, "And you think I do not know that?"

Michael was ever the peacemaker, "There is an easy solution, Sir John, I can take some of the new men to England and escort her back. Who knows we may be able to employ more men whilst in England and you know she will be safe with me."

He was right and the rest of the journey saw me in better humour. We would make the arrangements with Visconti and then make a rapid return to Lucca so that we could start to make the arrangements that would see me reunited with the daughter I was not sure I would even recognise.

Chapter 18

Milan 1377

Sometimes you can plan as much as you like but higher forces interfere. So it was on that visit to Milan. Bernabò wanted to impress me. He had lost my services once before and had no desire to lose them a second time. We were given sumptuous quarters in the ducal palace. Servants bathed us and our travelling clothes were taken away to be cleaned. The four of us wore clothes that rarely left our chests they were so fine but they seemed appropriate somehow. With hair and beards that were combed and oiled and smelling of rosemary and lavender, we entered the Great Hall. Bernabò continued to try to impress us. The great and the good from Milan were present and, as we entered, for we were the last, the guests of honour, we were applauded. That it was orchestrated by the Lord of Milan was clear but it pleased me. There were a sea of faces before me and most of them passed in a blur but one stood out. It was as though an angel had descended from heaven and landed in Milan. While I mumbled responses to those introduced to me by Bernabò I could not take my eyes off the vision in blue and silver.

"And this is my daughter, Donnina." I lifted her hand to kiss the back of it and found myself intoxicated by the perfume and then when I looked up, I fell into the two deep blue pools that were her eyes.

"I have heard much about you, Sir John, but I expected a much older man." Her voice was low and sultry, it belied her angelic appearance.

Bernabò clicked his fingers and said, "Antonio, change the seating arrangements, Sir John will sit next to my daughter, Donnina." I turned to look at him and he smiled, "My friend, it would take a blind man not to see the light that flows between you. You and I will have time to talk but when higher forces intervene it is a foolish man who tries to oppose them and whilst I am old, I am not foolish."

I found I could not argue. I was mesmerized by this vision of beauty before me. The girl looked to be the same age as John or Thomas and as I had seen more than fifty summers this would look wrong to others yet I found myself drawn to the girl as we were led to our seats. I knew not where my son was seated and, to be honest, I cared not. We were seated just four down from the Lord of Milan and I saw that William had been seated next to Bernabò. He might talk of higher powers but Bernabò was all about business. A servant placed a napkin over my left shoulder and handed me a pearl-handled knife, filigreed with silver to carve the meat. He poured a glass of white wine for Donnina and red for me. The glass was exquisitely made and I recognised it as Venetian. I could not bring words forth and I drank some wine to give myself time to think about how to speak.

Donnina smiled and the sip she took was like the sip a bee might take so delicate was it, "My father has often spoken of you, Sir John. When I was younger and he still visited my mother, he was full of your exploits."

"He no longer visits your mother?"

She laughed and then, covering her mouth with her hand leaned in to speak sotto voce, "My father likes pretty things and my mother aged too quickly, however since I have blossomed a little, he has visited us often." She smiled and bee-like drank more wine, "She is comfortable and he takes care of us. We have a fine house and servants."

I nodded and struggled for something to say, "I did not see you before, Donnina, but I would say that your bud has become the most beautiful of blooms."

She laughed again and I found her laughter made me smile, "Oh, sir, I am a maiden and unused to such flattery."

It was my turn to laugh, "And I cannot believe that you do not have many suitors."

Her face became serious, "When you are the daughter of Bernabò Visconti there are many men who make suits. Most either want the power for if you are associated with the Lord of Milan then you have power, or they seek money and assume that a Visconti daughter, even an illegitimate one such as I, will be given a fine dowry." She put her hand on mine and leaned in once more. I inclined my head to hear better and felt a thrill race through my body. "There will be no dowry. He will pay for the wedding but there will be neither land nor title. Do you understand?"

That was the moment that I saw behind the eyes and the beauty. Donnina Visconti had a mind as sharp as any warrior I had ever met. If I was Giovanni Acuto then she was Donnina Acuto.

She looked past me and said, "And that is your son?"

"My youngest, Thomas. My elder, John, is in England, He wishes to be a priest."

"And if he is as handsome as his younger brother that is a waste although I have known of some priests, cardinals and bishops especially, who are fond of women."

I began to feel jealous that she thought my son was handsome. It was wrong and I shook my head to clear the image that was forming in my mind.

"What is wrong Sir John?"

"Nothing but… my sons are older than you and…"

The first course had arrived and I sliced a piece from the pike. I offered it to Donnina who shook her head. I put it on the platter and then picked a succulent piece to eat. I needed time to compose myself.

Donnina took a bunch of grapes and taking one, sliced it delicately in two before eating it. "Sir John, when you entered the room, I did not see a man almost as old as my father, I saw a knight, a warrior. I saw a man who is used to power. A man who bends popes and dukes to his will. I liked what I saw and then I caught your eye when you saw me." She smiled and it was as though my heart melted at that moment, "The look you gave me was one who wishes more than to be friends, am I right?"

"I, er…"

She laughed again, "You are a man of war and the world of women is a mystery to you, is it not?"

It was my turn to laugh, "You are right. I am better with a sword in my hand than sweet words in my mouth." I wiped my fingers on my napkin.

"And you need no sweet words for me." She put her hand on her breast, "Your eyes speak here and they are more truthful than any poet's words intended to enchant a young girl."

"What are you saying?"

"I am saying that when you lie abed this night and think of me, and I know that you will, then ask yourself what it is that you want. The wine can often make our lips say that which we wish to stay hidden. On the morrow I will take you for a walk in the gardens, they are not at their best at this time of year but they are quiet and we can talk there without gossip." She nodded her head down the table and I saw eyes peering at us, "Already people are making up their own narrative for what goes on here." She patted my hand, "And now I will confuse them for I will talk to my half-brother, Rodolfo and you can endure a tedious hour with the Archbishop of Milan." She was a woman in a girl's body for she had a mind like a steel trap.

She was seated next to one of Bernabò's legitimate children and I knew he was just seventeen. Donnina Visconti was a clever girl and she was quite right, the archbishop just wanted to talk about the pope and how he wanted a new one. It was a test of my endurance and I fought hard not to keep turning around to look on the angel. Whenever a new dish was brought out and served, I took the opportunity to spend as long as I could carving the tastiest-looking piece I could. I still could not tell you the taste of any of the dishes for I was trying to glimpse her from the corner of my eye. The one piece of useful information concerned my old nemesis, Sir John Thornbury. He had taken every opportunity since we had parted to fight against me. I knew that he had fought for Milan and been quite successful in its war with Genoa. He had left and now I knew not where he was except that he had sought work with the pope.

When the archbishop tired of talking about the French popes he said, "I hear that Pope Gregory has employed another Englishman to replace you, Sir John."

"And who is that?"

"Sir John Thornbury." I tried to keep my face impassive as I nodded. He laughed, "I fear that he does not have a good word to say about you. He disparages you whenever he has the chance. It is said that it was his views that won him the contract. That and the fact that he is a friend of Robert de Genève."

The dull time I had endured with the archbishop had yielded me one valuable piece of information but I would rather have spoken to Donnina for longer.

When she, along with the other unmarried women, retired early I was mortified. The only good news was that it meant I could talk to Rodolfo. He spoke of wars and battles. He knew Ambrogio and I was held in high esteem. I found him easier to talk to than the archbishop but I still felt an ache for Donnina. I retired as soon as it was politic to do so. I did not wish to carouse until the early hours. William had already retired and I knew that William, Michael, and Thomas were only waiting for me to leave.

I stood and said, "Thank you, Bernabò, you did me great honour with this feast."

He came and put his arm around me. It was the most intimate gesture I had seen from the great lord. He spoke into my ear, "All these years I have been trying to throw a daughter at you and when you do succumb to the charms of one it is my favourite."

I spoke as quietly as he had, "Bernabò, she is younger than my sons."

"I am still fathering children with girls younger than my daughter. You English are so hidebound and worried about age and people's opinions. You live in Italy now. Embrace the Italian way. I shall see you at breakfast."

It was an order and I nodded.

Once in our chamber, I was assailed by questions. Thomas had been the furthest from me and he said, "Who was that beauty you were seated next to, father?"

"Donnina Visconti, an illegitimate daughter of the Lord of Milan."

"You were better off than I was. The woman and the priest next to me were the dullest people I have ever met. It is a good thing that the food was so good."

I saw the smile exchanged between William and Michael. They had seen more and understood. William said, "The contract will be a good one, Sir John, and will mean we can not only employ more lances but also have more money to invest. When we sign tomorrow, I can leave for Lucca and begin to plan."

Michael grinned, "And I can go with William and arrange for Antiochia to come to Italy. That is if you still wish her to?"

"Of course."

Thomas asked, innocently, "I thought we might be staying here longer."

Michael said, "I believe that you will be, Thomas. Your father will be in no rush to leave."

I was becoming irritated, "Enough, Michael, I am tired and it is time to retire. We have an early meeting with Lord Visconti and I wish a clear head."

That night I struggled to sleep as I wrestled with my feelings. For years I had fought off the attempts of Bernabò Visconti to marry me to one of his daughters. He had paraded enough of them before me over the years to turn my head before, yet I had resisted. What was it about this seventeen-year-old that was different? I was not an old man but I knew my body was no longer young. If I chose to pursue this young girl what would my sons think? What about my daughter? Michael was about to bring her to Italy. How would she view a stepmother who was younger than she? Exhaustion overtook me and I fell into a troubled sleep. Sometimes you see the dream or nightmare clearly as though it was painted on a canvas but at other times, and this was one, something horrible wakes you and you sit bolt upright in bed sweating. It was not yet morning but there was no way that I was risking closing my eyes and having my sleep assaulted by I knew not what. I slipped from the bed and dressed silently.

The Lord of Milan had sentries at the ends of the corridors. Assassins had been sent before now. I saw them tense as I approached them down the shadowy, sconce-lit passages. When they recognised me, they relaxed. I recognised one who had fought alongside me many years earlier. He smiled and nodded, "Good morning, Sir John. An early riser I see."

I smiled and lied, "I am an old campaigner and such habits are hard to break."

Although it was not yet dawn servants had cleared the hall the previous night and now it was being prepared for breakfast. The kitchens and the hall were far enough from the sleeping chambers for there to be a busy buzz of conversation. When I entered, they all stopped and bowed, "Carry on, I could not sleep. I will not hinder your labours."

Relieved, I think, that I was not some pampered popinjay who demanded some exotic food or drink they scurried about their business. The steward fetched me some fried ham on freshly made bread and a mug of ale. He smiled, "I believe this is what Englishmen like to eat of a morning, my lord."

"Indeed it is." There is something about the smell of warmed ham that makes a man hungry, even if he is not and this was thinly sliced ham, fried to almost a crispy consistency. It was delicious and, along with the strong ale, drove all thoughts of bad dreams from my head. It was Bernabò himself who descended first, just as the sun's rays began to appear from the stained-glass window at the end of the hall. I had not noticed it the previous night and guessed that it had been placed there to catch dawn's light rather than that of a sunset. The tables were already filling with breads, fruits, cold meats and the like but the arrival of the lord initiated a flurry of activity as hot dishes were fetched out.

The steward knew what Bernabò wanted and a platter was filled with dishes that reflected his unique taste, "Would you like more food fetching, Sir John?"

"I will choose my own, thank you."

"They have been looking after you, Sir John?"

"They have." I rose and took my platter to choose more hot food. I did not have to worry about what others thought as there was just Bernabò down as yet. I wondered if it was deliberate. Had he asked to be woken when I descended? To an old warrior, the variety of hot food was not to be wasted and with a laden platter, I returned. We both ate in silence.

Tuscan Warlord

That was out of respect for the food. However, once our platters were cleared and chilled wine infused with pieces of ice brought down from the mountains served, then Bernabò turned to me to speak.

"Sir John, you are a good friend and ally yet I would have you closer to me. As you know, for you have fought alongside Ambrogio, family is all to me. The ties of the family can be trusted when the bonds of alliances are broken. I would have you in my family. I have yet to speak to Donnina but from what I saw last night she would not be averse to marriage to you."

"I will be as open and honest with you as I can, my lord, and tell you that I am attracted to your daughter and that disturbs me for I am old enough to be her grandfather, let alone her father. Even if, as you say, she is attracted to me now will she still be so in a year or two?"

He smiled and drank half of the beautifully chilled wine which cleansed the palate well, "Let me tell you something about Donnina and her mother. They are both eminently practical women. Donnina wants a good marriage to someone who is rich. A powerful husband is also important to me. Such men are dukes and princes and even though she is the daughter of the Lord of Milan, the fact that she is illegitimate rules out such a marriage. You, however, are far more powerful than any man, save a duke or prince. Perhaps the Doge of Genoa or the Doge of Venice has more power but that is open for debate. Florence fears you so much that you are paid a stipend from that city and even though you are part of the alliance against the pope they fear you entering the city. If that is not power then I know not what is. As for money…I can only surmise your worth but as you have two banks and have managed to take plunder in every battle then I can assume it is a fortune. William is close-mouthed but he has let slip enough nuggets of knowledge to suggest to me that your worth rivals mine. You are the perfect choice for my daughter."

I finished the wine and shook my head when the steward came to refill it, "Yet there is still the age difference. Whilst I am besotted by her and confess it and you say she appears to be attracted to me, as she blossoms and blooms into womanhood I will age and fade."

He laughed and the laughter echoed around the hall, "You are full of life, Sir John. There are men your age who are doddery but you are like me. In my case, it is the pursuit of young beauties to take to my bed and in your case, it is the conquest of enemies. Donnina will not tie you to a home she will be happy to let you do what you do best and fight. You are a warrior. Men now call you a warlord and the title suits for you are a throwback to the times before kings when it was leaders who were followed and not someone who had a title."

It was at that moment others chose to join us for breakfast and the Lord of Milan became the genial host, greeting them as they entered. He pointed out the tastiest morsels and I was, seemingly, forgotten. I did not mind as I had much to think about. As I stood to leave Bernabò said, over his shoulder, "There are two men to whom you should speak, Sir John." He nodded to the two visitors who, by their dress, were not Italians. They were both looking in my direction. I was intrigued and suspicious. As Visconti had shown he was a devious man who often used deception to get what he wanted.

I wandered over and the two men confirmed that they were not Italian when they spoke in English, "Sir John, I am Sir Edward de Berkley and this is a diplomat, Geoffrey Chaucer."

There was something familiar about this Geoffrey Chaucer and as I struggled to recall it, he said, modestly, "Diplomat is an exaggeration, Sir John. I carry messages for John of gaunt and for the Duke of Clarence."

It was then I remembered where I had seen him, "I saw you when the duke was married."

He gave a flourished bow, "I was there but I met you earlier, my lord."

"I cannot recall."

He nodded, "And there is no reason why you should. I was a page at Poitiers, where you were knighted and I have followed your career since then. One day I should like to put your story into words."

"Words?"

Sir Edward smiled, "Geoffrey is a modest man but he is an accomplished poet. He writes verse and writes it very well."

Geoffrey shook his head, "Since I met Boccaccio I am in doubt about the sobriquet, poet, for compared with that wordsmith I am a writer of witty jokes."

I smiled at his modesty and liked him immediately. "It is an honour to meet you."

Sir Edward said, with a glint in his eye, "We intended to speak to you last night at the feast but you were somewhat preoccupied, Sir John." I felt myself colouring as they both smiled.

Geoffrey said, "I can fully understand why you swam in the pools that are the lady's eyes. She has the most captivating smile of any woman I have ever seen."

I was keen to leave their observations behind, "And what is the purpose of your interest in me, is it the pardon I requested?"

"Partly. The request has been granted and you are free to return to England at any time." I was relieved and it showed. "However, we would prefer it if you did not. You are of more use to England here in Italy."

"I do not understand."

"Let us take the morning air in the gardens where we can speak more freely."

It was as we were leaving that Donnina entered the hall. I stopped and bowed elaborately, "My lady."

She held her hand for me to kiss and when I touched it, she squeezed my fingers. "I can see that you are busy but when you are done with these gentlemen, I beg you to return here so that we may speak further."

The last thing I wanted was to leave the hall and speak to these two Englishmen but I had no choice. As we headed out into the cooler morning air Sir Edward said, "What we have to say will not take long Sir John."

Geoffrey smiled, "And then you can be a gallant knight and woo the beautiful maiden."

Sir Edward shook his head, "Poets are not practical men, Sir John." There was an arched bower and a bench beneath. We stopped there. "It is quite simple, Sir John, we would have you as an ambassador for England." He saw the shock on my face, "We know your history, how you fell out with Sir John Chandos and Prince Edward but both men are dead and King Edward is getting old and frail. The next king of England will be the son of Prince Edward. Richard is just a boy and there are many enemies in England. You are someone who could ensure that Richard becomes king and help to warn his government of dangers on this side of the Channel."

Geoffrey leaned forward, "What we do know about you, Sir John, is that you are a loyal Englishman. Despite provocation, you have never raised your sword against England and that has been noted. Sir Edward wants you to act as a sort of spy."

Sir Edward continued, "We all know that Bernabò Visconti is a great man but he is devious. He has been of use to England over the years but King Edward chose you to be our eyes and ears in Europe. Your involvement with the French Pope caused us some doubts but your joining of the anti-papal league now makes you someone who is vital to England's interests."

"I am happy to serve England. I am a loyal Englishman but I am not sure of how this will work." I confess that my mind was a whirl. Bernabò's words, the presence of Donnina and now this made me feel as though I was riding an unbroken stallion.

"It is simple. You have a daughter in England. You have lands in England. All we ask is that you send letters to Geoffrey here, whenever there is aught that you think we ought to know." I nodded. That was easy enough. William and I had been speaking for some time about investing more of our money in England. "By the same token, your new friend, Geoffrey Chaucer will send you letters asking about the situation here in Italy, France and the Empire. We know that you have a network of spies and intelligence about the political situation. Can you do this?"

I could not see a reason why I should not do this. "I can, although I think you believe me more important than I actually am."

Sir Edward smiled, "No, Sir John, we know exactly how important you are. You know that this means you will have to delay visiting England."

I nodded, "I am making arrangements for my daughter to visit with me here in Italy." I stood, "And now if you will excuse me…"

Geoffrey Chaucer laughed, "You are a true errant knight, Sir John. I look forward to our correspondence with great interest."

Once inside the hall I sought and found Donnina. She was seated next to her half-brother Rodolfo. Grinning he rose as I approached, "My lord, I have kept your seat warm and now I will join my other siblings." He picked up his platter and left.

As I sat down, I saw William, Michael and Thomas approaching. I shook my head and Michael guided them to the other end of the table.

Donnina smiled and nibbled on the delicate biscuit she held in her fingers, "You slept well?"

I shook my head, "My mind, my lady, was too full of you for a good night of sleep."

She mockingly put her hand to her mouth, "My lord, am I such a monster that I induce nightmares?"

I shook my head, "My lady you are as far from being a monster as it is possible to be. It is just that I wrestled with thoughts and urges I thought I was passed."

She put down the half-eaten morsel and wiped her mouth on her napkin. She leaned closer to me and my head was filled with her intoxicating perfume. "My lord, I believe that my father has spoken to you?" I nodded. "I may be young but in here," she tapped her head, "I have my father's mind. I am a practical woman. Aye, you may think me a girl but I am a woman, believe that. I am not one of these flighty young things who dreams of marrying for love. My father has spread his seed around half of Italy. There are more of us who are illegitimate than the ones born to his wife. I want a good husband. I want one who is strong, powerful and rich." She drank some wine to allow that to sink in. "Do I shock you?"

"Surprise me perhaps for your views seem eminently practical. And you would settle for me? Even though I am much older than you?"

"Even if I married your son, Thomas, handsome though he is, he would still be older than I am. What is age? You have experience that a younger man would not have. You will not struggle to give me the house I want and you have the money that will allow me to make you even more powerful. Our children will want for nothing."

I was taken aback, "Then you would marry me?"

"Of course."

When I had married Antiochia, my daughter's mother, it had been because she had been in love with me. I had liked her but not loved her. Now Donnina Visconti was marrying me even though she did not love me but I was besotted with her. Some higher spirit was toying with me but I could not fight it. I would be wed, for good or ill into the Visconti family.

Chapter 19

I was the only one who was surprised at the haste of the arrangements. Everyone seemed to see it as inevitable. A date was set and the marriage would take place in Milan. I hurried back to Lucca for Michael was needed to fetch back my daughter. She had wished to see me and I needed to speak to her before the wedding. He left from Pisa on a ship bought to take them all the way back to England. William paid for the ship and it was laden with spices bought from Giovanni Dini, a Florentine spice merchant who was friendly with William. The profits from the voyage would pay for the ship and more. Amongst those who travelled back was William Coggleshall who went to claim his inheritance. The others who went with Michael and William had similar reasons to make a brief return to England. As much as I wished to, I knew that my new role would prevent such a visit.

On our way back to Lucca I spoke to Thomas. I needed to know his views and I was also preparing to have a similar conversation with the daughter I barely knew. "What do you think of my marriage?"

"I think she is beautiful and any man would be lucky to marry her but…"

"But?"

"I cannot call her mother."

I laughed. I had spoken to Donnina about this before leaving Milan and the ever-practical daughter of the Lord of Milan had agreed. *Thomas, John and Antiochia are not my children. I hope that they will be my friends.* I smiled, "Thomas, she will not be your mother but she will be the mother of children as yet unborn."

"Good, a man should have many children. Do not worry about me, father. I am happy. You are not one who spreads his seed as Visconti does and I am becoming a man and know that a man has needs."

My leaders were equally happy. Robin and Giovanni were not married but they had both sired many children.

Tuscan Warlord

They saw nothing wrong with my marriage to Donnina. I had little to do with the preparations for the wedding but I had other duties to perform. We were now allied with Florence and I had been paid to protect her. When word came of a mercenary company led by Sir John Thornbury marching towards Florence, I needed no spur to make me don my armour and lead my company south. It had been almost a year since we had marched to war and my company was honed and ready to fight.

Sir John Thornbury did not lead papal soldiers but he fought for Pope Gregory whom, it was said, was dying. That explained why Robert de Genève was not in Italy. The company of Sir John Thornbury was modelled on the White Company and he had successfully sacked Siena. It would be foolish to underestimate him but I believed we had an advantage for I had fought in the lands around Florence more than any other condottiere.

Giovanni sent his light horsemen out to find the enemy. Unlike us, Thornbury's company were not all mounted and moved more slowly than we did. Having sacked Siena they had headed to Arezzo. A papal city, it would allow them to resupply and that meant I knew their route to Florence. It was neither the shortest nor the fastest way to get to Florence but it was the one that would keep them further from the White Company. We halted at Antella after a hard forty-mile ride. Had it been through an unfamiliar country it would have taken longer but we reached the town just after dark and we awaited the return of our scouts. I already had a plan in my head but it helped to talk through such plans with my leaders. As we sat around the table eating the stew we had bought from a farmer's wife I found that I missed Michael more than I might have expected. He was the youngest of my leaders and yet I felt very close to him.

We had a rough idea of the make up of Thornbury's company. He had English archers but fewer than we had. To compensate for the shortfall he had some hand gunners and crossbows. He had some English lances but the majority were Hungarians and Germans. Many had been with Paer and Sterz and knew how to fight against us. "Robin, if they come the way that I expect, along the main road that runs through here, then you should be able to send some of your archers and Giovanni's Italians and get around their rear. I think a hundred archers and a hundred horsemen should suffice."

Both men nodded and Robin said, "It is not the road for an army for it twists and turns through the forest and over the high ground but we could do it."

I shook my head, "Not you. I need a good leader to go with them but if Thornbury sees that you and Giovanni are missing, he will fear a trap. I need him to see you two. He will wonder at the absence of Michael but not as much as if he failed to see you two. I want you to be prominent in our battle line." I used my dagger to make a mark in the earth. I put a cross behind the line. "This is Antella. We make a line before the town and have our horses hidden from view. We have men at arms in the vanguard. Dai, you will be at the fore for the same reason as Giovanni and Robin but your men will be mounted and wait behind the town out of sight. That means there will be four hundred and fifty men missing and I hope that gives Thornbury the confidence to attack. We make a barricade before us. If they have, as I have been told, hand gunners then they may use them to attempt to blast their way through. He will seek to defeat me. I have heard that he has belittled me at every opportunity. He will want to humiliate me in battle. I want him committed and then the two hundred men in his rear can launch their attack. When they turn it will be time for Dai to appear and charge them from our left. The sudden appearance of four hundred and fifty men should demoralise them. I am counting on his expecting us to place our archers in the woods to our right."

"The signal you give for the attack must be clear."

"I know, Robin. Thomas, you can sound the horn five times. You will pause for the count of ten and then repeat it. Could you sound the horn that way five times?"

He grinned, "Of course and now that John has left us, I shall have the standard as well, shall I not?"

"Of course."

Tuscan Warlord

The scouts arrived back, exhausted, after midnight. I was woken and they were brought to me. They confirmed that the enemy warriors were on the Antella road. "They have camped twenty-five miles away. Their scouts will be here by the early afternoon."

I had the news I needed, "You have done well, get you to bed. Robin and Giovanni, we will send your men at dawn. They know who they are?"

"We chose them as soon as the meeting was over. They are ready to ride at a moment's notice."

"Good, then I leave that detail to you."

We spent the next morning making the ground before us as difficult as we could. We did not do a neat job. I wanted them to think that we had done so in a hurry. As an obstacle, it would only slow an enemy. It would not stop them. If Thornbury thought he was superior to me then I would do nothing to disillusion him. We used the obstacles to go all the way to the edge of the trees. Light infantry could easily pass through them and I hoped he would send his archers there to counter my own.

His scouts proved to be faster than Giovanni's men had expected. They arrived not long into the afternoon. We were ready but it showed that Thornbury was a good planner. He and his leaders arrived an hour later. Some of his scouts remained while the others had ridden back to warn the main body. I was on my wagon. My standard was propped up so that the slight breeze made it flutter a little. Thomas clambered up to lift it and wave it defiantly at the enemy. It was unnecessary but I was proud of the courage my youngest son showed. Thornbury and about five hundred lances were a quarter of a mile away from us. Had he wanted to then Robin could have sent arrows at them but there was no need to antagonise them. I wanted them to plan an attack so that they would be committed and when I gave the signal then we could close the trap about them. During the afternoon Thornbury's men marched up and he deployed them. I saw him looking at the sky and debating whether or not he should make camp. I could almost see his thought processes. I was known to favour night attacks and if he camped then he invited just such an attack. There was more than enough daylight for him to launch an attack and the sight of me, not mounted on a horse that I could use to flee but tied to a wagon that had no horses upon it must have been the deciding factor. It was too much of a temptation. I saw him wave and give commands.

"He has taken the bait. Now we need to hold him until he is fully committed." I tried to visualise what he would see. We were dismounted and had neither crossbows nor handguns. The mixture of men at arms, knights and men armed with pole weapons was before a thin line of archers. Their hats and longbows marked Robin and his men clearly but there were fewer of them than normal. He and his squire bravely rode to within bow range. He was expecting professional courtesy and I obliged for it suited me however Robin could have plucked him from his saddle had I given the command. I saw Thornbury examine the obstacles and when he turned to ride back to his men, I knew he had fallen into my trap. They looked hurried and insubstantial. He would think he had the beating of me. I was an old man who had passed his best days. He was confident and so was I.

The smoking linstocks for the handguns and the pavise being carried by the pavesiers were the first signs that the attack was about to begin. He had half of his men mounted and he had them placed on both flanks. Half of his archers were filtering towards the woods. Thornbury thought he knew me but he had not fought alongside me long enough for that. Robin saw the archers and he waved fifty of his own to counter the attack. It would be a duel to the death. The difference would be that my men knew this land well. We had fought here and hunted here.

The crack of the handguns and the snap of the bolts signalled the start of the battle. The lead stones thrown by the handguns smashed into the crude barricade and splintered it like matchwood. The bolts were sent to arc over the barricade. They hit shields but their force was lessened by their trajectory. In the trees, I heard the sounds of arrows flying through the undergrowth and then the cries as men were hit. I had to trust that Robin had sent his best men with

Tall Tom. As the barricade was destroyed so the men who would fight on foot began to move into position. Horsemen jostled to rein in their eager warhorses. So far, the only deaths had been in the trees but the wrecked and broken barricade must have seemed like signs of a victory. One problem with handguns was that they fouled easily. It was why I rarely used them. They were effective but unreliable and when the barricade was destroyed the handguns had to be cleaned. It was then that Sir John ordered his crossbows and dismounted men at arms forward.

Holding my shield close to my chest, I raised my sword. It was another trick for Robin would release his arrows when he deemed it right, while Dai and the men waiting at the rear of the enemy were waiting for my horn to signal the attack. The raised sword worked. The pavise stopped and the men at arms raised their shields and locked them in anticipation of an arrow storm. When I lowered my sword and sheathed it, I saw the whole enemy line brace. Even Thornbury, visible on his white horse looked confused. He turned to one of his leaders and said something. Even at a distance of a quarter of a mile, I saw the subordinate shrug. Thornbury's squire sounded the horn and the lines moved forward. When the pavise reached the line where the barricades had stood, they stopped and I watched as crossbows were raised. I lifted my shield so that only my eyes were visible.

I heard the creak of bows as they were drawn back and then Robin's voice as he shouted, "Loose!"

He must have drawn his own bow as a signal. Able to hold the full draw for longer than any other archer it was an effective signal. He timed it to perfection for the crossbowmen had risen to send their own bolts at our line of men at arms. Some arrows hit helmets but many hit either crossbows or bodies. An arrow hitting a crossbow can break or damage it. Flying splinters can blind a man. At the very least it upsets the aim and we had more archers than crossbowmen. Some bolts found their target but most did not. Robin sent five flights at the crossbowmen before stopping and when he did the number of crossbows had been halved. Again he did not shout an order but when the next flights flew, I knew that he had changed to bodkins and the targets were now the men at arms who were within range. Some of them had been so engrossed in the missile duel that their shields were not pulled tightly. As men fell so gaps appeared and the second flight found more bodies than shields.

It was then that the impatient horsemen took matters into their own hands. They spurred their horses and made an attack on our flanks. What they could not have known for even I did not know it, was that our archers had won the battle of the forest and the ones charging our right flank were showered with arrows. They were committed to the attack and it was time for my surprise.

"Thomas, the signal!" The five blasts echoed across the battlefield as the sun began to dip behind us. I saw my son counting and then another five blasts. So it continued. The horsemen charging our left flank were also about to get a surprise. Looming from the gloom from the north rode Dai and his horsemen to slam into the flanks of the charging horsemen. When arrows began to fall into the backs of the dismounted men at arms, I saw Sir John Thornbury turn. There were only one hundred horsemen but they were charging from the darkening east and he could not know that. He gambled and his own horn sounded as he charged towards us with his reserves, the men he led. He was coming for me. It was almost the endgame in this game of human chess and he would risk all and take the king; me. The men who were in our front rank had been carefully chosen. Led by Giovanni, they braced themselves for the attack. Thornbury's men were hampered by the pavesiers and crossbowmen who were trying to extricate themselves from the mêlée. The result was that it was not a solid wall of steel and wood that hit us and the pole weapons wielded by my men held the initial assault. The horsemen on the flanks were effectively out of the battle as Dai on one side and my archers on the other prevented them from joining the attack. It was left to Sir John Thornbury to try to make the breakthrough. It was a race against time for the archers sent to attack his rear were sending arrow after arrow into unprotected backs and the horsemen sent there were slaughtering those left to guard the baggage and crossbowmen trying to flee.

The weight of horses drove a wedge in the enemy lines and like the tip of an arrow, Thornbury rode at me. I could have used a pole weapon but instead, I held my sword. The wooden sides of the wagon protected my legs and his lance would have but one chance to hit me. I gambled that my experience would save me. My men at arms were good but charging war horses make discretion the better part of glory. The ones who survived the initial charge moved to the side the better to attack the flanks of this wedge of horsemen. I saw Giovanni leading his own men to come to cover the gap. He would not be able to reach me before the thrusting lance. The metal head came directly for my face. I braced myself and angled the shield so that although it was a punched strike from Thornbury, the angle of my shield took it away and the strength of my archer's arm diverted the strike. I hacked down at his shield. He had leaned forward to take advantage of his strike and my blow unbalanced him. He fell from his horse. He had the wit to let go of the reins and slip his feet from his stirrups but he still ended up in a heap on the ground. Before he could move Giovanni's sword was at his throat, "Yield, Sir John, and order your men to surrender." There were courtesies extended to fellow condottiere but they depended upon cooperation. Sir John saw the futility in refusing and nodded. His squire sounded the surrender and the weapons of our enemies were thrown to the ground. This was the first and the last time that I ever fought Sir John Thornbury and I was the victor. Perhaps I was trying to prove something to myself, that I was not too old to marry Donnina but whatever the reason I felt invigorated by the victory.

We had his baggage and after his men gave their individual surrender they were let go. The exceptions were the crossbowmen whose weapons were destroyed. The archers had their arrows confiscated by Robin and his men. He had lost forty archers in the fight but more than one hundred enemy archers had perished. He had proved himself

Tuscan Warlord

the best leader of archers. We took treasure with their baggage and more would be forthcoming when Sir John Thornbury's wife sent the ransom for him. He refused to speak to me as we rode back to Lucca and that made me double the ransom. The fact that his wife paid it within a week told me how rich he had become and when it was paid, he left Italy. He had made his fortune and he did what I had often promised myself, he returned to England. He was pardoned for any crimes he had committed and bought a huge estate and retired. I did not regret staying in Italy but Sir John Thornbury showed me what I could have done had not first Donnina and then Sir Edward de Berkeley not come into my life. I was now committed to becoming the *Inglese Italianato*.

Chapter 20

Michael made good time and by the time Sir John had departed for England my daughter had arrived. I had thought I would not recognise her but I had been wrong. She was the model of her mother. When she entered my hall, she fell into my arms and wept. I looked at Michael who said, quietly, "Both grandparents are now dead. She only has you, Sir John."

I squeezed her tightly to me, "And I shall never leave you again, my daughter. You shall want for nothing."

She pulled away and looked at me with wet eyes and cheeks, "I have always had everything I wished. My grandparents never neglected me for one moment."

Her words were like a dagger to my heart for even if she did not mean them to hurt me, they did. "I will try to make up for it now."

She forced a smile, "We will have to see, father. I do not know you and the odd letter you sent has not helped." She seemed determined to hurt me, "I must look like a mess. Where is my room?"

"Jack, take Lady Antiochia to her room."

"I am not Lady Antiochia, father."

I smiled, "You are now."

William Coggeshall said, a little hurriedly in my opinion, "And I will fetch your bags, my lady."

I was going to speak when Michael said, "A word, Sir John,"

"Of course."

He turned to Thomas, "And if you fetch in my bags there is a present for you, young Thomas Hawkwood."

Left alone Michael said, "I have to tell you, my lord, that William and Antiochia have become close on the journey here. You know what it is like aboard a ship. They were thrown together quite literally and they seem well suited."

I felt myself becoming angry, "I am not going to have some fortune-hunting lordling take my daughter from me. I have only just met her. I cannot let him take her from me."

He sighed, patiently, "My lord he has lands in England. He came to fight in Italy to get his spurs. Besides which, her grandfather left his lands to her. They are hers, my lord, and she can do with them as she wishes."

"But until then she is mine!"

Silence came between us but Michael broke it, "She is right, my lord, you are about to wed. Would you split your time between a young wife or a daughter you barely know? If you wish to be the father you have never been then tell Donnina you cannot marry her."

Any other man who had dared to beard me would now be lying in a heap on the ground but this was Michael and much as I hated it, he was right. I could not give up Donnina and if I tried to come between Coggleshall and Antiochia I would still lose her. I nodded, "The man will have to prove himself to me and I mean in battle. Thus far he has played at war. I want to see him make war before I give him his spurs."

"I have spoken to him and he does not want to be given spurs. He wishes to earn them."

"Good. I suppose I had better invite him to dine with us but not this night. You tell him that he can come tomorrow but this night he quits my hall. I will have you and my children here, that is all."

"Me, Sir John?"

"Aye, I do not know my daughter and it is clear that you do. You can keep me right."

It was clear to me that Michael was right, for Antiochia was displeased that William was not to eat with us. She sulked and pouted. She had clearly been spoiled by her grandparents. Even as the thought came into my head, I dismissed it. I had deserted my daughter, not the other way around. I could not complain about the way things had turned out. It was Thomas who saved the evening from becoming a silent gloomy affair and he lightened the mood with his questions. He was just a little younger than his half-sister and, I suppose, having lost his brother to the priesthood was keen to replace him.

"You are my sister yet I can see little of our father in your face."

Tuscan Warlord

I snorted, "And that is no bad thing, Thomas. She looks like her mother. She too was beautiful."

"You flatter me, father." The half-smile was the beginning of the thaw.

"And will you live here in Italy, sister?"

She shook her head, "My grandfather left me lands and estates in England. I came here for I was alone and felt deserted." She smiled, "Thanks to Michael, I now have hope in my life."

Thomas looked saddened by the news, "That is disappointing. Father, could we not go to England? John is there and you have lands. Do we need to stay in Italy?"

"You forget that I am to be married, Thomas and to an Italian."

Michael must not have mentioned the marriage for she looked surprised, "You are to be wed, father?"

"Yes, to the daughter of Bernabò Visconti. You should stay for the wedding."

"Will William be there?"

I sighed, "I suppose he could be included amongst the guests. Why, is it important?"

"Yes, it is for we love each other and would be wed."

"Are you not missing out on the part where my permission is sought?"

"I am almost nineteen years of age and this is the first time I have seen you. If you had any interest at all in me then you would have visited. Grandfather was always disappointed that you did not."

I had no answer to that and she was right. Michael came to my defence, "Antiochia, your father has been busy doing that for which he is paid. He is the leading general in this part of the world. His services are sought by popes and dukes."

"And that I know, Michael. I realised many years ago that his work as a warrior was more important than his duties as a father so, I say again that I would be wed and I will be."

"What if William's family objects?"

She laughed, "He has lands too. Not as many as I have but he has lands. We could wed here in Italy."

An uncomfortable silence filled the room. Thomas ended it, "Then if you wed, I shall have a brother-in-law. I like William. He has much to learn about being a warrior but he is keen."

I laughed, "Oh, so you are now an expert in matters martial?"

He shrugged, "Since you fetched us from Bordeaux, I have seen warriors, good and bad, being trained. Robin and Giovanni have shown me how to spot those who are warriors and the ones who come to take the gold and go. William is the former but he will never be a warrior like Michael, or me."

Michael and I laughed at his confidence and Antiochia said, "You are a warrior, brother?"

"I carry the standard and blow the horn. It is my job to stand close to our father and help to protect him."

"I can see that I have entered a world which is unfamiliar to me. I am tired now and I will retire." We all stood. "I hope, father, that we can become closer but eighteen years of absence cannot be filled with one meal, can it?"

She went to her room. Michael had bought Thomas a mace and after my daughter had retired it was fetched out to show me. I think it was deliberate on both their parts to allow me to speak of matters martial and not marital.

"An interesting weapon, Michael. What made you choose it?"

"For one thing the price, it was a bargain but the main reason was that it is a good weapon to use in close combat. I noticed at the Battle of the Pandoro River that Dai and his men at arms killed more men with pole weapons than blades. A mace is even better in close combat. It breaks bones and dents helmets better than any sword."

I liked that Michael had learned something from the battle that I had not. We spoke for a while abut battles and how Thomas might be used in the future. I was left alone when Thomas and Michael retired. I had thought the world revolved around me and now I saw that it did not.

I threw myself into the meeting and greeting of the new men the next day. I sent a message to William Coggeshall to invite him to dine but neither saw nor spoke to him. The new men all looked to be keen. Since the death of the Black Prince and with the decline in the king's health there was little opportunity for war in England and both archers and men at arms sought employment. If you were English then that meant the White Company. The brief life of Thornbury's company had diverted some but now they flocked to my banner. We could begin to exert our influence over a wider area. My lands and castles in Romagna were just the beginning. I would fight for the league against the Avignon pope but I would ensure that we profited too.

Jack knew how important the dinner was to be. He had the cook prepare all the dishes that I liked and he ensured that the table was perfectly laid and presented. I had also invited Giovanni and Robin. They would be my allies and moral support. It had been Thomas who had entertained his sister during the day and had shown her the sights of Lucca. Since his brother had left, he had demonstrated skills and traits that had lain hidden. I dressed to impress my daughter. On my return from Milan, I had hired a Luccan tailor who had made me clothes that ten years ago would have seemed far too expensive for a warrior for the working day. Now I had gold and I knew that I had to dress accordingly.

William arrived promptly and he and I were alone with Michael and Thomas until Giovanni and Robin came. I found it awkward. He was one of my warriors but I was forced now to see him as something different. Once again it was Michael who made life easier for he knew him from the voyage to England and back. They laughed and joked about some of the incidents on the ship and the antics of the sailors. I remained silent and spent the time examining the young man. I could see why my daughter had fallen for his charms. He was handsome and he was witty. He had a pleasant voice and manner. I knew that if he was not seeking the hand of my firstborn, I might view him differently.

When my two old friends arrived, I pounced on them for I wanted reassurance, Thomas and Michael were chatting at the far end of the table and I said, "What think you of this young lordling?"

I realised that they knew nothing about his relationship with my daughter for Giovanni looked puzzled and shook his head, "He is young and he is keen. In time he will be a good warrior."

"He seeks Antiochia's hand in marriage."

Robin laughed so loudly that everyone turned to look, "You have the luck of the devil, Sir John. You no sooner get lumbered with a daughter than you find a young man to take her off your hands."

Giovanni shook his head, "A little louder, Robin, the young lady in question might not have heard your bellowed shout."

Robin was not put out, "I am a practical man, Giovanni. Do you see Sir John as a caring parent? He only fetched his boys when he thought that they might be warriors and had not the girl's grandparents died do you think he would have stirred to contact her?"

I sighed for Robin's bluntness was not what I needed, "Robin, you are not helping."

He looked at me and said, quietly, "Have I said anything with which you disagree, my lord?" I shook my head, "Then stop pretending to be what you are not. Give them your blessing and that will please the girl and the young man."

It was just then that Antiochia swept into the room. She was stunningly beautiful, just as her mother had been. Even Robin looked impressed. I watched William. He had eyes only for her and she for him. They were all right and I was being a pig-headed and arrogant fool.

"Daughter you are as radiant as the sun."

"Thank you, father, and I feel special too, surrounded as I am by such handsome warriors."

Her words set the tone for the evening. I said little for the others chatted about England, the voyage and I was largely ignored. I did not mind for I was forcing myself to view all of this with the dispassionate mind that had brought me so many victories. It was when there was a lull in the conversation that I brought up the marriage.

"So William, you wish to marry my daughter?"

I saw Michael and Giovanni shake their heads in disbelief at my bluntness. Antiochia looked worried while William, probably because of my tone, looked terrified.

Thomas leaned over and said, "You will learn, William, that my father barks when he does not mean to. He is used to the battlefield. Do not be offended by the question but I beg you to be honest in your answer."

"Thank you, Thomas, I do not need others to make excuses for me."

Michael shook his head, "Yes you do, Sir John."

I glared at him but he was right. I forced a smile and said, a little more gently, "I believe that you wish two things from me, William, my daughter's hand and spurs."

"I do, my lord."

"As it appears that you have stolen my daughter's hand then my views on the former are moot but the second is most definitely in my hands."

"Yes, my lord, and I hope that my love for your daughter does not stop me from becoming a knight."

Even Robin looked at me as they waited for an answer. I drank some wine and wiped my mouth before I replied. "You see before you, William, a man of two parts. There is the condottiere who is feared in this part of Italy and you see a father. As a father, I suspect I am a failure but as a condottiere, I am without a peer. When we go to war and, once I am wed, we shall be, then you will have the opportunity to show me if you are worthy to be a knight. Michael was a squire and earned the right to be a knight many times over. I had to press him to accept the spurs. Your marriage to my daughter is immaterial in respect of your knighthood."

It took some moments for my words to sink in but it was Antiochia who understood them first, "Then we can wed."

"Aye, but not yet for my marriage comes first. Is that clear?"

She laughed and took William's hand, "I care not for I am to be wed and I can see your wedding and that will help me to plan mine."

Michael leaned over and said, "That was well done, Sir John."

"Perhaps, we shall see."

My wedding was a grand affair. The marriage of an illegitimate daughter would not have seen so many nobles at the wedding but the marriage of Sir John Hawkwood brought guests in their droves to the wedding. One of the guests was Geoffrey Chaucer. I had not invited him but the man seemed affable and was popular. Dukes and marquesses rubbed shoulders with men like Robin, Dai and Giovanni. We were wed in Milan Cathedral and the archbishop himself conducted the ceremony. Donnina looked stunning and I saw my daughter admiring both the dress and the composure of my young bride. The wedding feast was all that might have been expected in the ducal palace and hosted by the Lord of Milan. He sat on one side of me and Antiochia sat next to Donnina. The two young women seemed oblivious to my presence and chattered like magpies. I suspect that suited Bernabò for he had much to say to me.

"You know that Pope Gregory has returned to Rome." I nodded. Such information was important and William had told me as soon as he had learned of it. "He is not a well man and I have heard rumours that he is not expected to see another Christmas."

"And what does that mean for me?"

He spoke even more quietly than he had before, "The College of Cardinals still sits in Avignon and they are French. When Pope Gregory dies then there will be another Avignon pope."

"And?"

"Queen Joanna of Naples is opposed to the return of the papacy to Rome. However, she has allied to an old friend of yours, Robert de Genève."

That had surprised me, "The cardinal?"

"Who, it is rumoured will be the next Avignon pope. If so then our league loses a powerful ally. It means that we will have to fight Naples next."

"You mean I will have to fight Naples."

He smiled, "The Doge of Florence has been in touch with me. He sees you as insurance against the predatory Neapolitans. Perugia too recognises your skills. Florence would have you and my daughter live in Florence."

I laughed, "There was a time when they would not even let me into their city."

"Times change and they are more pragmatic. You know that Lucca is too isolated. Your company needs to be in the heart of Tuscany. That is the jewel that Robert de Genève and Queen Joanna desire. There is a rumour that the Duke of Anjou and the French king also support Robert de Genève."

"And that means that Milan is threatened from the north."

"Indeed, so you see, Sir John, you and I must act in concert or we could both lose everything. With Naples and the pope in the south, as well as the duke and the king to the north, we could be squeezed like an Amalfi lemon."

At the time I attended the marriage of Lionel Duke of Clarence, I had been amazed that after the wedding feast, the bride and groom seemed immaterial. My own wedding was the same. It was an opportunity for the women to gather and gossip while the men spoke of politics and war. The exceptions were my daughter and her intended who sat with Michael and the others who had come with me. William's wife along with Dai's were with the women and William and I sat with Bernabò.

Geoffrey Chaucer seized his opportunity, "Congratulations, Sir John."

"Thank you, Master Geoffrey, and how goes the poetry?"

He had a glint in his eye, "People say that poets get their inspiration from the people that they meet. Such an event as this is perfect for a poet. I watch and I listen."

The Lord of Milan said, drily, "And those skills also help a spy."

Geoffrey laughed and affected a shocked look, "A spy? No, my lord. Any observations I make and take back to England are like crumbs brushed from a wedding breakfast."

Bernabò leaned forward, "And what is England's view on the possibility of another French pope?"

Chaucer's face did not alter as he answered, "England will support a pope, of course, for he is the head of the church but it would prefer an Italian one."

"Then, when you return to England tell your king that there may be an Italian pope soon."

That was news to me and it showed on my face. The Milanese manipulator of men smiled, "Let us say that Cesena showed us the mettle of the man who will be a pope. I am not without influence and I am planning on having an Italian pope elected."

Geoffrey said, "But what about the College of Cardinals?"

"They are French. The papacy should be in Rome." He tapped his nose. "I pray you pass these crumbs on, Master Chaucer."

It was then that I understood a little more about the politics that affected the lives of common people who had no idea why things happened as they did. England opposed the French and therefore they would challenge a French pope and support an Italian one. It was why I would be the conduit that would channel the information from Visconti's court to England. William nodded at all the comments and I knew that his mercantile mind would be working out how best we might profit from such news.

Donnina told me when it was time to retire. Somehow, and I know not how, she made me turn to look at her as she chatted to Antiochia, Caterina and Bianca. She inclined her head and I understood. I rose, "If you would excuse me, gentlemen, my lord."

"I wondered why you were tarrying here, Sir John."

Geoffrey said, "In all his life to those who met his sight; he was a very perfect gentle knight."

I frowned, "What is it that you say, Master Chaucer?"

"Oh, just some lines of poetry I penned. They seemed appropriate to describe you."

I smiled and said, "Then you have never seen me fight for none would ever say that I was gentle."

"Ah, my lord, but this night we shall see a knight be as gentle as any, shall we not?"

Perhaps he was right. Certainly, he was a perceptive man. Donnina was the third woman I had bedded. It is true that there had been whores and doxies but I did not count those. Antiochia's mother and Elizabeth were the mothers of my children but Donnina, she was a revelation. I had been worried that my age might prove a problem but it proved not to be the case. It was as though the young woman who lay in my arms ignited such power in me that I felt like a young man once more. It was the precursor to a life I could never have imagined a year or so earlier. I found that leaving my home was harder now than it had ever been.

We left Milan after just a few days. We returned to Lucca but it was merely a stopover and I went with my leaders and bodyguards to Florence. I left Antiochia in Lucca but I wanted Donnina to choose our new home. The doge welcomed us as heroes. The Neapolitans were flexing their muscles and their armies were gathering to the south of Siena, Arezzo and Perugia. Even my old enemies in Perugia were glad to see me in the region. The house we bought was huge and elevated above the city. It was the one that Donnina wanted and the cost was immaterial. It was less than the stipend I received each from Florence. That done I sent for the company while Donnina set about making it the home she wanted. I was happy to let her do so. I had little interest in furnishings and wall coverings. A house to me was somewhere to eat and to sleep, nothing more. Donnina intended to make it a place that would be somewhere the nobles of Florence and beyond would visit.

It was while she busied herself with the house that the news came that we had two popes. Robert de Genève was now Pope Clement VII and the Italian clergy had elected a Neapolitan, Bartolomeo Prignano, the Bishop of Bari. He was Pope Urban VI and his election had been forced upon the church by the Roman mob who wanted the papacy back in their city. It hastened my return to war.

Chapter 21

When the news came, I joined my leaders for a council of war. Donnina did not wish us to clutter up her house. As Antiochia had now joined us the two were like two industrious bees and consequently, we were exiled to an outbuilding. It bothered none of us. Thanks to my conversation with the Lord of Milan and Geoffrey Chaucer, I had a better idea of what the news meant. The only aberration appeared to be that Queen Joanna seemed to be supporting the new Roman pope. All that meant, to me, was that there would be no sudden attack and that gave us time to prepare.

"Despite the fact that the new pope is a Neapolitan I think that she will not support him for she likes de Genève. We are opposed to Pope Clement and that means we have to support Pope Urban. We need the company to be ready to move south as soon as we have more information." I turned to Giovanni, "I think, Giovanni, that you and Michael should make a pilgrimage to Rome to visit with our new pope."

Giovanni smiled, "And if we can pick up intelligence on the way then that is no bad thing, eh, Sir John?"

"Exactly and then we can find somewhere that is closer to Rome so that we can intervene if we have to."

Robin asked, "We are being paid this time?"

"Florence had agreed to fund us and as we are ensconced in their city then I think it is in their interests to pay us. However, I will continue to fund the company from my own resources, if that is necessary."

"You have no need, Sir John, the men know that you have their interests at heart."

I smiled, "Dai, the day that I do not need to keep money to pay my men lies in my old age. For now, I have a new family. While she lives with me, I have Antiochia to care for as well as a new wife. What will keep them safe is a strong White Company."

Giovanni and Dai returned with the news that there was an uneasy peace in Rome. Pope Clement had taken refuge with Queen Joanna and that showed us her affiliations. As yet she had not expressed her hostility towards the new pope. I knew it could not last and we continued to prepare for war.

However, when we did go to war it was not in the south but to the north and Verona. Donnina's father sent a messenger to tell me that he needed me and a German company led by Lutz von Landau to claim the inheritance he felt his wife was due since her brother's death. She was the last of the siblings. Her nephews had claimed the money was theirs. Visconti's alliance with Verona was over and he was sending us to claim back the money. He sent our annual payment and so we were paid but I was reluctant to go. "What about protecting Florence and, more importantly, my wife?"

It was Giovanni who had the solution, "Leave Dai here with his company and half of our archers. With the men brought by von Landau, we should have enough to cow Verona and besides, it is paid work. Rome is quiet at the moment and Pope Urban is busy clearing out those who support Avignon. We have time for this."

He was right and knowing that there would be five hundred men to guard my family was reassuring. As we prepared to leave we had tears, from Antiochia for William was to come with us and the news that Donnina was with child.

In contrast to my daughter, Donnina was a strong-minded woman who shed not a tear at my departure, "See my husband, your seed is strong. By the time you return, I might have given birth but I would prefer it if you were at my side."

"Then we have reason to win this battle and return as soon as we can."

William parted from my daughter with the words, "And let us look on this, my love, as a brief interruption. I shall do great deeds and win my spurs and then we shall be wed."

I kept William close to me as we headed north. His parting words to Antiochia had made me uneasy. I wanted no reckless act that might endanger his life for I knew that Antiochia would blame me and having brought her back into my life I was loath to lose her. It helped as Michael and Thomas were able to continue their tuition of William. Thomas was younger than William but vastly more experienced. William was a brave and competent knight but he had not been trained well by his family. The ride to Parma, where we would meet with von Landau, became a classroom for him.

My future sone in law also had questions for me. He was an Englishman and did not understand the way things worked in Italy, "My lord, how can you fight alongside a man whom you defeated?"

"Ah, you are mistaking patriotism with what we do. When I fought at Poitiers I fought for England. Now I fight for the White Company. We are men without countries. We fought against Florence and now we fight for her. We fought for Pisa and we have fought against her. Visconti was my enemy and is now my friend. It is the way things work over here. We bear no animosity and whoever pays us is our friend. Von Landau was a worthy enemy and whilst I do not think that his men are the equals of mine they will do."

His company had no archers nor crossbows but he had some bombards and I knew that they would prove useful. We met at Parma, now a Visconti ally. Despite the fact that the last time we had met he had been defeated by me and ransomed he greeted me like a friend. "Sir John, it is good to see you and now, I hear, we are brothers, of a sort."

"Brothers?"

"Aye, for I married Elisabetta Visconti." I had heard of her. She was a legitimate daughter but von Landau had the good manners not to mention that. However, he could not help gloating, "A good marriage for she brought me the Castle of Constance as a dowry and 12,000 florins."

"You have done well, better than I did."

"Yet you have greater treasure than I do and a far more successful company. I shall watch and learn while we raid. Do we head directly for Verona and demand the money owed to our father-in-law?"

I shook my head, "They will be more amenable if we raid the lands around there so that when we reach Verona, they know our intent and will be more willing to talk. In addition, it fattens our purses. We will head for Valpolicella and Valpantena and then up to Roncà and Monteforte d'Alpone." He nodded, "One thing more, Lutz, I command."

"Of course, for you bring more men and have more experience."

Englishmen are experts at the chevauchée. The methods and skills we used were honed over generations in Gascony, Aquitaine and the Rhone valley. However, you needed mounted archers to be successful. Robin and his men were able to ride and cut off small towns and villages and give the heavy infantry of von Landau time to close with them. It worked well although William chafed at the bit for he was keen to show me his courage. I kept him close to me and we were merely spectators, "Be patient, William. Von Landau's men do this well."

"But all that we have done is ride and cut places off."

"And have we lost a man?" He shook his head, "Then we are doing what we do best."

After a month of raiding and with our loot sent back to our homes we headed for Verona.

However, our raids meant that being prepared, they had hired Hungarian mercenaries. We discovered this when we intercepted a messenger and he confessed all. It was Robin and his archers who found the men from the north east. They were between Lake Guarda and Brescia. It prompted a meeting with von Landau and my leaders, "Von Landau, we cannot afford to attack Verona while there are Hungarians threatening us. We must deal with them first and then conduct the siege."

"The Hungarians are safely tucked away in mountain valleys. We cannot transport the bombards over mountain roads. I will leave them here with a hundred men."

"Very well. Robin, find me the Hungarian camp."

Brescia was close to the mountains and the Hungarians had made a good defensive camp close to them. Robin and his archers soon found their camp and left some men to watch them. While I had told William that professional courtesy was often given to other mercenaries that did not apply in this case. Firstly, they were Hungarians and we had experienced unpleasantness before. Secondly, they had been hired by the Veronese and so they represented an enemy army. My intention was to make a sudden and surprise attack. Only half of von Landau's men were mounted. We had left one hundred with the bombards and now we left another one hundred dismounted men at arms to guard our camp. That meant we had Robin's archers and eight hundred mounted men at arms, the majority of whom were my men. I sent Robin and his archers to move as close as they could to the left flank of the Hungarian camp. When we charged their camp, they would send their arrows to strike them as they tried to prepare to defend against us. Robin's horse holders came into their own. They now knew how to fight and were an extra body of men we could use if we needed to. Having served with us they all aspired to be squires and, ultimately, men at arms. The pay was better.

We formed our mounted horsemen into three lines. I spread von Landau's men along the line but the better warriors in the front line were largely mine. Much to his chagrin, I had William in the third line. We used lances and we simply walked our horses towards the Hungarian camp. They did have sentries but they were three hundred paces from the camp and by the time they had shouted their warning we were already one hundred paces closer to a camp where men had discarded their mail to eat, drink and gamble. As Robin's archers' arrows fell there was clear confusion in the camp. Some men raised shields to face the archers while others prepared to fight the horsemen thundering towards them. When we struck the dismounted men at arms, we broke their spirit. I lanced one and Ajax trampled a second before they broke and fled for the mountains and rocks. Had we intended to slaughter them we could have but Verona was our target and all that we needed was to defeat them and take their horses. They could get more but I hoped that by then we would have defeated Verona and be on our way home.

When the last of them had fled we sacked their camp. Plate armour and weapons were as valuable to us as gold.

Although half of the horses had either been taken by fleeing men or had bolted, we captured enough to be able to mount von Landau's dismounted men at arms. We rode back towards Verona in darkness. My men were in high spirits for it had been an easy victory. We picked up the bombards from their camp and then marched to Verona, arriving at noon two days after our victory.

They knew we were coming and had prepared for a siege. We had lugged around von Landau's bombards and now they would come into their own. We surrounded the town, which had well-made walls and the German engineers made the bombards secure. I had rarely witnessed bombards in use and I went with von Landau as he inspected them. The engineers had made frames that angled them up. There were wedges to adjust the angle at which they fired. They had one man who loaded a stone ball, a second who looked to be the master gunner and measured out the powder and a third who had a metal rod in his hand. I asked one what it was.

"It is a touch, my lord. We put it in a brazier to heat it up and then thrust it into the touchhole. It ignites the powder and that sends the ball towards the target."

"You do not use a fuze like the hand gunners?"

"This is more reliable my lord and safer."

"I look forward to watching your bombards in action."

We gave the Veronese the courtesy of asking for the owed inheritance. They, of course, refused. "My brother Antonio and I owe my aunt nothing, Sir John."

"As you, my lord, Bartolomeo della Scala, are illegitimate, therefore I believe the Lady of Milan is the rightful heiress of Verona."

"When she married the Lord of Milan then all such rights were lost. My father, Cansignorio della Scala was fond of his sister but my brother and I have no such affiliations. If you wish to take the inheritance it will be bought with the blood of your men."

I nodded, "Verona has been kept safe all these years by the friendship of the Lord of Milan. A sacked city is not a pretty sight. You have a beautiful city, surely the payment is a small price to pay for its safety."

Tuscan Warlord

He shook his head, "We are done. Come no more."

With that, we were dismissed. I had no intention of wasting men assaulting walls and Lutz and I returned to the bombards. "Well, Master Gunner, you may begin your work."

Our rude dismissal had angered me and I wanted them shocked into submission. I had been fired on by handguns and bombards but they did not prepare me for both the noise and the stink. I now understood why gunners wore cloths about their ears and noses. The stink of gunpowder and the smoke made me retire well behind them. I was able to watch as they methodically began to break down the gatehouse and gates. Once the gunners had the range and that took more balls than I thought was necessary, they kept up a regular bombardment. It was slower than I had anticipated but by dark, the top of the gatehouse had been badly damaged. Of course, they would repair it at night but the repairs would involve wood and wood burned. It took three days for the bombards to effectively destroy the gatehouse and as soon as they did then one of the two lords of Verona appeared. He came with the archbishop and his brother Antonio.

"Sir John, can we talk with you and Count von Lutz?"

"Of course. You wish to surrender and pay the inheritance?"

They both looked to the archbishop, "We have another solution, an offer if you will." The archbishop leaned in and said, "We have two chests, one for the two of you. They each contain 75,000 florins. If you take them and an annual stipend of 10,000 florins would that make you forget your loyalty to your father-in-law?"

I was not sure but von Landau surprised me and agreed for us both, "Bring out the chests and we will leave this very day." I shot him an angry look and he shrugged. He put his head close to mine and said, "It is my bombards that have brought this about. I will take my chest. Can you take the walls without losing men if you have neither bombard nor trebuchet?"

He was right, "It is not my way, I never break my word."

"You did not. It was me who agreed." He softened his action with a smile, "Besides, this way we get away before the Hungarians come looking for vengeance."

I shook my head, "The Lord of Milan will not see it that way. He will blame both of us equally and want his wife's inheritance."

However, it was done. The carrot was out of the ground and the gold was delivered. I suppose I must have a noble streak somewhere in me for none of my leaders found anything wrong in what we did. However, the parting from von Landau was not as pleasant as the initial meeting had been. Our two companies separated and he headed north to Castle Constance while we headed south.

We were still three days from Florence when one of von Landau's men found us. His horse was lathered and he had blood on his surcoat, "Sir John, I was sent to warn you. We were ambushed in the passes close to Castle Constance. We lost our bombards and many horses. Von Landau barely escaped with his life. He is now besieged in his castle but he wanted you to know that the Hungarians are coming for you."

That meant the Hungarians had either been reinforced or we had not hurt them as badly as we had thought, "Thank you, my friend. Are you hurt? We can have your wounds tended to."

He shook his head, "No, my lord, this was from the battle. It is the blood of dead men. Now I must return to my company. We will have revenge on these Hungarians."

His arrival had brought my leaders close to me and as he galloped off, we discussed what it meant, "Was he just unlucky, Sir John?"

"Perhaps. Riding to Castle Constance would have taken him close to the Hungarian camp. Let us be pessimistic however and see a plan in this. I think that we should anticipate an ambush sometime soon."

Giovanni said, "You may be right. The Hungarians see Naples as their own. Charles of Durazzo has some claim to be king and there is still resentment about the murder of Prince Andrew who was briefly married to Queen Joanna.

This may not be simply a company of mercenaries but something more sinister, a Hungarian army intent on taking Naples."

William always managed to come close to us when we were talking, For the rest of us everything that Giovanni had said made sense. We had warred through the scandals of Naples.

"I am sorry, Sir John, but I do not understand. Firstly, why should Hungarians think they have a right to Naples and secondly surely that helps us. If Queen Joanna shelters Pope Clement, then she is our enemy."

I sighed as I explained, "The Hungarians have historic links with Naples and the Kingdom of Naples and Sicily is the largest kingdom in the whole of Italy. The only kingdom," I corrected myself. What Giovanni means is that it may not be a company such as ours that is in this part of Italy but something worse, an army and the taking of the White Company and its destruction would make it easier for the Hungarians to take over Naples." I had explained myself enough, "Robin, scouts out. Dai, protect the baggage train. From now on we ride armed and ready for war."

Thomas had my helmet ready and after pulling up my coif I donned it. He handed me my shield and I let it hang on my left side. The guige strap would hold it there. "Do you need a lance, father?"

I shook my head, "My sword will suffice. Make sure that you are well protected, Thomas, and stay close to me. The standard can stay in the wagon. We need not trumpet our identity for they will know where we are."

They were waiting for us south of Bologna. The cities in the area still reeled from the Cesena massacre and our raids there. It was the shortest way back to Florence but not necessarily the safest as the only help we could expect would come from Modena and we had passed through that safe haven the day before. It was not an ambush but a planned attack; they were waiting for us in battle lines. They chose a section of the road that lay between two woods. Four hundred paces wide it afforded enough room for them to pack their dismounted men at arms and crossbowmen in the gap. We could have declined battle and headed back to Modena but my sharp mind wondered if that would then initiate an ambush closer to Bologna. With laden wagons, we could not travel quickly and so I decided to fight this battle on prepared ground of the Hungarians' choosing.

When Robin had brought news of the waiting warriors, he had left his archers who dismounted, to prevent an attack. He and my other leaders gathered around my horse. Each of them was a good leader but they always deferred to me. They might offer suggestions but the battle plan would be mine.

"How many men face us, Robin?"

"I would say equal numbers but we know not how many are hidden beyond the woods. They invite battle, Sir John and that worries me. They know our skills and yet they just stand there. Perhaps it is like a conjuror at a country fair. He shows us one hand but keeps the other hidden. They simply wait and made no attempt to discourage us."

Dai nodded, "And we cannot go around them for that would expose our baggage."

Michael said, "We could abandon the wagons. The extra horses mean that we are well mounted."

Robin growled, "Let a mob of hairy-arsed Hungarians have our treasure without a fight? I think not, Michael."

"It would not do to run, Michael." I rubbed my chin. We had trained our squires well. Many of them were almost ready to become fully-fledged men at arms. They were, however, only protected by leather brigandines and short hauberks. We could use those as they would be dismissed by our enemies as would the archer horse holders. "Robin, have your horse holders bring their horses here."

William could not help asking another question, "But how can we shift them?"

I ignored him and turned to Michael, "You know the squires better than any. Is there one who is a natural leader?"

"Ned of Lincoln."

"I want him to command a quarter of our archers and all of the squires and for them to make their way through the woods to our right. On the sounding of the horn, they will harass and attack the Hungarians on their left. They are not to take risks but make noise and try to fool the Hungarians into thinking that we have a flank attack with men at arms. In the darkness of the woods the shadows that are squires may appear like the spectres of mailed men at arms" He nodded. "Robin…" My captain of archers had sent a deputy to obey my command.

He had anticipated my words and nodded, "Ralph of Rugby was an archer but he was wounded and he leads the horse holders. He has a good mind. You want him to do the same on the other flank?"

"I do. It will take time for them to get into position. While they do so we will spend time forming battle lines. Robin, you will initiate the attack with an arrow storm with the half of the archers that we show to the Hungarians and then we will attack with lances. When you have done with the arrows your men will make out as though you are fleeing but I want you and your archers to divide into two and support the horse holders and the squires."

"Aye, my lord, but you realise that you are gambling all in this one ruse. If it fails then you lose everything." Giovanni was not telling me not to attack but asking me if I had thought it through.

He was right, of course, "Tell me, have we ever tried anything like this before?" They all shook their heads. "Then the Hungarians will never have endured such an attack. Giovanni, we have to try new things if only to keep enemies we might fight in the future wondering what we intend."

The nods from all told me that they were happy with my decision. I turned to Thomas and William. "William, you will protect Thomas. I want them to know where I am. I will use a lance and you two will ride behind me. I will not need a second lance. We either break them or lose. Giovanni is right. We gamble all."

I saw the fear not on Thomas' face but on William's. The only reassurance I would give him would be the truth, "William, this is what we do. There is no guarantee that we will survive any battle. We have the skill and we are good warriors but as Michael will tell you we have buried good warriors who fell in battle. You need to decide if you wish to be a husband who lives in England and farms his lands or a warrior who goes to battle not knowing if he will return alive." He looked stunned. "For today, fight as though not only your life but mine and Thomas' depended on you, for they do." He looked resolutely at me and nodded.

Our formation meant that I would be slightly ahead of my four bodyguards, two on each side, with Thomas and William flanking Ajax's rump, Thomas had learned how to hold the standard and blow the horn whilst using his knees to guide his horse. The young acquire such skills quickly. I turned to look at William. He held his lance aloft as we all did. I had not seen him use a lance in battle and I gave him advice. I did not care if he thought me patronising, I did not wish to break the news to my daughter of the death of the love of her life.

"When we charge keep your shield high and angled along your body. When you strike with your lance pull back and punch. You may see me stand in my stirrups. Do not try that as you may become unhorsed. Lower your lance when you see men and my bodyguards do so. Stay alive, William."

"I will, my lord. I am only just beginning to see that what you do is not as easy as you make it look."

He would do. Once we had our line one hundred men wide, I looked down the line. Only the middle fifty of us would have an obstacle-free passage. It was another reason for our formation. I would be the tip of the arrow and the rest would echelon behind me as they negotiated bushes, saplings and low walls. It would encourage the Hungarians to try to flow around our flanks and I wanted that to happen as it would present backs to my squires and horse holders who would already be in position in the woods. Many of the Hungarians had breastplates but not back plates. Even a badly swung sword could act as an iron bar and break a backbone.

I nodded to Robin who had his men move forward. They would have to endure an attack of crossbows and they spread themselves out to make a more difficult target. They knew how to avoid bolts. Robin would hope to win the duel as the crossbows, slower to reload, were whittled down. Our attack would be initiated by his retreat. We had practised the manoeuvre many times and what looked complicated to others was easy for us. The Hungarians had far fewer crossbowmen than we had archers and they had no pavise before them. Instead, they stood behind a wall of dismounted men at arms who held their shields as a wooden barrier. It afforded some protection but Robin knew how to get around that. The Hungarians loosed their bolts somewhat prematurely while our archers were still marching. The archers saw the bolts coming for they were not like arrows descending from a white sky. I saw one lucky bolt slam into the head of an archer and another half a dozen were hit by bolts but that was nothing and it allowed Robin to halt his men, nock, draw and release in one easy motion. The disadvantage of the Hungarian formation was that they were tightly packed behind the front rank of crossbows and men at arms. Five flights fell before the crossbows had reloaded and those three thousand arrows hit more than they missed. Some hit crossbowmen while others hit men at arms and spear men in the rear ranks. Many arrows hit plate and mail and bounced off. Such arrows were often not wasted as they ricocheted into flesh. Others hit the lightly armoured crossbowmen while the majority slammed into the men in the fourth and fifth ranks, many of whom had no armour. They all pressed forward into the rear of their front rank for security, hampering the surviving crossbowmen.

I heard Robin shout, "Bodkins." The next five flights were devastating. They pierced helmets and plate armour. Only those who raised shields had any protection and the front rank, guarding as they did the crossbowmen could not do that. As the last flights flew Robin, shouted, "Back! Let us get more arrows." I smiled at the ruse. He did not need arrows and the Hungarians would know enough English to make out his clearly shouted words. The archers pulled back and I said, "Ready, Thomas?"

"Aye, my lord." I wanted the horn to sound and then for us to charge. He would need his hand on his reins. He sounded the horn and I led my lancers forward. I was depending upon two unknown leaders to command the flank attacks. I had to trust that all our training had been worthwhile. I had to ensure that Ajax did not do as his nature wished and charge off down the road which was clear of obstacles. As Robin and his men filtered between us to then disappear into the trees I tried to keep as straight a line as I could. There were still some crossbowmen who sent their bolts at us but with horses and men protected by mail and plate the chances of one hitting were slim. The Hungarians quickly pushed spears and pole weapons over the men in the front rank. They had to be confident that their packed ranks would hold us. The ones in the front rank might die but their second and third ranks would do far more damage. I saw, out of the corner of my eye, my racing archers as they rushed through the woods. They would not be able to launch a concerted arrow storm but they would each loose when they had a target. They would take great delight in choosing victims who would die. Competitive to a man they would relive the battle around the campfires when all was done and every arrow would be recalled. I had been an archer and done so myself. The Hungarians were preoccupied with the wall of horseflesh and steel that hurtled and thundered towards them. They were brave and doughty warriors but a charge by heavy horsemen is not something to be dismissed lightly.

    Timing was all and I waited until we were fifty paces from the Hungarian line before I lowered my lance and spurred Ajax. He leapt forward. It was at that precise moment that I heard a wail from the Hungarians at the rear of their front lines. My squires and horse holders allied to my archers had begun their attack. I had never been in the position of the Hungarians but it must have come as a shock to see an attack at the fore and then find that the enemy was around your flanks and rear. Heads that had faced us now looked over their shoulders and that was the death knell for the front line. Lances jabbed and speared into heads and chests which had shields held too low thanks to the distraction of the well-timed flank and rear attack. My lance rammed through the plate and into the chest of one

Hungarian who, dying though he was, tried to pull the weapon from his chest. I had a strong grip and his lifeless body slipped from the head of my lance. It was then that the Hungarians sprang the surprise that Robin and I had suspected. They too had a reserve and two hundred lancers appeared at the rear of the Hungarian line. Had it not been lightly armoured squires, archers and horse holders whom they attacked the Hungarians might have slaughtered many men but my men simply fled swiftly back into the safety of the trees. There they could still harass and attack the Hungarians but they would be safe from the horsemen.

The dismounted Hungarian men at arms broke by the time my lance shattered on the plate armour of one of those in the third rank. Ajax had trampled a number of wounded men and our lines were still largely intact. It was too early to say if we had won but I felt we held the advantage. The archers in the trees now had the protection of the swords and spears of my horse holders and squires. They picked off the heroes and the leaders. Whoever led the Hungarian horsemen saw his chance for glory and he spurred his horse and the rest of his lancers to come directly for me. I was still the tip of the arrow and the nearest warrior to their horsemen. They rode directly at me. Some still had lances but most had suffered the same problem as me, they had broken and there were no replacements. This would be sword to sword. It would be their leader who fought me. The defeat of Sir John Hawkwood, especially in single combat, would be something that would make any knight's reputation.

As we slammed into each other's lines I braced myself for the swing of his sword. He was strong but not as strong as I was. The blow did little to hurt me. I am a tall man and the Hungarian was a squatter and solidly built man. I stood and brought the sword down hard. He tried to bring up his shield but he merely slowed the speed of the strike and not the force. He reeled and I spurred Ajax as I regained my seat, so that he snapped and bit at the Hungarian's horse. Ajax was the victor and the enemy horse also tried to wheel away from the snapping teeth. It turned to its right and while the

Hungarian knight was still protected by his shield he was unable to use his sword. Even worse for my opponent was that he was in danger of overbalancing and was struggling to keep his saddle. I lunged over the top of his shield. He had an open bascinet and although he had a coif, I made contact with his nose with the point of my sword. As the sharpened tip slid through flesh and scraped on the bone it diverted the blow towards the eye. He could do nothing about it and my sword entered the orb and, thanks to the pressure still applied by Ajax, drove into the skull and thence the brain. He fell from the saddle but his death grip on his reins meant that he pulled his horse over.

My bodyguards were still around me, having followed me into this deadly duel. I saw that Roger was hurt but still fighting. I swept my sword backhand against the man he was fighting and it was then I saw the dismounted man at arms run at my son's horse with a glaive. He hacked, not into the head, which was protected by mail, but at the unprotected leg. The glaive is a wicked weapon and it sliced through the flesh and the bone. Thomas' horse reared and I saw my son tumble. He should have dropped the standard to save himself but he did not for he knew that a falling standard would dishearten our men. I tried to wheel around to protect my son. It was a foolish move as it exposed my back but I could not allow Thomas to be butchered and it was clear to me that the Hungarian with the glaive intended to decapitate Thomas who lay prone on the ground. Even though it exposed him to an attack in the flank William gallantly galloped towards the Hungarian and rammed his still unbroken weapon through the man's back.

"Sir John!" Michael's voice made me turn and I was just in time to see the war axe slicing down to hack into my back. My sword was too low and even as I tried to raise it, I knew I would be too late. Tall Tom's bodkin struck the back of the helmet and head of the Hungarian and drove so far through that it almost drove into the fletch. I knew it was Tom's arrow for I saw him in the distance, nocking another and looking in my direction. I raised my sword in thanks.

I completed my wheel and then spurred Ajax. There was no banner behind me but my men were still intact and as we all rode at the survivors of the Hungarian attack they broke. Their leader was now dead and Sir John Hawkwood was leading the White Company to victory. The dismounted men at arms were already running to get to their horses before we did. I knew from Ajax's heavy breathing and lathered coat that pursuit was out of the question and so I stood in my stirrups and shouted, "Hold! We have won! Sack their camp!"

I sheathed my sword and rode back to Thomas who was just pulling himself from his dead horse.

"Are you whole?"

He nodded, "Just shaken." He knelt next to his horse and stroked its head. "I feel as though I have lost a friend."

I nodded, "And I would feel the same." Turning to William I nodded, "Well, William, you have earned not only our thanks but your spurs. I shall knight you this night."

He shook his head, "With respect my lord, I would wait until Florence. I would have Antiochia see the ceremony."

"I understand."

We had lost men but not as many as von Landau for we held the field and von Landau had been forced to flee. I owed him a debt of thanks for his warning had saved us. Once more we took horses, plate armour, and treasure. We buried our dead and headed back to Florence where our victory had preceded us. Although we had been fighting for Visconti and not Florence the fact that we had defeated a Hungarian army made us heroes. I knighted not only William but Tall Tom too. It was rare for archers to be knighted but he had earned it. Ned of Lincoln had also performed gallantly and he became Sir Edward. Many of the squires became men at arms and a large number of the horse holders replaced them as squires. It was how we grew as a company.

Epilogue

Our safe return showed me how much my daughter loved William. She wept as she hugged him and thanked me for bringing him safely home to her. Now that he was a knight he could be wed. Donnina arranged the wedding of my daughter and Sir William. It was a double-edged sword for although it was a glorious day and all enjoyed it, I knew that it heralded the end of my daughter's time in Italy. I had enjoyed her company for a brief time and now she would return with her new husband to England. William had achieved what he wished and he was honest enough to tell me that the life of a mercenary did not appeal. His courage was not in doubt and my leaders approved of his choice of a safe life in England. He wanted a life in a country he knew, with the woman he loved. Not everyone was cut out for a life as a sword for hire. It was also sad for when he returned to England, he took Thomas with him. It was not to leave my service but to raise a company for me in England. He would be a leader like Michael and the others but the company he raised would be his and it would take time to attract archers and men at arms. He would live with William and Antiochia while he did so. The new men would be part of the White Company but I had seen that we might need to diversify. We were growing larger as a company and needed the flexibility to use smaller warbands. That was what we were, a warband and I was the warlord. Visitors from Venice had told us of a Mongol leader called Genghis Khan who had conquered huge swathes of land by using warbands led by good leaders. I would emulate the Mongol but instead of horsemen loosing arrows from the backs of horses we would use lances backed by arrows and billmen. My warband would be the envy of every other condottiere.

Bernabò Visconti did not forget what von Landau and I had done. He withheld our pay and relations became soured. We had taken treasure and for my part I could endure the patent hostility. I wondered about Donnina however, but when she gave birth to our first child, Giannetta, then her father was forgotten.

"Husband, we have a beautiful daughter and you are successful. You were sent to collect money not for my mother but my father's wife." She shrugged, "I do not want you hurt fighting for her. Do what you do and I will use my skills to make us richer than my father ever was."

"Are you sure?"

"I owe Bernabò Visconti nothing. You owe him nothing and if he is so foolish as to fail to pay you then shame on him. You continue to take Florence's money and to do what you do best, be a leader of men."

She was right and I knew that I had been more than lucky to marry not only a beauty but a beauty with a mind and together we would be a formidable weapon.

The End

Glossary

Battle- a military formation rather than an event
Bevor- metal chin and mouth protector attached to a helmet
Brase- a strap on a shield for an arm to go through
Brigandine- a leather or padded tunic worn by soldiers; often studded with metal and sometimes called a jack
Centenar- the commander of a hundred
Chevauchée – a raid on an enemy, usually by horsemen
Cordwainer- Shoemaker
Cuisse - metal protection for the thigh
Faulds - a skirt of metal below the breastplate
Feditore-an Italian warrior
Gardyvyan- Archer's haversack containing all his war-gear
Ghibellines – The faction supporting the Holy Roman Emperor against the Pope
Glaive- a long pole weapon with a concave blade
Greaves- Protection for the lower legs
Guelphs- the faction supporting the Pope
Guige strap– a long leather strap that allowed a shield to hang from a knight's shoulder
Harbingers- the men who found accommodation and campsites for archers
Jupon – a shorter version of the surcoat
Mainward - the main body of an army
Mêlée - confused fight
Noble- a gold coin worth about six shillings and eightpence
Oriflamme – The French standard which was normally kept in Saint-Denis
Pavesiers - men who carried man-sized shields to protect crossbowmen
Perpunto- soft padded tunic used as light armour during training
Pestis secunda – second outbreak of the Black Death in 1360-62
Poleyn – knee protection
Rearward- the rearguard and baggage of an army
Rooking - overcharging

Tuscan Warlord

Spaudler – shoulder protection
Shaffron – metal headpiece for a horse
Spanning hook- the hook a crossbowman had on his belt to help draw his weapon
Trapper – a cloth covering for a horse
Vanward- the leading element of an army, the scouts
Vintenar- commander of twenty
Vambrace – upper arm protection

Tuscan Warlord

Historical note

John Hawkwood was a real person but much of his life is still a mystery. At the end of his career, he was one of the most powerful men in Northern Italy where he commanded the White or English Company. He famously won the battle of Castagnaro in 1387. However, his early life is less well documented, and I have used an artistic licence to add details. He was born in Essex and his father was called Gilbert. I have made up the reason for his leaving his home but leave he did, and he became an apprentice tailor. It is rumoured that he fought at Crécy as a longbowman and I have used that to weave a tale. It is also alleged that he was knighted by Prince Edward at Poitiers.

The problem with researching this period is that most of the accounts are translations and the interpretation of the original documents leaves much to be desired. In one account the battle of Rubiera occurs in 1372 whilst in another in 1370. All I know is that von Landau was defeated and captured by Sir John and that the battle came about because he was still fighting for the Visconti family. As this was the last time he fought for the Visconti for some time and was employed by the pope to fight against Milan and Florence in 1371 I have had to adjust what I know. The dates might be open for debate but the battles and the outcomes are not. Until I manage to get a time machine this will have to do.

The massacre at Cesena happened. Sir John was ordered by Robert de Genève to massacre the population. He was acting on the pope's orders. Sir John saved many of the population. He was always, it seemed, trying to get payment for services and that explains his freebooting activities. There is no doubt that he acted like a warlord. He captured and kept castles in lieu of payment. There were many occasions when the employers of the White Company failed to pay them for their services. The White Company proved to be very loyal as it was Sir John Hawkwood who paid them from his own purse.

I know that Hawkwood's marriage when he was in his fifties to a girl who was just 17 will make some people uncomfortable. However, it happened many times in the Middle Ages and to be fair to them they stayed together and appeared to love each other. Donnina bore him children and seemed an equal partner in the marriage. She was a strong woman and, unusually for the time, took charge of his finances.

Von Landau's livery

Visconti constantly hired mercenaries to do his work. Von Landau and Hawkwood did go to Visconti's ally to get his wife's inheritance. They accepted bribes to depart and then von Landau was badly handled by Hungarians. The White Company also fought the Hungarians but was more successful.

Queen Joanna is a complicated character and the involvement of the Hungarians in Italian politics was a key one, at least until Queen Joanna died.

There will be at least one more book in this series. Sir John Hawkwood's greatest and most famous victory came when he was in his sixties at Castagnaro. The story will continue, at least until then.

Griff Hosker
November 2022

The books I used for reference were:

- French Armies of the Hundred Years War- David Nicholle

- Castagnaro 1387- Devries and Capponi
- Italian Medieval Armies 1300-1500- Gabriele Esposito
- Armies of the Medieval Italian Wars-1125-1325
- Condottiere 1300-1500 Infamous Medieval Mercenaries – David Murphy
- The Armies of Crécy and Poitiers- Rothero
- The Scottish and Welsh Wars 1250-1400- Rothero
- English Longbowman 1330-1515- Bartlett and Embleton
- The Longbow- Mike Loades
- The Battle of Poitiers 1356- Nicholle and Turner
- The Tower of London-Lapper and Parnell
- The Tower of London- A L Rowse
- Sir John Hawkwood- John Temple Leader
- Medieval Mercenary: Sir John Hawkwood of Essex – Christopher Starr

Tuscan Warlord

Other books by Griff Hosker

If you enjoyed reading this book, then why not read another one by the author?

Ancient History

The Sword of Cartimandua Series
(Germania and Britannia 50 A.D. – 128 A.D.)
Ulpius Felix- Roman Warrior (prequel)
The Sword of Cartimandua
The Horse Warriors
Invasion Caledonia
Roman Retreat
Revolt of the Red Witch
Druid's Gold
Trajan's Hunters
The Last Frontier
Hero of Rome
Roman Hawk
Roman Treachery
Roman Wall
Roman Courage

The Wolf Warrior series
(Britain in the late 6th Century)
Saxon Dawn
Saxon Revenge
Saxon England
Saxon Blood
Saxon Slayer
Saxon Slaughter
Saxon Bane
Saxon Fall: Rise of the Warlord
Saxon Throne
Saxon Sword

Medieval History

Tuscan Warlord

The Dragon Heart Series
Viking Slave *
Viking Warrior *
Viking Jarl *
Viking Kingdom *
Viking Wolf *
Viking War
Viking Sword
Viking Wrath
Viking Raid
Viking Legend
Viking Vengeance
Viking Dragon
Viking Treasure
Viking Enemy
Viking Witch
Viking Blood
Viking Weregeld
Viking Storm
Viking Warband
Viking Shadow
Viking Legacy
Viking Clan
Viking Bravery

The Norman Genesis Series
Hrolf the Viking *
Horseman *
The Battle for a Home *
Revenge of the Franks *
The Land of the Northmen
Ragnvald Hrolfsson
Brothers in Blood
Lord of Rouen
Drekar in the Seine
Duke of Normandy
The Duke and the King

Tuscan Warlord

Danelaw
(England and Denmark in the 11th Century)
Dragon Sword *
Oathsword *
Bloodsword *
Danish Sword

New World Series
Blood on the Blade *
Across the Seas *
The Savage Wilderness *
The Bear and the Wolf *
Erik The Navigator *
Erik's Clan *
The Last Viking

The Vengeance Trail *

The Conquest Series
(Normandy and England 1050-1100)
Hastings

The Aelfraed Series
(Britain and Byzantium 1050 A.D. - 1085 A.D.)
Housecarl *
Outlaw *
Varangian *

The Reconquista Chronicles
Castilian Knight *
El Campeador *
The Lord of Valencia *

The Anarchy Series England 1120-1180
English Knight *
Knight of the Empress *
Northern Knight *
Baron of the North *

Tuscan Warlord

Earl *
King Henry's Champion *
The King is Dead *
Warlord of the North
Enemy at the Gate
The Fallen Crown
Warlord's War
Kingmaker
Henry II
Crusader
The Welsh Marches
Irish War
Poisonous Plots
The Princes' Revolt
Earl Marshal
The Perfect Knight

Border Knight
1182-1300
Sword for Hire *
Return of the Knight *
Baron's War *
Magna Carta *
Welsh Wars *
Henry III *
The Bloody Border *
Baron's Crusade
Sentinel of the North
War in the West
Debt of Honour
The Blood of the Warlord
The Fettered King
de Montfort's Crown

Sir John Hawkwood Series
France and Italy 1339- 1387
Crécy: The Age of the Archer *
Man At Arms *
The White Company *

Tuscan Warlord

Leader of Men *
Tuscan Warlord *
Condottiere

Lord Edward's Archer
Lord Edward's Archer *
King in Waiting *
An Archer's Crusade *
Targets of Treachery *
The Great Cause *
Wallace's War *
The Hunt

Struggle for a Crown
1360- 1485
Blood on the Crown *
To Murder a King *
The Throne *
King Henry IV *
The Road to Agincourt *
St Crispin's Day *
The Battle for France *
The Last Knight *
Queen's Knight *

Tales from the Sword I
(Short stories from the Medieval period)

Tudor Warrior series
England and Scotland in the late 15th and early 16th century
Tudor Warrior *
Tudor Spy *
Flodden

Conquistador
England and America in the 16th Century
Conquistador *
The English Adventurer *

Tuscan Warlord

Modern History

The Napoleonic Horseman Series
Chasseur à Cheval
Napoleon's Guard
British Light Dragoon
Soldier Spy
1808: The Road to Coruña
Talavera
The Lines of Torres Vedras
Bloody Badajoz
The Road to France
Waterloo

The Lucky Jack American Civil War series
Rebel Raiders
Confederate Rangers
The Road to Gettysburg

Soldier of the Queen series
Soldier of the Queen
Redcoat's Rifle
Omdurman

The British Ace Series
1914
1915 Fokker Scourge
1916 Angels over the Somme
1917 Eagles Fall
1918 We will remember them
From Arctic Snow to Desert Sand
Wings over Persia

**Combined Operations series
1940-1945**
Commando *
Raider *
Behind Enemy Lines

Tuscan Warlord

Dieppe
Toehold in Europe
Sword Beach
Breakout
The Battle for Antwerp
King Tiger
Beyond the Rhine
Korea
Korean Winter

Tales from the Sword II
(Short stories from the Modern period)

Books marked thus *, are also available in the audio format.
For more information on all of the books then please visit the author's website at www.griffhosker.com where there is a link to contact him or visit his Facebook page: GriffHosker at Sword Books or follow him on Twitter: @HoskerGriff

Printed in Great Britain
by Amazon